LAURA KAY

Wild Things

Laura Kay is the author of *The Split* and *Tell Me Everything,* both published by Quercus in the United Kingdom. *Wild Things* is her first novel published in the United States. She lives in East London.

Wild Things

Wild Things

A NOVEL

Laura Kay

VINTAGE BOOKS

A DIVISION OF PENGUIN RANDOM HOUSE LLC

NEW YORK

A VINTAGE BOOKS ORIGINAL 2023

Library of Congress Cataloging-in-Publication Data
Names: Kay, Laura, [date] author.
Title: Wild things / by Laura Kay.
Description: New York : Vintage, a division of
    Penguin Random House LLC, 2023.
Identifiers: LCCN 2022038301 (print) | LCCN 2022038302 (ebook) |
    ISBN 9780593470053 (trade paperback) |
    ISBN 9780593470060 (ebook)
Subjects: LCGFT: Romance fiction. | Novels.
Classification: LCC PR6111.A936 K39 2023 (print) |
    LCC PR6111.A936 (ebook) | DDC 823/.92—dc23/eng/20220824
LC record available at https://lccn.loc.gov/2022038301
LC ebook record available at https://lccn.loc.gov/2022038302

Vintage Books Trade Paperback ISBN: 978-0-593-47005-3
eBook ISBN: 978-0-593-47006-0

Book design by Nicholas Alguire

vintagebooks.com

Printed in the United States of America
10 9 8 7 6 5 4 3 2 1

For everyone I've ever had a crush on.
Thanks for all the material.

Wild Things

CHAPTER ONE

I look down at my phone and watch with relief as the ticks turn blue. She's typing. In the moments before her reply appears, I reflect on how profoundly tragic it is to be seeking company on WhatsApp in this situation. Truly a dark moment, even for me.

I've forgotten to switch my phone to silent mode and cringe at the loud message alert tone. I don't know the etiquette in this situation—perhaps it is like being at the cinema? No one appears to notice the disturbance.

What do you mean you feel like a spare part?! Just get involved! Put yourself out there!

I glance up briefly at the scene unfolding in front of me and then back at my phone. That's easy for her to say. Ray is an extrovert. She loves getting involved. I've never really been a "group activity" kind of gal.

I literally am a spare part, Ray. It was fine at first but then I just sort of became surplus to requirement.

So what are you doing?

Messaging you! I'm just . . . watching?

Oh god, El! I mean cool if that's what you're into.

I'm not into it! I don't want to just watch. I wanted to get involved. This is my wild year! I'm being wild!

I place my phone down on the desk at which I'm sitting, a statement which, under the circumstances, feels very bleak indeed. I notice a framed, faded photograph of a man crouching down, his arms wrapped around both a golden retriever and a child wearing a pair of shorts and an enormous sun hat. I turn it facedown. The respectful thing to do. No father or golden retriever should see their child doing this.

I glance back at the couple on the bed and sigh. It would perhaps be better if they were fucking. Doing something obscene. But they're doing only what I can horrifyingly describe as *making love.*

How did I find myself here—silently observing a couple of strangers having sex from the comfort of an ergonomic office chair? Well, it's the fourth month of my Wild Year, a self-inflicted challenge born out of a drunken New Year's Eve fifteen long weeks ago. It's the resolution that just keeps on giving.

"I'm stuck in a rut," I'd said at Ray's house party, flinging my arm in the air hopelessly, wine sloshing out of the top of the bottle I was holding. The four of us—Ray, Jamie, Will, and I—were in the garden getting some fresh air (smoking) and a much-needed break from the people inside. I honestly don't know why we ever bother inviting anyone else, it always ends

up just us, willing them all to go home. I was especially grateful for the break from the chatter inside that night. I had been
starting to feel like the only person in the room who didn't have
something exciting to contribute to the conversation—a fabulous professional achievement, a baby, a sordid affair, a divorce
even. Oh, to be a glamorous divorcée! But no, I had nothing.

"Don't be so dramatic, El," Jamie said. He could talk. He'd
borrowed someone's faux fur coat to wear into the garden as
well as a pair of stilettos that he couldn't walk in. I'd heard him
announce only moments ago that he was going to "literally die"
if the rumor that we were running low on ice turned out to be
true.

"I can't believe that's another year of my life gone," I carried
on, ignoring him. "Everything stays the same. I dated Greg for a
hundred years. I feel like I've been doing this job I fucking hate
since birth. I've lived in that flat for three years now and every
single day I want to throw myself out the window."

I'd taken a clumsy drag on a badly rolled cigarette and
coughed dramatically. Ray rolled her eyes at me and took it
from my hand, shaking her lighter and relighting it. I know
smoking is very bad, not cool in any way, but the way Ray does
it—sorry, she should be on adverts, everyone would be taking
it up.

"Well, you do live on the ground floor, El, so . . . ," Ray said,
blowing smoke into the night air.

I saw Ray lock eyes with Jamie and exchange a look, the
briefest flicker of a smile.

"I'm being serious," I said. "This is what I do! This is my life!
Just the same, always, always the same. I never do anything different or interesting or, or . . . brave!"

It was partly incoherent, drunken rambling, but it came

from somewhere real and deep and guttural. This feeling of utter stagnation so intense sometimes I'd wake up in the night gripped with it, seized by panic.

"You broke up with Greg," Will said, dropping his own cigarette end to the ground and squashing it under his foot. "That was brave."

I don't think sweet Will would know bravery if it slapped him in the face. As we spoke, he popped a piece of chewing gum in his mouth so his girlfriend wouldn't know he'd been smoking.

"It wasn't brave to break up with Greg," I said.

It really wasn't. It didn't feel brave in any way. It felt essential. Vital to being able to go on living. Like shedding the weight of the world. Sorry, Greg.

I was drunk enough in that moment that I nearly said what I really thought would be brave. The reason I feel like a coward most of the time. It was on the tip of my tongue. But I chickened out of course. Thankfully, I suppose. Or unfortunately. I can never decide. Instead I said:

"I'm going to do something about it next year."

I poured white wine confidently and generously into my mouth directly from the bottle as the others cried out in indignation. In hindsight, I don't believe it was mine.

"I have to do something that scares me every day, something brave, something *wild*. Wait," I said, screwing up my face, reworking the math, "not every day, every month. I mean month, obviously."

Ray laughed in my face, taking the bottle from me to pour the dregs into her glass.

"El, you couldn't even *think* of twelve wild things," she said, "let alone do them." She didn't mean it unkindly, she said it as a matter of fact—as surely as she knew the sky was blue she knew that Eleanor Evans was not a wild woman.

It felt like a punch to my stomach. The wine threatened to make a reappearance. Is that really what she thought of me?

"I can," I said indignantly, looking around at the others. "I can think of loads of wild things. I can be wild, don't you think?"

Will squinted and looked into the distance, like he was concentrating on something far away and couldn't hear me.

"Babe," Jamie said, "earlier you told me that you'd been doing a lot of research into memory foam pillows because 'it's not a decision to be taken lightly.'"

"That's just good sense," I said. "You only get one neck, Jamie."

"El," Ray said, "you're fine just as you are. You don't need to do anything differently. We like you like this—healthy necked and sensible."

It is deeply humbling to be described by someone you fancy as "healthy necked" but on that night it only added fuel to the fire.

"No, Ray," I said, "I'm not fine as I am. I know there's a better version inside, a wilder, more exciting one. I'm going to show you."

"Yeah?" Ray said, looking at me in that maddening way, that twinkle in her eye, that cockiness.

I hate myself for it, but it just does something to me. Instead of grabbing her and kissing her, which is what I wanted to do, I reached out and poked her in the side with my index finger. Nursery school flirting. She didn't respond at all, probably because she is twenty-eight, not six.

"OK," she said, and held out her hand.

I took it and we shook.

"A year of wild things. Really wild though, El. I'm going to hold you to it. Proper out-of-your-comfort-zone stuff."

I nodded as I watched her fingers slip from mine. The way she looked at me, amused, with pity almost, and then up at Jamie to share a knowing glance. She didn't think I could do it. The concept cemented in my mind.

I have never wanted to prove someone wrong so badly.

I'd like to say I was overflowing with ideas for my new adventures but, actually, my immediate thought was of the new notebook I would treat myself to so I could journal my progress, perhaps a new pen. Highlighters, even. The thrill of new stationery! Yes, this was definitely something I could get into.

So now here I am. After a minute or two longer of waiting to be subbed in, I admit defeat, get up from the desk chair, and start pulling on my jeans. I wonder if this will remind the couple that I'm here, that I've been here the whole time. That I'm the person they took out for drinks. The person they kissed in the back of an Uber. That they took these jeans off in the first place. They remain oblivious to my existence.

I catch a glimpse of myself in the mirror leaning up against the wall. Jeans undone, black lace bra chosen especially for other people to look at, my freshly cut hair disappointingly unruffled. There is a flush of red on my chest, my internal discomfort making itself known. I take a couple of deep breaths and press the back of my hand to my chest, trying to cool it down. I give my reflection a grim smile. It's going to be a good story at least. Well, a story.

Once I've pulled my T-shirt back on and ordered an Uber, I hover by the bedroom door. I'd love to just walk out, but I am physically incapable of leaving any social situation without first profusely thanking the hosts for their hospitality.

"Um, I'm just going to . . . I'm heading off. Thank you so much for having me, um, well not *having* me but, um, your flat is lovely. Very"—I run my hand over the doorframe as though I might be admiring the timberwork—"sturdy."

I hardly recognize my own voice; for some reason I'm speaking in a sort of reverent, hushed tone like a librarian.

They both turn their heads, one on top of the other.

"No," the girl says with no conviction whatsoever. "You should stay."

"Yeah, stay," the man says.

"Oh, no. I have . . . some work to do. So good to meet you though!"

I run out of the flat and onto the street. The door slams behind me, and I burst out laughing. A passing dog walker glares at me, but I don't care. I'm free. My heart is racing. I'm relieved at the laughter; I feel dangerously close to crying. It could have gone either way.

It's a long way from the couple's flat in Barnes to my own in Leyton—£55-in-an-Uber long. I check that I have enough money in my account. I do, just. Luckily, I transferred all my "savings" into my current account at the beginning of the week. That £134, the total of my assets, has now disappeared with nothing to show for it but the memory of a couple of great Pret sandwiches and the beginnings of a savage hangover.

I clutch my phone in case it turns out I need to play one of those TikToks that makes it seem like your burly boyfriend is waiting for you at home, but I don't look at it, as I'll get carsick. The driver appears as relieved as I am that I'm not going to be chatty and that he can listen to talk radio in peace and so, after a few minutes of not being murdered by him, I decide to take the risk and close my eyes. I rest my head against the window and let it vibrate against my skull.

My Wild Year has not been a great success so far, if I'm being honest. I am starting to think there is a reason that up until the age of thirty I had not spent my time doing wild things, but I'm in too deep now. The idea of Ray patting my hand gently, telling me it's OK that I failed, that maybe I could take up a different challenge—sewing or sudoku or something—is too much to bear. I want it to be like the ending of *Grease*, my own Bad Sandy moment, in which Ray sees me and practically falls over in shock at how sexy and cool I am. Yes, Ray is John Travolta in this scenario. Don't think about it too much.

To be fair, it was hard to be wild in January, when this all began. It was cold, and the daylight hours are so short. There's no real time for it. I got drunk on tequila on a Wednesday night and was so violently ill the next day that I had to call in sick for work. After that I decided that I could only really afford to be wild on the weekends.

In February I got a tattoo of a butterfly on my left hip. It is very delicate and tiny, and in truth, I quite enjoyed the experience. Going to get a tattoo is much like going to the dentist, only with far more forms to fill in. I'd taken a deep breath just before the woman began, prepared to feel what others had described as "broken glass being dragged across your skin," but as I felt the first scratch, I was pleasantly surprised. It was methodical, sharp. When she finished after just a few minutes, I was almost disappointed. I left the shop with strict instructions to buy diaper rash cream and felt distinctly unwild.

In March I tried MDMA for the first time. The first time I have taken illegal drugs of any kind. I split a pill with Ray and felt like I was the conductor for all the electricity in the world. Like every part of my body was more receptive to touch and sound and light than anyone else's had ever been. My shoulders relaxed for the first time in my life. I felt free of myself, my overworking brain, my tired muscles. The freedom lasted for about five hours, after which I felt crushing, and I mean *crushing* sadness. Anxious thoughts and made-up memories roaring through my body like flames. I am grateful for that brief window of wildness, although I am not interested in revisiting it.

So here we are. The end of April. The month of the threesome, something I have always wondered about when I'm alone. Something I previously thought could be fun and exciting. Something that other people do, exciting people. Tonight was the first date I've ever been on with two people. "Looking for a third," they'd said. Well, that could not have been more accurate. I've never felt more like the third wheel in my life.

When I get home, I struggle to open my bedroom door. I jiggle it about and realize there is something heavy directly behind it. When the door eventually gives way enough for me to squeeze through, I see that the offending object is an enormous tent. My brother, Rob, must have dropped it off while I was out, and instead of coping with it in our hallway for a few hours, my roommate, Amelia, has dumped it in my tiny bedroom, so there is now not enough room for me to fully open my door or indeed get into bed. I gather the tent up in my arms and chuck it onto the bed. I bundle it up so that it fits on the left-hand side up against the wall. Turns out I will be sharing my bed tonight after all.

I make as much noise as I possibly can in the bathroom, hoping that Amelia is sitting in her much larger, much nicer room, boiling with rage. This is technically Amelia's flat, or, more accurately, it's Amelia's parents' flat. They bought it for her, but part of the deal is that she has to pay the mortgage, which necessitates her having a flatmate. She feels that this is deeply unjust. Since she can't punish her parents for it because presumably they'll evict her or take away her pocket money, she punishes me by being unbelievably passive-aggressive or, in Ray's words, "a little bitch."

I pull on some fresh pajamas and climb into bed next to my tent boyfriend. I give it a little kick to try to make some more space, but it springs back, bulkier than ever. I hate it already.

I am not the sort of person who likes to be outside. A brisk walk between tube stops, yes. A cocktail at a sidewalk café on a sunny day, sure. But I have never found trees and fields and exposure to the elements to be as restorative as other people claim to find them. In fact, if anything, I find the outdoors stressful. All those bugs, the wind, miles and miles of nothingness. Blisters. Lukewarm bottles of water. No Wi-Fi.

This weekend I am going camping. Because of a girl.

Ray is not just any girl though; she is *the* girl. She's been my closest friend since we met—day one of our internship at the newspaper we both still work at. We were sitting in a sweaty conference room in an open-plan office, the glass walls adding to the feeling that all of us were on display to the rest of the company. That was before the budget cuts, when they moved us to a smaller, grungier office with no air-conditioning and the lingering smell of a thousand different microwaved lunches.

"Which one are you?" Ray had whispered to me.

I frowned, and Ray pointed at the handout we'd been given detailing the company's extensive diversity program, of which we were both now a part.

"Ah." I picked up my pen and, after a moment's hesitation,

circled the *B* in the LGBTQ section. I'd squirmed a bit in doing so. I don't particularly like labels, but I quickly realized that being here meant that we were our labels first and foremost.

I passed Ray the pen to do the same. She grinned and circled *L* and then drew an arrow to the bit where it read "working class."

She pointed at herself and mouthed, "Common." She has a London accent, but at that moment I couldn't place exactly where she was from. Later, I learned it's South East, where her family still lives.

I grinned.

"Any questions can be asked at the end. OK?" the blond woman at the front giving the induction said loudly and pointedly in our direction.

We both nodded, biting our lips to stop ourselves from laughing.

I watched Ray while we all sat back for an inspirational talk from a former intern who had now worked his way up to an entry-level position. He kept calling us all "guys" and was sweating profusely.

Ray had short blond hair, all wavy and long on the top, which meant she had to push it out of her eyes every few minutes. She had piercings in mismatched places all the way up her ears and a smattering of freckles across her nose. She was wearing a white shirt tucked into jeans, and she had rings on some of her fingers. Plain gold bands. None of them, I noticed, on her ring finger. That pleased me for some reason and was, looking back, the beginning of the end for me and my then boyfriend, Greg. Poor Greg.

Ray's name tag, printed out with the company logo emblazoned on it, read "Ramona," and I had called her Ramona all day until we'd been standing outside the building chatting, about to head home.

"Do you fancy going for a drink?" I'd said, not ready to leave Ray yet, wanting to stretch out our time together for as long as possible. "I feel like I need to decompress after that."

"Sure," Ray said. She was so distracted trying to unpin her name tag, she pulled a thread from her shirt and twisted it around in her fingers.

"Ramona," I said, "it's a lovely name."

"I don't think that anyone has called me Ramona since I was about five years old," Ray said, smiling. "Apart from maybe my nan."

"Oh! Shit, sorry."

"How would you have known? I've had it stamped on my chest all day."

I found myself looking at the place where the name tag had been. I just knew I'd gone pink.

"Everyone calls me Ray," she said.

"That's lovely too."

Ray had looked up and flashed me a smile, and from that moment I was hooked.

Now, in the afterglow of the threesome that wasn't, I lie on my back, my arms on my pillow above my head, and sigh. I hope to hear Amelia up and about, disturbed, but our flat is silent apart from the hum of the fridge, which always sounds like it's right on the verge of exploding. The people in the flat upstairs are playing Lithuanian power ballads, but it's not so bad. At this point I'm so used to it that it's essentially white noise.

Before I switch off the light, I pick up the journal next to my bed, where I've been keeping track of my Wild Year. Next to April I write *Threesome month!* and in the "Notes" column I write, *Underwhelming. Did not actually have sex, which I believe is usually considered essential to the full threesome experience. I did kiss two people in one evening though. Quite wild, actually. Good work overall. 6/10.*

I read it back and then add, *Would not repeat.*

CHAPTER TWO

I have worked at the newspaper for almost four years. Five if you count the internship, which actually I should because that was the year I worked the hardest, believing that if I barely slept and proved myself to be tenacious and ruthless in my pursuit of groundbreaking stories, then I would rise high up the intern ranks and straight into a reporter role. I even thought I might be an editor by now.

I screenshot the recipe I've been reading on my phone and glance back up at my computer screen. My eyes blur taking in the spreadsheet in front of me, a roster filled with different blocks of color denoting time zones, people's holidays, shift patterns. I have been working as an administrator for the newsroom ever since I left the internship. When the job came up, I was encouraged to go for it because I was "so organized" and "always had solutions," so I did. I always saw it as a foot in the door. It was just a matter of time before I was working as a journalist again. Well, the door has stayed firmly closed on my foot. Absolutely no movement there. I know that I am lucky to have survived budget cuts (although my salary has remained the same for the past three years), so I remind myself to be grateful. I tell myself how exciting it is to be in such close proximity to the action. And I spend a decent proportion of my day staring out the window, which, you know, is a nice way to spend my time, in the grand scheme of things.

"Got any plans for the weekend, Eleanor?"

I jump. Despite wearing huge Doc Martens, Mona, the terrifying Frenchwoman in charge of all the administrators in the building, always manages to sneak up on me. I have no idea where her desk is or if she has an office or if she is even based on this floor. I don't even know if she works full-time. She just appears like magic when I least expect it and frightens the life out of me.

"Oh," I say. "Um, no. Nothing special at the moment. Maybe camping."

I don't know why I said maybe. We are, unfortunately, definitely going camping. While I'm talking, I slowly pull the hood of my sweatshirt down from my head. I try to do it subtly, as if I'm adjusting my hair. I realize that sitting at my desk with my hood up is probably not very professional, but it's not my fault the office is freezing cold; it's like working in an igloo. I keep this hoodie under my desk, an upgrade from my previous "work cardigan"—essentially a giant gray blanket—which I eventually retired after people kept asking me if I was OK.

"Camping?" Mona says, her eyes lighting up.

Oh no. Of course she loves camping, she strikes me as the kind of person who enjoys recreational torture.

"Do you like camping, Eleanor?"

"No. Um, I like"—I gesture around me at the fluorescent light above my head, the empty can of Diet Coke in front of me—"the indoors."

Mona glares at me and shakes her head, her thin eyebrows disappearing under the front of her bowl cut.

"Eleanor Evans, spending time doing the things you enjoy is very important," she says, frowning. "You have to have something to look forward to or how will you ever cheer up?"

"I don't need cheering—"

"You're just always so sad," she says. "It would be nice to see a smile on your face. Good for morale."

This is very fucking rich coming from Mona, who walks around the office waiting to chastise people, dressed like an army sergeant. I don't think I've ever seen her so much as smirk.

I plaster a huge sarcastic smile on my face, which seems to be good enough for her. She nods seriously and glides away to silently accost her next victim. I know I'll see her again only when I'm at my most weak and defenseless. Probably when I'm staring out the window wishing I was one of the pigeons on the street below—eating chips off the pavement, fighting—really living.

A reminder crops up in the corner of my screen announcing that I have a "weekly admin audit" coming up in ten minutes. I've had this meeting, a block of two hours every Thursday morning, in my work calendar for years, and no one has ever asked me what an "admin audit" is. I'm not sure I'd know what to say if they did.

I take a notebook, a pen, and a highlighter as well as my

phone, which I frown at as if I am receiving an urgent email even as I move just a single inch from my desk. This would actually be impossible because despite company encouragement, I refuse to set up work emails on my phone. My phone is my respite from the tedium; I do not need Gareth from payroll sending me emails with PLEASE READ in the subject line. Or worse, when he means something is very serious or pressing, he changes the font color to red. Dire.

I push my chair in without saying a word to anyone around me. They don't look up from their screens anyway.

Instead of turning left toward the row of meeting rooms, I turn right, go through the barrier, and let myself out of the building and onto the street. Across the road, waiting for me, are Ray and Jamie.

Jamie was a diversity intern too. That's how Ray and I met him. He'd looked lost at lunchtime, and so we'd trundled off to Pret together and have pretty much been trundling off to Pret together ever since. Jamie describes himself as a diversity triple threat—mixed race (his mum is first-generation Thai, born in Australia. She met his dad, and they moved here before Jamie was born. He will never forgive them for raising him in Manchester and not Bondi Beach), gay, and anxious. Ray says he is a quadruple threat because he is also a massive pain in the arse. I don't think he's a pain in the arse, not really. Just sometimes *quite a lot*. And sometimes, although she'd never admit it, so is Ray. We started off just tolerating him tagging along with us but ended up loving him the way you love a little brother. We're very protective of him. A man in a shiny suit once deliberately stood on Jamie's foot in Pret, so Ray threw the man's tuna baguette out onto the street.

"I love that you wear that round your neck," Ray says when

I reach them. She grabs the ID pass on my lanyard and pulls slightly, so I'm forced to step closer to her.

"It means I don't lose it twenty times a week, like you," I say, batting her hand away.

"Come on," Jamie says, glancing nervously at the building as though it might suddenly spot us and set off some sort of truant alarm. "Let's get out of here."

We hurry along the street and walk to our chosen "audit" spot, which is just far away enough to guarantee we won't bump into our colleagues. We stop when we reach the Scandinavian café that serves the biggest cinnamon buns and the bitterest coffee. The staff are outrageously rude, which we have chosen to find charming.

Once we've ordered and taken our usual table right at the back, next to the stock cupboard and the "staff only" door, Jamie puts his hands on the table and says, "There's only one thing I want to talk about."

I roll my eyes, sensing what's coming. I look at Ray, and she grins, confirming she's already told him. Ray and Jamie are both copy editors and sit next to each other on the floor above me, so are able to gossip about me to their heart's content.

"What do you mean?" I say, just as the waitress comes over.

She slams the cups down on the table so hard that coffee spills over the edges. Jamie's cinnamon bun slides off his plate, but he has perfected the art of catching it just in time.

We all thank her profusely, and she stalks off, scowling.

"You know exactly what we mean," Ray says, picking up her coffee and wrapping her hands around the mug. I watch her hands intently. You know you have a big stupid crush on someone when you have, at times, wished that you were the inanimate object they are holding. It's relentlessly humiliating.

"It was ridiculous," I say. "Honestly, there is basically nothing to report. When we got back to theirs, I think they realized they were very into the *idea* of me being there but not particularly sure about the reality. Nor was I, to be honest."

"Hmmm," Jamie says, taking a big bite of his cinnamon bun and then continuing to talk with his mouth full, "does it really count as being wild, then?"

"It does count, I think," Ray says. "Because the intention was there."

"It counts because I went on a date with two people! I kissed two people in one night!"

They both smile at me kindly.

"Right," Ray says, glancing at Jamie and giving him a look that says, *Bless her.* "And because you kissed two people."

I roll my eyes and take a sip of my scalding-hot coffee. As usual, it is disgusting. It's so strong that I know I'll be having heart palpitations for the rest of the day. I stir in a spoonful of sugar in an attempt to make it more palatable.

"So what's the next wild thing?" Jamie says. "May's wild thing?"

I shake my head.

"Not sure yet. No tattoos. No drugs. No sex."

"You're not going to have sex in May?" Ray says, looking up from her phone, a smile playing on her lips.

"No," I say haughtily, refusing to look at her.

"You'll think of something," Jamie says. "I mean thinking long and hard about the wild thing is half the wildness anyway. Being wild is all in the planning."

I kick his foot under the table. He blows me a kiss.

"Anyway," I say. "I don't want to talk about being wild. I need a break from it."

I blow over the top of my coffee.

"Tell me what's going on with you two."

Jamie sighs heavily. He picks up the tiny spoon in the bowl of brown sugar in front of us and drags a line through the middle of it.

"Don't judge me, OK? I went for a drink with Dale last night."

Dale is Jamie's ex-boyfriend. They were together for a year, and I swear in that whole year I did not hear Dale string an entire sentence together.

Ray and I both groan.

"Jamie," Ray says. "No."

"Yeah," Jamie says, "I know. It's just . . . it's so *bleak* out there. And Dale was really nice, wasn't he?"

"He was nice," I say. "But also, Jamie, and this is important, he was very boring."

Ray nods vehemently in agreement. "He was absolutely dead," Ray says. "Just nothing going on in there whatsoever."

Jamie smiles, but it doesn't quite reach his eyes. "I'm just so tired though. I hate dating. I hate the people I meet on apps. I hate the apps themselves. It's all so nasty, especially if you don't fit into this really particular bracket of like—muscular and masculine and *white*. And you know, Dale would marry me tomorrow if I wanted him to. And it sounds pathetic, but that is what I want." He sighs. "Not to marry Dale necessarily, but I want to be settled. And he would settle with me."

"Jamie! Obviously he would marry you tomorrow," I say. "Because you're a solid ten. And he'd do well to lock you down."

"If I'm a ten," Jamie says, "then why does no one else want to marry me?"

I glance at Ray, and she just raises her eyebrows at me. I'm on my own with this one.

"You just haven't met the right person yet."

I hate to say it, because it sounds so empty, even though I really mean it. When people say it to me, I always want to give them a little kick on the shin.

"Well, maybe I have and maybe it's Dale. He owns his own flat in Sydenham. It's got a garden."

Ray and I nod. He has a point. The flat and the garden are probably Dale's most enticing attributes. They make him about 50 percent more attractive.

We're all quiet for a moment, chewing and listening to the sound of the waitress scolding someone in Swedish. It still sounds quite nice, all singsong, even though she's clearly furious.

"What about you?" I say to Ray. "Anything to add to the meeting agenda?"

Ray shrugs. "Oh, you know, I've just been babysitting Will."

I grimace.

Ray first suggested this weekend's camping trip as a way to cheer up our friend Will, her housemate, whose grandmother died and then his girlfriend dumped him, all in the same weekend.

To be fair, his girlfriend had said she didn't know his grandmother was going to die. And she'd had it planned for ages.

This was not of much comfort to Will. In fact, it was so devastating knowing not only that she didn't want to be with him but that she also didn't want to be with him so badly and for such a long time that even a dead grandmother wasn't going to stand in her way, that Will had decided that his room contained "too many memories of her" and set up camp on the sofa, which he has not left since. So the truth was that while our upcoming camping trip is absolutely about cheering up Will, it is mostly about removing him from Ray's living room.

"How's he doing?"

"Not great," Ray says. "He just keeps watching *Legally Blonde* and crying. I don't think he's eaten anything apart from Maltesers since the breakup. And not little bags, the boxes of them that you get at Christmastime. It's quite weird because as far as I know he's not been outside. So where are they coming from?"

"It's quite gratifying, really, isn't it?" Jamie says.

"What? Will killing himself slowly with Maltesers?" I say.

"Yeah! Well, no, I obviously hate Will being sad, but it's quite nice that it's him going through it for a change instead of one of us. He and Melissa were always so . . ."

"Smug," Ray says just as I'm saying, "full of themselves."

Will and Melissa were one of those couples who, despite only having been together a couple of years, behaved as though they'd been married for forty and treated everybody else accordingly, by which I mean with deep condescension. From the outside it had seemed like everything was perfect. In reality, Will had been desperate to move in with Melissa for the past year but she refused to move out of her parents' home in Hertfordshire. She believed renting to be a "total waste of money" so had stayed put, saving for a deposit while Will continued to "throw his money down the drain" in the damp terrace in Stratford that he shares with Ray and their absent housemate, Thea, whose boyfriend won't let her move in but will let her sleep over seven nights a week.

"It'll do him good to get away," I say. "Get some country air. Do some bracing walks."

"It will do me good to get him away," Ray says. "He's driving me mad."

"Have you seen much of Kirsty recently?" I ask. I dig my

fingernails into the palms of my hands. A neat, sharp pain
to distract from the emotional torture I am about to subject
myself to.

"Yeah, I've actually stayed at hers a few nights just to get
away from Will." She pauses. "That sounds bad. I mean, I've
always cracked a window, made sure he has access to plenty of
clean water."

I smile weakly.

"So are you sort of . . . back on?" I ask. I can't bear to look at
Jamie. He knows how I feel about Ray. I confessed to him once
when we were both drunk about three years ago. He has, on
multiple occasions, described me as "gay for Ray" despite how
many times I've asked him to stop.

Ray shrugs.

"I mean we're not on, we're not off. You know what it's like."

I make a noncommittal sound as if I'm not particularly
interested in her love life, as if I didn't just specifically ask.

Kirsty and Ray have been on and off for a long time now.
At least a year, perhaps even longer than that. It started off as
a casual thing, got a bit serious, ended, and then sort of half-
heartedly started back up again with neither of them defining
the terms. Kirsty has never been anything but lovely to me,
which sort of makes everything worse, it makes it much harder
to dislike her, though I do try. I see myself so painfully clearly
in her. She is deeply in love with Ray, and Ray is maddeningly
casual about her. As though she simply has no idea what effect
she has on people. Or chooses not to know.

We make our way back to the office and go back inside a
couple of minutes apart from each other as if anyone is actually paying attention to what we're doing. Reggie, the security
guard, rolls his eyes at me when I walk back in. As I approach

my desk, I hold my phone up to my ear and say, "Yes, yes, fine. OK," in a harried voice and then hang up and sigh heavily. I log back in to my computer and start typing ostentatiously so that everyone on the entire floor knows that I'm at my desk. I fire off a couple of pointless emails with very important people cc'd in to make a point of how present I am today, and then, checking the time on my watch, I grab my jacket and head out for my lunch break.

Late in the afternoon, just as I'm wondering if I can get away with logging off for the day, one of the senior editors asks that I print off his daughter's school project. It is 120 pages long. She wants it in color.

The editor winks at me when he asks, which makes me want to vomit. I smile tightly instead of answering, and nod. We're not allowed to discuss salaries here, but everyone is quite literally paid to be professional nosey parkers, so we all know how much everyone makes. I happen to know this particular senior editor will make more this month than I will make in the next four, maybe even five. He has a printer at home is what I'm saying. He probably has a computer suite. An entire library.

The copier room is in the basement. I descend the flight of stairs and push the door open. There's a keypad on it which hasn't worked since we arrived but it's enough to put most people off bothering to come down. I pretty much always have the place to myself. One of the fluorescent lights flickers on when I press the switch; the rest remain off. It's hard to report the broken lights to maintenance because they're not actually consistently broken. They switch on and off at will. They do their own thing down here. It's not my business.

I swipe my card over the printer and lean against the wall next to it, closing my eyes briefly, listening to the whirring. When I open them, I see that someone is pushing open the door. I assume it's going to be one of the other admin assistants and get ready with my knowing smile, prepared to roll my eyes at their stories of whoever's being the biggest dick to them today. There are a lot of senior people here who think they're extremely important and are therefore above things like basic manners and respect.

My heart leaps when I see that it's Ray.

"Well," she says, smiling at me, "fancy seeing you down here."

"I live down here," I say. "You know that. I'm the office troll."

"Do I need to answer your riddles in order to get something printed?"

"For you?" I say. "No riddles."

Ray smiles and swipes her card over the black-and-white printer. She rests one hand on the top of it, as if testing if she could lean her whole weight on it, before turning to me and grinning.

"Train ticket," she says, "in case I lose my phone."

I laugh, but I'm actually impressed. This kind of foresight is rare. Ray loses her phone all the time, which is even more stressful nowadays since it's her bank card, her Oyster, her ticket to everything.

"Very smart," I say.

She taps the side of her head. "Not just a pretty face, my friend."

She picks up her piece of paper and comes to lean against the wall beside me.

"You all right today, El?" she says.

"Oh, you know." I gesture around myself. At the crumbling

walls of this damp basement where I am doing secretarial work
for a twelve-year-old.

"It is what it is," I say.

Ray sighs and puts her arm around my shoulders. She
squeezes gently, pulling me closer to her.

I wait a moment. I have long perfected the performance of
being unmoved by Ray's charm. After a couple of beats I let
myself relax into her. I briefly rest my head on her shoulder and
take a deep breath. Ray smells like the same scent she's worn
every day since we met. It's full of notes of ridiculous things
that it doesn't really smell like—leather and tobacco and for-
ests. I bought it for her once, and the sales assistant asked if it
was a gift for my boyfriend. I looked her right in the eye and
said no, it was for a woman.

"Oh, sorry," the sales assistant said, "your girlfriend."

I hadn't corrected her.

"It's fine," I say, pulling away before she does. I always do
that. As if to prove that I care less. That it's nothing when she
touches me.

"Just think," Ray says, pulling her phone out of her pocket
and frowning slightly, "we'll be at one with nature tomorrow.
And there's even meant to be some sun."

I want to look at her phone. To see what made her frown. I
just know that it's from Kirsty.

"I want to be at one with a bottle of wine," I say.

Ray laughs and stands up straight, putting her phone back
into her pocket and making a move to go. As she does, the one
working fluorescent light flickers again and then switches off
entirely, plunging us into darkness.

This happens pretty regularly but still never stops being
part alarming, part totally thrilling. Like when someone leans

on the light switch in assembly in primary school. My primal urge is to scream, delightedly.

"Oh shit!" Ray grabs the top of my arm as if to steady herself. I turn to face her. We're so close. I can feel my heartbeat in my ears. Sometimes, I'm sure she must feel the electric current between us too. I don't know how it can just be me, crackling with it, all by myself.

"It's happened before," I say, whispering as if the light can hear me.

Ray's grip has loosened slightly, but her fingers are still digging into my skin.

"You usually just have to wait a—"

As if by magic, the light above our heads flickers back on.

She grins at me and squeezes my arm gently before letting it go.

"It's spooky down here, El. Don't hang out for too long moping about."

"I won't," I say, fully intending to do just that.

"See you later!" she says, bounding up the stairs and out of sight.

"See you," I say, as the door slams shut behind her.

Once she's gone, I turn to face the wall and bang my forehead against the cracked plaster. Not enough to hurt. Maybe just enough to knock some sense into it. Five years and she is still making my heart race. Will I ever get a grip?

CHAPTER THREE

I'm having dinner with my brother, Rob, and his girlfriend, Polly. I chose to live in Amelia's flat partly because it's not too far from theirs and it means I can spend a lot of time being their third wheel. They've chosen the restaurant, a tiny place on Broadway Market that does small plates of vegetables cooked in complicated ways and cloudy wines with sediment in them. I always roll my eyes when Rob tells me where we're going, but I secretly love it. The food is delicious and wine is wine at the end of the day, plus Rob always pays.

When I arrive, slightly sweaty from the bus, they're already sitting at a tiny table outside the restaurant. The waiter drags up another chair for me. There's not really enough room, and the chair isn't the same as the ones they have. It's raised, almost like I'm in a high chair.

I kiss them both on the cheek and grab a cashew nut from the bowl on the table. It's got about six coatings to get through before I get to the actual nut, chili and honey and something else I can't quite identify. I am sure this one nut costs about five pounds. I hold it in my mouth and savor it.

"How have you been?" Polly says as she pours me a glass of wine.

Polly and Rob have been together for years, long before I moved to London, and no offense to Rob, but she is too good for him. She's got dark hair and green eyes and always looks healthy and glowing like she's just back from a beach holiday. However much exercise Rob does, or however much time he spends in the sun, he always looks a bit peaky. So do I. It's in the Evans genes.

"I'm good, thanks, how are you both?" I say, taking a sip of the wine. It tastes like strawberries and faintly of a farm, but in a good way.

They pause before answering; Polly glances at Rob, and she nods at him like, *You answer.*

"Oh, you know," Rob says, turning back to me, "same old, same old. We've been sorting out the spare room. Doing a bit of a clearout." He coughs slightly, as if the words are catching. "We're thinking of maybe turning it into an office at some point."

"Maybe," Polly says, concentrating on her wine, "or something. It just needed sorting; it's been left for way too long."

"Mm," I say, taking another nut and raising my eyebrows. "Fun!"

Polly looks up at me and laughs. She puts her head in her hands, and I notice when she looks back up that she looks tired.

"How did we get to a place where our news is that we're decorating an office?" she asks.

Rob shakes his head at her as if in disbelief, but he smiles. They're both so comfortable with each other, in their lives together, it makes me feel hopeful when I spend time with them that I might have that too one day—but also, if I'm honest, it makes me feel a little bit sick.

We talk about my upcoming camping trip; Rob gives me very strict instructions about the tent, which I forget immediately. The waiter brings over endless tiny plates until there is not even an inch of space left on the table. We have to transfer the wine onto the floor.

We move the conversation onto Mum and Dad, our favorite subject.

"Apparently they're going on a cruise," Rob says, rolling his eyes.

"What? Where?" I'm eating a tiny piece of cheese balanced on a tiny piece of bread. The bread is gray for some reason, but it tastes heavenly.

"All over, they're gone for four months apparently," Rob says. He glances at Polly, and she shakes her head despairingly.

"Bloody hell. I wonder when they were going to tell me."

I can't say I'm too shocked; they're always up to something.

"They were probably just planning to call you from Antarctica. They only told me because I rang them to check they were still alive, and Mum was all 'Ooh must dash, darling, I'm dropping Bernard off at his countryside retreat.'"

Bernard is Mum and Dad's long-suffering poodle-cross. They should have got a fun little dog that they could carry around with them on their stupid adventures. Bernard, much like Rob and me, is a bit of a disappointment to them. He's quite serious, he likes things to be in order, and he is distinctly unspontaneous. Whenever they jet off on one of their later-in-life gap years,

Bernard gets sent to a dog hotel in the countryside. I think he has a lovely time. Much more peaceful. I wouldn't mind going to a dog hotel myself now that I think about it.

"I'll text them later," I say. "Maybe ask them to confirm they haven't drowned once every few weeks."

"Ha," Rob says. "We'll get a postcard in a couple of months if we're lucky."

We can laugh about this now. At what sometimes feels like Mum and Dad's almost total indifference to us. It wasn't always very funny. They're great people, Mum and Dad. The life and soul of the party. My mum is a florist; she owns her own shop, and everyone knows her. She was born in Connecticut but moved here when she was eight years old. This small fact hasn't stopped her from retaining a subtle East Coast twang and telling everyone she's from New York City. My dad is a photographer; when he was younger, he traveled the world working for magazines, and now he does weddings. It suits him even better, I think. The receptions anyway—those late nights, the socializing.

They used to look at Rob and me, getting on with our schoolwork, requesting fruit and vegetables, coming home before our curfews, and wonder out loud what happened. How on earth they could have ended up with children so different to them. If it could really have been possible that they took two of the wrong babies home from the hospital.

"My little alien," my mum would say sometimes. "Where did you come from, eh? Dropped off from another planet onto my doorstep."

She'd stroke my hair as she said it, marveling at me. They loved us, it's not that I ever doubted that, but what they don't realize, and maybe never will, is that Rob and I are like this *because* of them. Cautious and risk averse and comfort seeking. We wanted them to visit our planet once in a while, or to meet us halfway at least.

When Rob met Polly, it was the moment his life really started: he opened up, and it felt like his world expanded. She loves his seriousness, his nerdiness. I panicked that he would leave me and our little team, but he never has. We've done Christmas just the three of us a few times now because Mum and Dad like to go on long-haul holidays to sunny places. Apparently, "it's so depressing in England at Christmas," even though that's where their beloved children are. I've even been invited to Polly's parents' house to spend the holidays with them once or twice.

When I feel sad about Mum and Dad, which I do sometimes, I try to feel sad *for them* instead. That they miss out on this, on us.

"So how's the Wild Year going, El?" Polly asks. She has been studying the dessert menu, though there are only two things on there—a gelato and a cheesecake—and I know that we'll end up ordering them both with three spoons.

"Erm," I pause, trying to think about whether I want to talk about the ins and outs, as it were. I decide best not and settle on a simple, "It's good!"

In January, when I told Rob and Polly I was planning to be wild for a year and showed them my notebook and color-coded system for categories of wildness and the ways they could be cross-referenced, they listened politely, smiling and nodding in all the right places. I could tell they didn't think it would last, but that's fine. I had nothing to prove to them. I mean, I love them, but these are people who have a special drawer for their thermal underwear and camping socks. Hardly the barometer for fun.

"Good," Polly says, smiling, "as long as you're enjoying yourself, that's all that matters."

If it were just the two of us, I'd probably tell her everything, but I'm pretty sure Rob would die if I told him about the failed threesome. Just immediately stop living.

I'm right, Rob does pay. He also hands me a tote bag as I'm heading off. It's filled with bits and pieces they've picked up in their new local deli. I squeeze them both extra tight and make a mental note to bring them something next time.

I decide to walk home. It's getting dark, but there are plenty of people still milling about, and it's a nice route through Clapton, past all the huge houses and through the park where people are cycling and jogging and slightly drunkenly walking home. It is one of those nights where London feels like the center of the world. I can't imagine that anyone lives anywhere else. I can't even imagine how there is anywhere else other than here.

Rob and I grew up in a small town in West Sussex. Mum commuted into Brighton, where her shop was, and my dad often got the train into London for meetings or to photograph corporate events. It felt like we were so close to everything, right on the edge of the action. I once saw where we grew up described as peaceful in an article about commuter towns. Peace is relative though, isn't it? I used to stare out my window over our garden, over our neighbor's identical garden and onto the street behind ours, and feel this deep sense of longing. Although I didn't know what I was longing for. Something bigger or better or more exciting. Somewhere I fitted in, or somewhere I didn't. Something that terrified me.

I still feel like I've been thrown out of my tank and into the ocean. The filthy, expensive ocean. Mostly I'm happy to be here though, kicking furiously, just trying to keep my head above the water.

Amelia's out when I get home, but I head straight for my room just in case she's on her way back. It's not possible once I hear the key in the lock to get out of the living room and to my bedroom fast enough to avoid seeing her. I know, I've tried.

I get into bed and rifle through my tote bag of treats from Rob and Polly. I unwrap a block of slightly soft white cheese and sniff it tentatively. The smell is appalling but in that morbidly intriguing way where you can't help but keep going back for more. My room will probably never smell of anything else but this cheese again. I dip the corner into the jar of chili jam, pausing for a brief moment before I take a bite as if I might not. As if I might go and get a plate and a knife, maybe a glass of water. A small amount of self-respect. I take a huge bite of the oozing cheese, rich and ripe on my tongue.

I pick up my phone to thank Rob again and see that I have a message from Ray.

What are you up to?

I wait a moment, taking another, smaller bite of cheese. I stick a finger into the jam jar as a chaser and lick it before wiping my hand down the front of my sweatshirt.

I'm sitting in bed, eating cheese dipped in jam.

Ray replies instantly.

Literally a sext. I'm jealous.

I can't help but smile stupidly, my mouth still full, my gums glued together. She is not flirting with me, I remind myself. She is flirting with cheese. If it was Jamie messaging me I'd send him a photo of myself with my cheeks stuffed like a hamster, but because it's Ray, I don't. I don't reply at all to allow for the air of mystery, for the possibility that she is actually thinking about me in bed and picturing me looking stunning, gorgeous. Sexy, even. I unwrap a packet of poppy seed crackers and put one in my mouth whole, letting it melt on my tongue slightly before crunching down. Some crumbs escape from my lips, tumbling down onto my bedsheets. I brush them onto the carpet. The people upstairs switch on their speakers, the bass vibrating through my ceiling. I roll onto my side, close my eyes, and listen to my neighbor singing along to a guitar solo. I wish Ray were here with me, laughing and singing and feeling sick from too much cheese. She'd come if I asked. But of course I don't. Because it wouldn't be the way I want it, the way it is in my head. It never is.

CHAPTER FOUR

"This is a good spot," Ray says, hands on her hips, surveying the patch of grass that is going to be our home for the next two nights. She is wearing denim shorts, a white vest top, and a red-and-white lumberjack shirt with the sleeves rolled up. She looks like she might go into the forest with an ax and start chopping wood at any moment. Something I would quite like to watch if I'm honest.

The "good spot" is actually the only spot left. The campsite Ray has booked, an hour from London on the train, is packed with families, screaming children, and loud groups of people unpacking cars full of enough furniture to re-create their entire homes in this field.

"Is it?" I say. I hold my phone up to the sky and close my eyes briefly, a silent prayer to the gods of mobile phone reception. Nothing.

"Eleanor, put your phone away."

She's only sort of joking. I know there's a note of seriousness whenever she full-names me.

"Everything you need," she says, gesturing at herself and then opening her arms out wide to include the field and, I suppose, perhaps, the toilet block, "is right here."

"Stop acting like you're so happy. I know you hate camping too," I say, begrudgingly putting my phone in my back pocket.

Ray likes to give the impression that she is an outdoorsy person. The truth is that she is even more impractical than me. Mice have her standing on chairs screaming. Rain messing with her hair has ruined entire nights out.

"I am happy!" she says. "Will's off the sofa. The sun is shining. Come on, El."

"I know, I'm sorry. I'm getting into it. I promise."

We spot the boys in the distance, heading toward us. We'd brought a couple of bottles of wine with us but as soon as we arrived, Will and Jamie left Ray and me to deal with the tent so they could walk the mile down the road to where Google Maps had promised a co-op. As we watch them now, they look like they're arriving at Glastonbury. Both have their arms wrapped around huge boxes of beer. Will even has a bottle of wine poking out of each jacket pocket.

When they reach us, they drop the cases of beer at our feet with an alarming clatter.

We greet them with the kind of enthusiasm one might reserve for Olympic gold medalists or war heroes.

"Yes, boys! You've done us proud!"

"Amazing job! You can relax now. It's over. It's over," I say as the boys drop to the ground, exhausted.

Jamie lies down flat on his back in the grass, a hand to his brow. He opens his mouth as if to speak but then closes it again, simply shaking his head.

Once they've recovered, we set up the disposable barbecue that we've brought with us and proceed to smoke out everyone within a twenty-meter radius. This works very well as a child repellent. No one dares come near.

We cook vegetarian sausages, which we eat in soft buns. Dry. No one had thought about condiments, only alcohol. We also attempt to cook corn on the cob; however, two hours in, it is still rock solid and cold. Fortunately, all of us had bought Percy Pig gummy sweets at the station, so for dessert, we put them on the barbecue as the embers are dying. Will perks up every time an ear slides off or an eye disappears into a little pink head. Disturbing, but nice to see him smile.

"Honestly, thank you," Will says as he takes a swig from a bottle of Malbec. None of us remembered to bring cups either. "I really appreciate this."

We're sitting in a semicircle on a "blanket" we've cobbled together out of jackets. We have two bottles of wine open that we're passing back and forth between us, and each of us has a warm beer, which we're taking occasional sips from. The sky is perfectly pink and orange—you couldn't ask for a better sunset—and I'm at that perfect level of drunk where I feel like nothing in the world could stress me out. The office is but a distant memory.

"Of course, mate," Ray says. "I'm glad you're enjoying yourself. You seem better for being out of the house."

"I am. I am." Will sighs. He looks tired. Will is one of those people who has always looked young for his age, something about him being so tall and skinny, but the past few weeks seem to have caught up with him. He has deep bags under his eyes and lines on his forehead when he frowns, which is often. He looks even thinner than usual, despite the Malteser habit.

"It knocked me for six," he says. "It's not just missing Mel and what we had. It's missing everything I thought we were going to have. I just thought that was my whole future. And now it's gone."

None of us really know what to say. Jamie passes Will the wine.

"We were going to buy a house. That's what we'd been saving for. I don't understand how she let us get so far into it if she was always going to . . . We found this big project—it's out in the countryside but near enough to London that we could commute. Nearish to the seaside. Close enough that we could drive there on weekends. I mean, it's a wreck, but it was going to be . . . to be . . ." Will swallows back tears. "It was going to be our wreck."

"I'm sorry, Will," I say. "It's so unfair. You didn't deserve this."

"Do you know what else is funny?" Will is completely grim-faced. "My nan. Which I'm upset about as well." He looks at us, and we all nod seriously to confirm that we understand how upset he is. He's clearly feeling guilty for crying more over Melissa than Beryl.

"My nan left me some money. Enough money to cover the entire deposit for the house. More than. So we could have used all of Melissa's money for the renovation. Or, like, pay for a really great . . . a really great . . . wedding."

His bottom lip wobbles.

"Will," Ray says. She puts her hand on his knee and squeezes it tightly. I know that knee squeeze. She's doing it partly to comfort him, partly to encourage him to get ahold of himself.

"If you love the house so much, then what's stopping you from buying it yourself?"

Will pauses, holding the wine bottle in midair, inches from his mouth. He frowns.

"I can't buy it by myself."

"Why?"

"Because, because . . ."

He reaches around for a reason and looks relieved when he manages to land on one.

"I can't get a mortgage for it with just my salary. It needs to be two of us. I don't earn enough."

Ray raises her eyebrows as if to say, *Fair enough.*

A naked toddler shoots past us tailed by a very stressed-looking man who is waving a towel at him.

"Or it could be four of us," Jamie says quietly as we watch the pair run into the distance.

"What?" Will says.

Jamie looks at him for a moment.

"Four of us could buy it," he repeats.

We all look at him like he's lost his mind, which I think he might have.

"Hear me out," Jamie says, sitting up a little bit straighter as the idea takes hold, placing his beer down on the ground. "It actually makes total sense if you think about it."

I look at Ray, expecting to exchange bewildered looks with her, but she's watching Jamie intently, her brow furrowed, picking at the label on her beer bottle.

"We all have decent jobs," he says.

I honk with involuntary laughter.

"We all have jobs," he corrects himself. "And we all earn some money. But also none of us have actually got any money. No savings. Nothing to show for it. At the end of the month it's zero, right?"

He looks around the group, and we all nod.

"Less than zero, actually," I say, "I'm always dipping into my overdraft."

I usually have to dip into my overdraft a few days after pay-day, so it would probably be more accurate to say that I live in my overdraft.

"Right," Jamie says. "So if we're all working these jobs where we don't earn any proper money and can't save any of it, then when will we ever be able to buy a house? When we meet a partner who has loads of money? If we win the lottery? I don't know about you, but I personally am going to inherit shit all when my parents die."

"Same," Ray says. "My parents don't own their house. Also they're, like, not even sixty, so, what? Even if they did own it I wouldn't stand to inherit anything until I'm like . . . seventy? I mean, I'd hope at least that," she says, clarifying, "obviously I hope they never die."

"Same," Jamie says quickly, "obviously."

"I mean, I think I might get half of my parents' house," I say. "Although they keep saying that they're going to sell it and travel the world. Their motto is 'You can't take it with you.'"

Rob and I have suggested a few times that although they can't take it with them, typically parents take some pleasure out of leaving some amount of money, if they're able to, to their children to give them a helping hand in these uncertain times. They always laugh like they've never heard anything so ridicu-lous. I mean, to be fair, I can't complain too much. If I called them now and told them I needed financial help, they'd lend me money. It just would never occur to them to offer.

"OK," Jamie says, "so, I think the answer is: we will never be able to buy a house. Or at least not until we're very old. But what if . . ."

Jamie looks around the group, I've never seen him so animated—I make a mental note to tell him he should go into motivational speaking—as he continues. "We find ourselves in a situation where one of us"—he jabs Will in the arm—"finally gets lucky."

"Well, my nan died," Will says, frowning, but Jamie carries on as if he hasn't heard him.

"And the rest of us are in a position to make it happen. What I'm saying is . . ." He pauses before the big reveal, even though we can all clearly see where this is going. "We club together. And buy the house."

"Like a commune," whispers Ray.

"What?" Jamie says.

"A commune, like . . . a queer commune."

Every single time there's one of those articles in the *Metro* about a small island for sale for a tenth of the price of a parking space in London, Ray sends it to me and Jamie in an email, often with the word *urgent* in the subject line, and suggests that we buy it and turn it into a commune.

"But also a straight commune," Will says, pointing at himself, and then on seeing Ray's face and hearing the words *straight commune* said out loud, says, "No, a queer commune, yes, you're right. Fine."

"Will, you're not actually thinking about this, are you?" I ask.

Even as I'm saying it, I can see that he is—and if I'm honest, so am I. One half of my brain is dismissing it as fantasy, but the other half is already packing up my room and waving goodbye to Amelia forever.

"I sort of am," he says. "I mean, would you lot really want to do it? It's a lot of work, and it's obviously not in London. Although it is only forty-five minutes on the train, so you can think of it as zone twenty-five."

"But are you sure you didn't just want to do it with Melissa?" I ask. "You don't think you're going to be sad that you're with us and not with her?"

"Honestly, no, I don't want to do this without Melissa," Will says. "But that isn't an option anymore. And I put so much time and effort into finding this house, and mentally, I feel like I'm already halfway there, you know? I was so ready for the change. I felt like I was on the brink of starting my new life, and now I've been dragged ten steps back."

"That's what I'm saying," Jamie says. "I'm ready for a change. Aren't we all? Don't we all say this all the time? I am sick of my life in London. I am sick of men and dating and all the horrible bullshit. I just feel like I'm done. I'm tired. I'm over it. I want to start again. Meet a rugged country man. It'll be like *Brokeback Mountain* or *God's Own Country* but, like, just really romantic and no one dies. But by myself, a new start in the countryside quite literally isn't an option. It's not an option for any of us by ourselves. But together"—Jamie pauses for dramatic effect, closing his eyes—"we can do anything."

Normally I would roll my eyes at this kind of speech from Jamie, and perhaps it's all the wine, but I actually find myself quite moved. I feel that it deserves a round of applause or a standing ovation.

"Maybe we could really do this," Ray says. She's wide-eyed, staring at Jamie. His speech clearly worked on her too. "I mean, if you don't mind putting your money into it, Will? I don't think any of us have anything significant to add to a deposit."

Ray looks around the group, and Jamie and I shake our heads.

"I mean if I move around some assets, liquidate a few things, maybe like a hundred pounds," I say. There are some clothes I've got to return. I could sell my old phone, that's at least a tenner, isn't it?

"It isn't my money, really, is it?" Will says, ignoring my pathetic offering. "I mean, up until a couple of weeks ago I had less than five pounds in my savings account. It feels like it's Monopoly money. Nan had it from Grandad's pension. A payout from when he died twenty years ago. It has just been sitting there."

"Let's go and see the house next week," Jamie says. "Can we do that? And then just go from there?"

"Sure, yes. Let's do that," says Will. He gets out his phone as if he's going to set up an appointment this very minute and then remembers that it's ten on a Friday night and he doesn't have any signal. "I'll arrange it first thing Monday morning."

"It can't hurt to look, can it? I mean, we may as well. It doesn't mean that we're committing to anything," Ray says, glancing at me. She's biting her lip now, the dream plan perhaps becoming slightly too real.

"Ray," I say, "you have lived in London your entire life. Just think about the reality of not living there anymore."

She frowns slightly, a flash of worry across her face. Gone before most people would have a chance to register it.

"But . . . it's zone twenty-five. Will literally just said. I have done hour-and-a-half-long commutes on the tube before. Forty-five minutes is nothing. It would feel like nothing."

"True," I say, "but it's not just the distance. It's what it's actually going to be like to live in a village and not a city. It will be really different. So quiet. The people aren't going to be the same. Well, I mean, the people are all probably going to be exactly the same—as each other."

I've never actually lived in a village, but I have watched a lot of *Midsomer Murders*, and I really think I've got the gist of it. I know small-town life. And I know Ray—easily bored, restless, a city person through and through.

Ray shrugs. She's in one of those moods where I could tell her that the village is also the world's biggest rubbish tip and she'd be like, *That's amazing though, I love rubbish.*

"I know. I know it would be a big change," she says. "But maybe I want a big change. I'm stuck in a rut. With work, with Kirsty, with everything. I'm sick of living in a fucking horrible damp house for thousands of pounds a month. I want something else, you know? Something better. At the very least this would shake things up."

"Exactly," Jamie says, "a big shake-up is exactly what we need. Instead of just complaining about everything all the time. Actually *do* something about it."

"Plus, think of the house parties," Ray says. "We could even start our own festival."

"Um," Will interjects, "I said it's in the countryside, I didn't say it was an estate."

The ridiculousness of this plan. The hugeness of it. The life-changing-ness of it is overshadowed by the idea of living with Ray. It makes me feel sick. In a good way, I think. I would get to see her every day. Her room could be next to mine. But if I live with her, how will I ever get over her? Will I just moon about after her for the rest of my life? Following her around the commune like she's a cult leader and I'm one of her sad wives?

"To a new way of living!" Ray says, and lifts her bottle. She smiles knowingly, like we're all in on a big joke. And yet when we clink our bottles and cheers, we're all quiet for a while, contemplating the possibility.

Rob's tent is split into three sections. There are two separate compartments off the middle where we've laid mats on the ground. They're meant to be very comfy camping mats that Will borrowed from his friend at work, but to me, they look like yoga mats. We don't actually discuss where everyone's sleeping. I'd sort of wondered if Ray might stay with Will and I'd go with Jamie, but the boys throw themselves into the right-hand compartment and one of them almost immediately starts snoring. I suspect it's Jamie, who is technically allergic to red wine but has still put away at least a bottle of it.

I've slept in a bed with Ray before but there is something distinctly more intimate about sleeping next to someone in a pod I can't stand all the way up in, our sleeping bags unzipped laid out next to each other like a giant duvet, the uneven ground underneath our yoga mats tipping us toward each other. I turn my back to her as I pull my jeans off and swap them for pajama shorts. I'm not sure why I've brought shorts, I'm not used to camping, and I sort of forgot about the sleeping-outside part of it. I don't see if Ray changes her clothes too. I hear her shuffling around, but when I turn back, she has the sleeping bag pulled up over her chest and the hood up on her gray sweatshirt.

"Can I switch this off, El?" she asks. We're using the light from her phone flashlight as our "lamp"; the entire tent is pitch-black apart from one blinding beam.

"Yes," I say, climbing under the sleeping bag duvet. The sensation of the fabric against my bare legs is unpleasant, static. I wriggle, trying to get comfortable. It is as though I am lying flat on the earth: I swear I can feel every single blade of grass digging into my back. I sigh, resigned to a night of no sleep. I'll be treated to the experience of being conscious during both the feeling of the alcohol wearing off and the hangover setting in. I run my tongue over my teeth, and despite having just brushed them they still feel slightly fuzzy, my mouth stale. I'm thirsty, but that's because I'm deliberately dehydrating myself so I don't have to go to the toilet block alone in the night and wind up murdered by a campsite strangler. I feel around in the dark for my water bottle and allow myself one small sip, letting the water run into all the crevices of my mouth.

"Are you all right?" I say to Ray. Well, I say it to the darkness, to the polyester ceiling above our heads.

"Yeah, why wouldn't I be?" she says.

I can feel her wriggling next to me, obviously also deeply uncomfortable. I know I must be drunk because I can feel the words spilling out of me before I've even really decided to say them.

"You're not wishing Kirsty was here?"

I can sense that Ray is smiling next to me. I feel her shift. I bet she has her arms up behind her head.

"Not really. I'm not sure she'd be having a nice time. Plus, you know there's no one else I'd rather be sharing a yoga mat with than you."

I can't help but smile. It's such a throwaway platitude. I hate myself for knowing that I'll be replaying and reading into it for weeks.

"Ha," I say. "I'm sure."

"I mean it, El. If we get murdered out here in the wilderness . . ."

"Surrey."

"Then at least we're going together."

"Perfect."

"Are you OK?" Ray asks.

"Yeah, I'm OK."

"You're stressing about this house thing," Ray says.

"I'm not *stressing*, I'm just thinking about it, that's all. It's a huge decision. I don't think I can make a decision like that in five minutes after I've been drinking. I don't think any of us should."

Ray's quiet for a moment; some of her earlier buoyancy about the plan has worn off. Somewhere, in a not-too-distant tent, a baby is screaming.

"It would be pretty wild," she says eventually.

I laugh.

"It would. Maybe it would be wild enough that I wouldn't have to do any other wild things for the whole year. . . ."

"Ha," Ray says, "it doesn't work like that. But nice try."

She reaches under the sleeping bag to squeeze my hand and then grabs it with both of hers, rubbing them together.

"You're freezing! Why didn't you say something?"

"I don't know. I'm fine."

I snatch my hand back. This sometimes happens. Feeling irrationally furious at Ray. For what? Not being telepathic? Not throwing herself at me? Not declaring her undying love?

We've been friends for five years, and I've never given her any reason to think I see her as anything other than a friend. Well. Nearly never.

"You're not fine, you're freezing. You should put your jeans back on."

"No," I grumble, "I'm not sleeping in my jeans; they're scratchy."

I just know she's rolling her eyes.

"Turn over, then."

"No! Ray, I'm . . ."

Ray grabs my hip and shoves so that I roll over onto my side, and before I can protest any further, her body is wrapped around mine. I have no choice but to be her little spoon.

I'm too tired and too tipsy to resist. To go through the routine of trying to wriggle away before relenting. Instead I take a deep breath and relax my shoulders. Her hoodie has ridden up slightly under the covers, and the feel of her stomach on the small of my back is so intimate that for a moment I feel like all the breath has left my body. I close my eyes and focus on the feeling of Ray's fingers on my hip and her mouth at the nape of my neck and think how perhaps, if I never moved, we could stay like this, tangled up in each other, forever.

Sometimes I think about what it would be like to tell Ray how I feel, but the longer I wait, the more impossible it seems. The longer I wait, the better friends we become, the more we confide in each other. I meet more of Ray's girlfriends. I witness the way she feels about people, how casual she is. How quickly she's able to discard them. The thought of being discarded by Ray is so painful that it makes the idea of putting myself in that position absurd, masochistic even. I'm safer where I am. An indispensable friend.

I did say something once. Early on. We'd known each other only a few months. It was the first holiday party at work that we ever went to, and it was a big one, before the cuts, before the holiday party became a sad slice of turkey in the cafeteria. We were on a rooftop in central London drinking glasses of free champagne. It was a beautiful still night and there were so many heated lamps that it was almost too hot. I distinctly remember a lot of people fanning themselves with napkins. I was just the right side of tipsy, that sweet spot after two glasses where you feel like the best version of yourself—my conversation was sparkling, my quips delightful; I felt beautiful. The timing was perfect. Ray and I were standing next to each other, alone, looking at the view across the city. She was smiling at me a lot, more than usual. It felt that way anyway. We were giddy. So pleased with ourselves for being there, among all these important people doing important work.

"I have something to tell you," I'd said.

Ray turned away from the view to face me, leaning against the glass barrier. She lifted one hand to push her hair away from her face. I wanted to reach out and do the same so badly. She was so close. I tipped up the last of my champagne and drained the glass.

"OK," she said, "what?"

I took a deep breath.

"I have a huge crush on you."

I said it to the city, not quite able to look directly at her.

There was silence for a couple of moments. Then she laughed. Not an unkind laugh. A laugh as if we were both in on the joke.

"No you don't, El."

"I do."

She shook her head. "I'm just wearing a nice suit and you've had a bottle of champagne."

I laughed too, then. I didn't know what else to do. My insides had turned to ice.

"And," she said, gently prodding my forearm with her index finger, "remember Greg? At home?"

"I know," I said. "I know."

The truth was, I didn't really remember Greg at home. Not at that moment. Not in any moment when I was with Ray. I'd been with Greg for eight years. We met during freshers week, and that was that. He was exactly the kind of boy I'd always fancied—slightly brooding, a bit pale, and interesting. I'd told him that I also liked women. He thought that was cool. He thought maybe he was bisexual too. We got together on a night out. I remember kissing him in a grungy club while the Arctic Monkeys played and thinking how this was it. I'd found it—love. I thought that Greg was the One. Until I didn't.

"Hey, I'm going to go and get us another drink and one of those crab things. Do you want a crab thing?" Ray said.

I nodded.

She reached out her hand to take my empty glass from me, and when I passed it to her, our hands touched, briefly.

She paused before walking away and then leaned forward and kissed me on the cheek, gently. It felt like an electric shock.

"Be right back."

For the rest of the night we acted like it had never happened. Jamie came over, and we talked about Christmas and the price of trains home and where we were going to go for food once the party was over. My confession drifted off, floated over the rooftops and out into the city. We never spoke of it again. Mostly I think she's forgotten about it but sometimes

I swear she looks at me and there's a flicker of something, like she's thinking about it.

When I finally fall asleep, I dream about living with Ray in a house so big and rambling that no matter how many corridors I run down, how many doors I try opening, I simply cannot find her.

CHAPTER FIVE

On the Monday following our camping trip I am sitting at my desk listening to a podcast where people talk about their favorite foods. The guest is describing the best oysters they've ever had, creamy and sweet. The overnight oats I'm eating for breakfast taste of the Tupperware I carried them to work in. My packed lunch is a box of crackers and the half block of cheese I couldn't finish in bed the other night.

I am in the process of marking every single email in my inbox as read when I get a WhatsApp notification from Will. I used to have WhatsApp up on my computer screen when I had a desk where no one could walk past and see what I was up to, but now that I'm at the end of the row I have to be more careful. I often think about how rich I would be if I could invent an app that disguised WhatsApp as an Excel spreadsheet.

Will has created a new group and called it *The Commune*. The image is of Will and Ray standing in a field looking vaguely outdoorsy. If you zoom in, you can clearly see that they are in a park in the wilds of zone two.

Morning, folks, I hope you've all recovered from the weekend. Thank you again for everything. I feel miles better for having got some perspective and some country air. You'll all be pleased to know I am back to work today and no longer living on the sofa.

So, I don't know if everyone's actually serious about the house or if it just seemed like a good idea at the time. Maybe it was just the wine talking . . . but it's worth going to take a look together, don't you think? At the very least we get a day trip out of it. I can sort it for Saturday if you want to go. I haven't told the estate agents or my solicitor or anyone actually that Mel and I have broken up. I couldn't bring myself to say it out loud . . . might end up being a stroke of luck, eh? Let me know what you think!

I tap the screen with my fingertips while I think about my reply. Honestly, I didn't expect Will to follow up on it. I don't know why. He's a man of his word. Maybe it's more accurate to say there was a part of me that hoped he wouldn't. That we wouldn't chase this thing that would so drastically disrupt the status quo. That maybe we could just forget the conversation ever happened.

Underneath that, though, the protective practical layer, there is a part of me that is thrilled. A real, proper step out of my comfort zone. A real wild thing. My fingers are practically twitching at the prospect of writing it down in my journal.

I'm free on Saturday. I don't see the harm in taking a look, I reply.

OK I'm in if you're in! As you say, no harm in looking. Thanks Will.

Me too! Can't wait! You're right—it's a day trip if nothing else.

Ray's and Jamie's replies come in at exactly the same time. Clearly they're upstairs discussing it together. I had sort of expected for some of the excitement about this plan to have worn off by today. For one of them to have thought of a reason they couldn't possibly leave London. Obviously I was wrong.

"Keeping busy, are we, Eleanor?" Mona says.

I jump and throw my phone facedown on the desk.

I don't know how she can be so sneaky in her massive boots. It makes no sense.

"Hi, Mona, yes, just quickly checking an appointment."

I gingerly reach out and turn my phone back over. Nothing to hide here.

I look back up at my monitor to see I've been inactive for so long that the screensaver has kicked in.

"Worse things happen at sea," Mona says.

"What?"

She is always coming out with stuff like this.

"You are always looking so down, Eleanor," Mona says. "Cheer up, it's a beautiful day."

She says this all without smiling once; the effect is eerie. I honestly wouldn't be surprised if she turns out to be a robot. I give her a weak smile, and she nods, satisfied that another team member is having a fantastic time under her watchful eye.

I don't end up seeing Ray and Jamie at lunchtime. Jamie has work to catch up on, and Ray is going swimming. That she can go through the rigamarole of getting changed and dry and back to the office again in an hour is fascinating to me. I simply couldn't do it.

I pass her on the stairs as she's heading back into the office, and I'm on my way out to buy a Diet Coke. She's all pink from walking quickly, and her hair's still wet. She has her backpack slung over one shoulder with her towel stuffed into the top of it so it isn't quite closed. She's wearing a white T-shirt that is clinging to her still-slightly-damp skin. I'm sure I see at least two other women check her out as they walk past her.

"Give us a smile, Eleanor," Ray says, deadpan, slightly French. Her best Mona impression.

She passes me before I can respond. I grin all the way to the cafeteria.

Every Monday after work I volunteer. This gives the impression that I'm a better person than I actually am. Or at least a different kind of person than I actually am.

I never intended to become a volunteer, that's the thing. A few years ago I wanted to write a piece for the newspaper about the rise in LGBTQ+ homeless youth and why these young people who were so at risk were most likely to go under the radar. I went to interview the founder of a small grass-roots organization who turned out to be a brilliant woman named Lisa. Lisa is tiny, not more than five foot tall, and she's always perfectly put together, all pearlescent lipstick and sweet smiles. I don't think she's ever left East London in her life, she smokes like a chimney, and she calls everyone sweed'eart. She is also ferocious. Sort of somewhere between a rottweiler and Peggy Mitchell from *EastEnders*. I swear I've seen her growl at people.

Before I really knew what was happening I'd agreed to

become a mentor in their program, and I've gone back every Monday night since. I mentored someone called Jack for nearly four years, and when their time was up, Lisa and the project were so woven into the fabric of my life that it never occurred to me that I could leave. Not that I had the chance. Lisa simply assigned me someone else without asking and told me where to go. She frightens me so much that I will probably be volunteering there until the day I die. She'll outlive me for sure.

I've been meeting with Rozália now for six months. She's eighteen and achingly, intimidatingly cool. She's lived in the UK for five years. She moved here from Hungary with her family, who, when she came out to them last year, told her in no uncertain terms that homosexuals were not tolerated under their roof. If she wanted to be queer, she was going to have to be queer somewhere else. And so that's what she did.

Rozália is waiting for me at a table outside our favored coffee shop in Hackney. She's smoking a cigarette and barely looks up from her phone when I sit down. She has a new tattoo on her forearm, so new that it's still in plastic wrap.

"That's new," I say.

She looks at her arm and then at me.

"Yes," she says.

She smiles at me kindly and pushes her sunglasses up onto her head. I do sometimes get the impression that she considers this *her* community service, to spend some time with an elderly person once a week.

I order us both coffees, and she rolls her eyes when I make mine a decaf.

"Won't you be up all night if you have a coffee at six p.m.?" I say.

"I'm going to be up all night anyway," she says. "I'm going out."

"On a Monday?"

"Yes!" she says. "When do you go out? Friday?" She says *Friday* as if it's the most embarrassing idea she's ever heard of.

"No," I say. "Obviously not. I mean, Thursday though?"

Rozália raises her eyebrows and snorts, amused by my basicness.

When the waitress puts our coffees down in paper cups, Rozália spins her cup round to show me that hers has got a phone number on it.

"Whoa," I say. "That's quite presumptuous, isn't it? I could be your girlfriend sitting here."

"She probably thinks you're my mum."

"OK."

I take a sip of my coffee.

"I got a message from Lisa saying she might stop by and say hello since this is our six-month anniversary, so she can see how things are going," I say.

"Right," Rozália says.

I don't bother to point out that this is where a lot of people might say how great it's been or that they can't believe it's been six months already because it feels like we've known each other forever. I'm not absolutely certain she's not going to tell Lisa that I've been taking her to conversion therapy or something, just because she thinks it would be funny.

"How's your week been, then?" I say.

"Yeah, good," Rozália says. "A table at work left me an insane tip. Like, insane."

Rozália works at a restaurant in the city. She has to deal with a lot of terrible men, but the combination of her being absolutely beautiful and thoroughly repulsed by them means she's very popular. No one gets better tips than Rozália.

"And have you started the book yet?"

"Um," she says. "Sort of. No, not really. I'm waiting for inspiration to strike."

Rozália's supposedly been working on a children's book since I met her. Since long before I met her, actually. She's been very cagey about it, but I know that the reason Lisa matched us is because Rozália is a writer and so, supposedly, am I.

"She's a real fucking talent," Lisa said to me, and then she'd frowned and pointed her perfectly manicured pink talon in my face. "Don't you dare let her give up."

"How's it going in the house?" I ask. Rozália's in a house share with two other queer young people.

"Fine," she says. "Although, do you know how much council tax is?"

I nod. "I do know."

"What am I paying for?"

"Um," I say, "bins?"

"Is that it?"

"Yeah."

She shakes her head and stubs her cigarette out in the plant pot in front of us before I can reach out and stop her.

"Mad," she says. She fixes me with a look. "So, you got a new job yet?"

"No, not yet."

"You looking?"

"Yeah, I'm always looking, aren't I?"

"Pshh," Rozália says, leaning back in her chair, "not hard enough."

"All right, well," I say, "we're not here to talk about me, so . . ."

"What was your wild thing this month?"

I put my head in my hands. Telling Rozália about my Wild Year was a huge mistake. I thought it might be an icebreaker—we'd been meeting for a couple of months by that point and she's a tough person to crack. I thought that telling her that my life isn't perfect, that I'm still trying to figure out who I am too might get her to open up to me. I mean it did in a way—when I'd shown her my butterfly tattoo, she'd actually taken my hand and squeezed it, like she was so touched that someone could do something so pathetic.

"Um . . ." I absolutely cannot tell her about the threesome that wasn't. "I might move into a house in the countryside and turn it into a queer commune."

Rozália nods, raising her eyebrows. "Now that," she says, tipping up her coffee and draining the last of it from the cup, "is very interesting."

"Do you think? I don't know if it's going to work out. I mean, for a start, my friend who's buying it is a straight man."

Rozália rolls her eyes at me.

"I don't know though. It could be fun. It's something different, isn't it, at least."

"Let me guess," Rozália says. "Ray is going to be living there too."

"Yeah, I mean, of course, she's my best friend. . . ."

"My best friend!" Rozália repeats in a high-pitched voice.

"She is!"

"Sure."

"I don't know how we got onto this," I say. "We're meant to be talking about you."

"What are you talking about instead?"

I nearly jump out of my seat. Lisa sits down next to me and immediately lights a cigarette. She sits back in her chair as she takes the first drag, closing her eyes as she exhales as if she's been holding her breath and she's finally got access to oxygen. She pushes her sunglasses up from her face to balance on top of her freshly blow-dried hair. Her talons, at least an inch long, are painted deep purple.

"Nothing," I say. "I mean, hi, Lisa."

Lisa ignores me and looks at Rozália. "What are you talking about?"

Rozália nods in my direction. "Eleanor moving to the countryside with one of her many lovers."

"Is that right?" Lisa says, looking at me and frowning. She points at me with her cigarette. "You want to watch out, there'll be wolves and bears and all sorts."

"I really don't think there are any wolves in—"

"Anyway," Lisa says, "we're not here to talk about you, we're here to talk about our lovely Rozália. How are you doing, darling?"

"All right," Rozália says. "Yeah, good. I was actually just trying to tell Eleanor, if she would let me get a single word in"—she pauses to glance at me, the briefest raise of an eyebrow—"that I heard from my younger brother at the weekend, which was nice. I haven't heard from him in a long time. Since I left actually."

"That's amazing news," I say. "Might you see him? Would he come and visit, do you think?"

Rozália shrugs.

"In time," Lisa says, "all in good time. It's a start, isn't it? You feel good about it?"

"Yeah," Rozália says. "It's something."

Lisa takes another long drag on her cigarette and smiles at the barista bringing her coffee in a takeaway cup.

"Cheers, darling," she says, blowing out smoke and pulling her cat-eyed sunglasses back down and patting her hair.

"You got somewhere to be?" I say.

"Always," she says. I can't see her eyes behind the glasses, but I'm sure she's winking at me. "Right, then, girls, this is working, then? No complaints?"

"It's working," Rozália says. "I think I am really helping Eleanor find her feet."

"Fantastic," Lisa says, before I can even open my mouth to respond. "I knew you two would get along. So we'll leave this little arrangement as is. Take care of yourselves, girls. No trouble, all right?"

We both nod as Lisa gets up from the table, picks up her coffee, and puts her phone to her ear.

"Bye, Lisa," I say, "it was really good to . . ."

She's gone, her back turned, cackling down the phone to someone else before I can finish my sentence.

We watch as she totters off down the street in a cloud of cigarette smoke. Rozália shakes her head in awe.

"I fucking love her."

Just as Rozália and I are leaving, after we've briefly hugged goodbye to go our separate ways—me to the tube station, her to her bike, which she rides without a helmet in the middle of the road while she's on the phone—she stops me.

"Hey, um, I just wanted to check . . . if you move to the queer commune owned by a straight man."

I nod.

"You're not . . . it doesn't mean . . ."

She gestures to herself and then shoves her hand in her pocket, unhappy about displaying any vulnerability.

"I'll be here every Monday," I say. "Whether you like it or not."

Rozália nods and spins on her heel to get away from me as quickly as possible.

When I get home, I see that I have been treated to a lovely note from Amelia. A pink Post-it on the fridge.

Hi Eleanor, if you borrow my milk please replace it. I know it was almost full last night and I was surprised to see this morning that it's half gone. Thanks:)

I think the smiley face is what I hate the most. Amelia does not have a smiley face in real life. I'd have had more respect for her if she'd drawn a patronizing little smirk. Or a knife with blood dripping off it.

If I could be bothered I'd write a note back saying that cow's milk is murder and I wouldn't ever touch it and that perhaps her sad boyfriend drinks it, maybe in the middle of the night when he's standing in the kitchen staring into the abyss wondering what on earth he's doing spending his one precious life with her. But actually I did use her milk to make my depressing overnight oats and honestly I'm about to use it again on the granola I've got for dinner. Instead I leave the note where it is so that when she comes home she won't be sure if I've seen it or not and then I set a reminder on my phone to buy milk in the morning. I'm not a monster.

I climb into bed with my granola and see that I have an email from my mum. Well, it's not actually from her. She has forwarded me and Rob an email from Bernard's dog hotel. It's a photo of him standing under a huge tree in the sunshine and some information about what he's had for dinner, which sounds significantly more nutritious than what I'm having. I must buy some apples tomorrow, or some multivitamins.

I'm not entirely sure why she's sent it to me because she hasn't taken the time to add a note, a "lots of love" or even a "kind regards," but I'm glad she has. When I see Bernard under that tree, free from the shackles of his terrible roommates, I also see myself. I too could be having a lovely time in the countryside— no passive-aggressive Post-its there, unlimited milk, nutritious home-cooked meals. A new life just like Bernard's. So close I can almost taste it.

CHAPTER SIX

When we assemble at Liverpool Street station at ten on Saturday morning, we barely even speak about why we are there, as if discussing practicalities might burst our bubble, ruin the magic. We get on the train with our coffees and Pret croissants and talk about pretty much everything else apart from the house. Will was out last night with the boys from work but had come home early so he could get up and go for a run before we caught our train. Jamie had spent the evening watching all the Twilight films back-to-back with his housemates and is severely sleep-deprived. Ray had stayed at her family's house last night. It was her nan's birthday; she was ninety-three. They'd had a party that sounds more raucous than most twenty-first birthdays. Ray sips her oat milk latte carefully, keeping her sunglasses on even once we're on the train.

I had spent the evening alone in my room trying to watch a true-crime series about a man who snuck into women's houses at night, cut off all their hair, and made it into wigs that he wore when he visited his next victim. I'd kept touching my hair just to check it was still there and definitely not being worn by a psychotic but highly skilled craftsman. I couldn't properly concentrate because Amelia was in her room having boring sex with her boring boyfriend all evening, which was incredibly distracting. I thought about banging on the wall but couldn't bring myself to be that miserable. I should have been having Friday night sex instead of eating Amelia's posh protein cereal for dinner and being titillated by stories about creepy wigmakers.

When we arrive at the station, only a handful of other people get off the train. They head off in the direction of the car park.

"It's only a mile up the road," Will says. "A twenty-minute walk, max."

"It would be quick on a bike," Ray says.

"Exactly," says Will, "that's what I thought we'd do. Me and Mel, I mean. We thought we'd do a lot of cycling around here."

Will, Ray, and Jamie have all got bikes that they whizz about London on, resulting in me having to send near-constant texts every time we part ways saying, *Are you alive?! YOU SAID YOU'D TEXT.*

I don't have a bike because cycling in London has terrified me ever since I once decided to use a Boris bike and someone in head-to-toe Lycra called me a "stupid bike bitch" for stopping at a pedestrian crossing. I feel that could all be different here, though; everyone will ride around on bikes, probably with baskets full of flowers and fresh loaves of bread, waving and bidding each other good day.

The pavement up from the station toward the village is narrow, so we have to walk single file. It feels slightly like we're on a school trip. At one point we cross over a bridge and look down to see ducklings. It's picture-perfect, like the world they jump into in *Mary Poppins*. So bright and green, it's almost cartoonish.

The village is pretty, even prettier than I'd expected. Lots of higgledy-piggledy houses in different muted pastel colors. The windows and doors are tiny. I think even I, at five foot five, would have to duck to go inside. We turn off the main path and up a steep road, and at the top there is a house. The house.

We stop in the front driveway (driveway!) and stare.

It's bigger than the other houses in the village but not huge. It doesn't feel imposing. It's detached—the nearest house is at the bottom of the hill—and it is surrounded by fields. The windows are single-glazed and grubby. They look like they might never have been washed. The front garden is overgrown, but there is a wooden front door that looks in decent condition, and growing in large pots on either side of it is lavender, which I can smell from where we're standing.

The estate agent emerges from his smart car. He is wearing loafers with no socks, and when he walks, I can see where they're rubbing his skin raw. His ankles will be bleeding by the end of the day.

He speaks only to Will, as if the rest of us might be Will's kids. Certainly he has decided we're inconsequential. This works out quite well because once we're through the front door, Ray, Jamie, and I are free to go and explore by ourselves without having to nod along to the man in the shiny suit.

We are hit immediately by the smell. It is not unpleasant necessarily. Not stale or musty like you might expect an unlived house to be. It's earthy though. Almost as though we're outside still, like soil after rain.

On the ground floor there is a huge kitchen where there are ancient-looking cabinets and a stove that looks like it's been there since the seventies. The paint is peeling off the walls, and the linoleum floor is ripped at the edges. There is a slug making its way across the back step and under the sink. The floor is streaked with silver.

There's a tiny bathroom off the kitchen with just a toilet and a small sink. The tap is rusty. There's a small, cracked window, and outside I can just about make out the most overgrown garden I've ever seen. A mass of green all tangled together. It appears to go on and on.

There is an enormous dining room with brown, red, and yellow floral wallpaper. Half of it is hanging off and half looks to be so stubbornly pasted on that I wonder if we would ever be able to remove it. There is a thin, faded red carpet on the floor, but when you peel it back at the corners, which Ray does, you can see that there are wooden floorboards underneath. They are not damp to the touch. Jamie jumps up and down, and they don't collapse.

At the front of the house there is a living room the size of Amelia's entire flat that has a huge open fireplace. So big that you can step into it. The person who lived here previously, albeit presumably a long time ago, has left an ancient beige sofa, which Ray kicks tentatively with the very tip of her foot. None of us say anything but assume the kick to mean, *We'd have to get rid of this.*

Upstairs there are four bedrooms, a box room, and a bathroom. There are rickety stairs leading up to an attic, as if someone once started a conversion and then just gave up. One of the bedrooms is smaller than the others but not by much. All of them are painted different garish colors. There are filthy net curtains on the windows. We open a cupboard in the smallest room and inside there is a framed portrait of what look to be two Victorian children. We close it again very quickly. Jamie, a self-pronounced atheist, crosses himself.

Everything in the bathroom is brown and, horrifyingly, it is also carpeted. Ray opens the medicine cabinet above the sink. The door squeaks horribly. It's empty inside, which is somehow both a disappointment and a relief.

We trudge back down the stairs to meet Will, who is standing in the garden talking to the estate agent about football. The garden feels less unmanageably overgrown and more excitingly junglelike once you're actually in it. Like perhaps it only needs a bit of taming, not necessarily an entire revamp. It's so long that you can barely make out where it ends and the fields begin. I've never had a garden that wasn't surrounded by other gardens before. It's quiet out here.

Once we've assured Will that we've seen what we need to see, we walk back through the house, and the estate agent leaves us standing dumbstruck in the front garden next to an out-of-control lavender bush.

"So," Will says, turning to the three of us. "What do you think?"

We're all quiet for a moment. I take a deep breath.

"I think I love it," I say quietly, surprising myself. "I think I want to live here."

"I do too," Jamie says quickly, looking at me.

Ray turns, looking back at the house and then at Will. She bites her lip and then breaks out into a grin.

"I think we might be doing this thing," she says, and then looks round at all of us. "Are we doing this?"

"I can't believe I'm saying this." I swallow, my mouth dry, my throat sticky. "But yes, I really think I want to do this."

"Christ," Will says. "I need a drink."

We walk down the hill and back into the village, talking at one hundred miles per hour, the enormity of the decision and the absurdity of it making us near hysterical. We laugh about the seventies wallpaper, about the brown bathroom suite. Ray starts talking authoritatively about sanding floors and we all shout at her that she has no idea what she's talking about. Instead of getting in a mood about it she just bursts out laughing.

There's just one pub in the village, the Swan. It's on a winding street, wedged between two houses. Will strolls right in, but the rest of us wait a fraction longer, a brief assessment about what kind of pub this might be, what kind of welcome to expect for a brown man wearing pink shorts and a woman with short hair wearing a tank top meant for men.

"Come on," I say after a couple of beats, walking in front of them like I'm their shield. "We don't want to lose Will."

The pub is quiet: it's midday and there's just one table occupied by two elderly men sipping pints in silence. The man behind the bar doesn't bat an eyelid at us walking in. I suppose he might be used to day-trippers from London.

Will orders us all pints of some local ale that the man assures him recently won a very prestigious award, and we traipse out into the small courtyard to sit around a picnic bench.

We cheers, tapping our glasses together, but we don't say to what. It feels too precarious to toast the house just yet.

"So," Will says, grimacing slightly after tasting the ale and then clapping his hands together. "I have to admit that I've done a bit of research this week into exactly what we'd need to do house-wise. Just in the eventuality that you all came here and loved it as much as I do. Which I had a feeling you might. Well, I really hoped you might."

"Oh god," Jamie says, taking a sip of his drink and then reeling back as if it had poisoned him, "good news or bad news?"

"Good!" Will says. "Obviously. I wouldn't have let you see it if I didn't think it was possible. So Mel and I . . ." Will pauses briefly and sighs. "Mel and I got quite far into the process. Basically all the way through the process, to be honest. Surveys are done, we were just waiting for the last bits from the solicitors and we were good to go. Obviously the main issue now is the mortgage. So what I need is for one of you to apply, and I think because I'm already approved we could end up doing this quite quickly."

"Can all four of us do it, then?" Ray says. She's been rooting around in her backpack for her sunglasses and has found them at the bottom, no case. She rubs the lenses on her shirt and then puts them on. I can see that they're covered in scratches.

Will shakes his head.

"Well, we could. But it's a bit trickier. Ideally I'd just have one of you do it and then we figure out a system between the four of us. What we pay into it, what we get out of it at the end, that kind of thing. I really don't want this to feel like my house that you're all living in. This is *our* house. Every penny you put into it, you'll get back. I just feel like it's a great investment for us all." He pauses and then smiles. "And a great adventure!"

I feel a surge of affection for Will. His generosity to this motley crew. I picture him privately, obsessively researching this all week. He looks so tired.

"Who should it be, then?" I ask. "I mean, I'm not actually even sure I can get a mortgage on my fixed-term contract to be honest."

Or with my overdraft.

"Well, I was thinking . . ." Will turns to Ray. "Just because, you know, we're so close and we already live together and know each other so . . ."

"Will!" Ray says, resting her head on his shoulder. "It would be my honor to be a homeowner with you."

"Is that all right?" Will says to Jamie.

"That's fine by me," Jamie says. "Wait, so then we'll split the payments four ways? And renovations? And then, what? When we sell it . . ."

"Four ways," Will says. "One hundred percent. I can get it drawn up. We'll get it in writing. I mean apart from my deposit, which I'll take back if that's OK with you. . . ."

Jamie nods slowly and then breaks into a huge smile.

"I can't fucking believe this," he says. "I mean, yes, it will be weird not to live in London anymore, but I mean, we're super close right? That took no time today."

"We're so close," Ray says. "Like, yes, it will be an adjustment. But that's life, isn't it? Sometimes you've got to make big moves."

"And we always complain about it," I say. "We've been saying that we need a change for such a long time."

My heart soars just thinking about telling Amelia that I'm moving out.

"Maybe I'll meet my future husband here," Jamie says wistfully, looking around the empty pub garden. "I could be a farmer's wife."

"I'm sure," Ray says, "that the village is crawling with homosexuals."

"Fingers crossed," Jamie says.

I volunteer to go inside and get more drinks. All of us, including Will, are ready to move on from the local ale. When I step inside from the sunshine it takes a moment for my eyes to adjust to the shade. It feels tiny in there, ceilings and doorways built for people hundreds of years ago when everyone probably had scurvy and only grew to four foot tall.

The man is gone from behind the bar and has been replaced with a woman who I'd guess was around my age. She has dark hair cut into a bob and is wearing a white summer dress with sunflowers on it. She's holding a cloth in one hand as if she's going to spring into action and clean the bar at any moment. In her other hand she's got a battered paperback that she is thoroughly engrossed in.

She looks up when I approach the bar and places the book facedown, pages still open.

"Sorry," I say, gesturing toward the book.

"Oh no, don't worry," she says, "I'm not meant to read behind the bar anyway."

"Have you guessed who did it?" I say.

She smiles broadly, and I find myself smiling back.

"Have you read it?" she says delightedly.

I nod. "A long time ago." I've read all the author's books, actually.

"I mean I think I've guessed, but I'm never right about these things. . . . Don't tell me!" she says.

"I won't," I say. "It's a good one though. I'll say this, it isn't who you think. . . ."

"Ah, intriguing!" she says, and then, "It never is."

I order four pints of lager, and she studies me as she pulls them.

"I haven't seen you here before."

"No," I say, "I'm just visiting for the day from London . . . my friend, I mean . . . my friends and I might be buying a house here."

The words sound so ridiculous that I worry she might laugh, but she just raises her eyebrows.

"Ah, cool."

"Do you . . . I mean, have you worked here for a long time?"

"All my life," she says. She puts the final glass down in front of me and pauses before going to the till.

"It's my mum and dad's pub," she says. "I was living in London until recently, but I'm back here for a bit."

"Bit of a change of pace, right?" I get my card out of my back pocket and hold it out while she frowns at the card machine.

She nods, holding it out for me.

"Just a bit," she says. "But I like it here."

She insists on helping me carry the drinks outside despite my protests.

"It would be good to see some natural light," she says. "You're doing me a favor."

We put the drinks down on the table and just as she's about to head inside she turns back to us.

"So you might move into the house up there?"

She gestures in the direction we just came from.

"Yeah," I say. "We hope so anyway."

"Well," she says, "I really hope you do too. It'll be nice to have some new faces around here. I'm Rachel, by the way."

She smiles at us all.

"Let me know if you need anything else."

She lifts a hand and goes back to the bar to a chorus of *thank-yous* and *nice to meet yous* from the group.

"Look at you," Ray says, nudging my knee with hers under the table. "Making new friends already."

We decide to go for one more drink back in London, all of us still effervescent with excitement and not quite wanting to let one another go. I don't know about the others but I don't want to give my brain the opportunity to let doubts begin to creep in, or any counterarguments to our decision. Ray suggests going to their house because of its proximity to Liverpool Street and the fact that they've got all the leftover camping beers.

"We've got to start thinking about being more frugal," she says, "now that we're going to be homeowners."

We laugh. It feels like a joke even though she's probably right.

We pile onto the packed Central line. Will and Jamie end up standing in the middle of the carriage wedged in by a group of teenage girls who are wild on Red Bull and reeking of too-sweet perfume.

Ray and I are at the end of the carriage. She gestures for me to lean against the side, and she stands in front of me, facing me, her hand resting next to the right side of my head. When the next crowd of people get on at Bethnal Green, she presses against me so closely that our thighs are touching. I can feel that I've gone pink and it's nothing to do with the Central line being hotter than the sun.

"Mad day, right?" Ray says, leaning in close to talk to me. She smells faintly of her perfume but mostly now of just her.

We've been out all day and sweating. It is intoxicating. It is truly a miracle that I'm able to lean back and speak to her as if she's not causing me actual cardiac complications.

"Mad," I say. "I think I still need to process everything. It feels like a dream."

"Hmm?" she says, leaning in again, not able to hear me over the roar of the tube.

"I just need to . . . I need to process."

"Yeah," she says. "For sure."

She gets out her phone at Mile End and starts typing furiously. When the train sets off again, she puts it into her back pocket and looks at me. Properly looks at me like she's only just registered that I'm there in front of her. She smiles.

"You suit your hair like that, El."

I lift my hand to my head as if I've forgotten what hair I have. It's pulled back in a ponytail. I did it earlier without thinking, sick of feeling hair on my neck in the heat.

"Oh, thanks."

"Yeah, it looks good, you should do it more often."

She reaches down and pushes a piece of hair away from my face and then leans back as if to admire her handiwork. When the train pulls into Stratford she leaps up and off the train as if she hasn't just left me swooning behind her. Just walks away as if she goes around pushing hair off girls' faces all the time, causing explosions of the central nervous system everywhere she goes. She probably does.

As we're walking to Ray and Will's house, I feel high. Completely jubilant about the house, the wildness of it, the joy. About how much I love my friends. Mainly I am high from the physical proximity of Ray, and I let myself believe that, perhaps, she too is feeling high on life, on me, and that maybe tonight will be the night we'll end up confessing our love to each other. She'll turn to me and say, *When I touched your hair on the tube just now near Mile End, that changed everything for me.* I don't let myself have this particular Ray fantasy often, the close-to-reality one, the "it could all change in one instant" one. But I can feel it take over this evening, and I let it. It washes over me like relief.

In their kitchen Ray puts on some music and turns it up loud; it sounds like Haim, but it's not. It will be someone Haim-adjacent that I've never heard of and Ray has just discovered. She starts chopping up a lime into wedges to stick in the top of everyone's bottles of beer. She absentmindedly licks her fingers when she passes me a bottle, and when she catches me watching her, she grins.

"I could just eat a whole lime like an orange, is that weird?"

"Quite weird," I say, grinning back at her stupidly.

"You'll have to get used to living with all my weird habits."

"I feel like I know them all," I say.

She raises her eyebrows and smiles.

"I do keep some things to myself, you know."

My breath catches in my throat, and I grin stupidly back at her, unsure how to respond. She's flirting, right? That's brazen flirting. Or is she just trying to tell me there are other citrus fruits she'd eat whole? Because I'm feeling giddy I open my mouth to ask her what else she's keeping from me, or to warn her that all the enamel on her teeth will rot if she's not careful. But before I can even decide whether to flirt with her or lecture her, there's a loud knock on their door. Ray puts her beer down on the counter next to me. When she returns, she has Kirsty attached to her hand.

"El," Kirsty says, "*so* good to see you."

She detaches herself from Ray to give me a loose hug. She pats me on the back a little, like you might to comfort a small child you don't know well. I hate when she calls me El. It is far too familiar for someone I'd like to keep at arm's length. Worse, when she pulls back, I see that Kirsty looks great. Her hair looks freshly cut, hanging just above her shoulders, and although she hardly wears makeup, her skin is glowing. Flushed slightly as if she might have jogged here.

"*So* good to see you too," I say. I press the lime into my drink and it fizzes down my hand.

"I've been trying to track this one down all day," Kirsty says, poking Ray's upper arm. "And it turns out she was literally purchasing a house! I can't believe it!"

Kirsty's eyes are sparkling; she is the picture of breeziness. There is a slightly manic edge though, the manic edge of someone desperately trying to be cool about something they are very not cool about. I imagine the boundaries of their not-relationship do not extend to being able to have an opinion about this sort of thing. I almost feel sorry for her.

I don't stay long at Ray and Will's once Kirsty shows up. I feel myself deflating, my buoyant mood dissipating, and by the time I'm finishing my drink and ordering an Uber, I am decidedly flat.

"You're not going, are you?" Ray says. "Stay! We'll order some food or something."

She is standing behind the chair Kirsty is sitting in, absent-mindedly playing with Kirsty's hair, running strands of it through her fingers.

"Honestly, I'm so tired. It's just the day. Big day. I need time to process it all. You know me," I say, as lightly as I can.

Ray smiles.

"I do know you. So please don't go home and spend all evening stressing."

"I won't, I promise," I say, gritting my teeth, the tension headache already setting in, preparing myself for a full night of worrying about everything.

Jamie comes and stands outside with me while I'm waiting for the car.

"You all right?" he says.

"Yep," I say, refusing to look at him, rummaging in my bag instead, searching for a lip balm I know isn't in there.

"Is this going to be a problem?" he asks, jerking his head toward the house. "Are you sure you're going to be able to live with her?"

I look at him then, meeting his eyes. I want to snap at him, but seeing his genuine concern, I find my irritation melts away.

"I don't know what you're talking about," I say.

He raises his eyebrows at me.

I sigh.

"It won't be a problem. I'm on top of it," I say. "I promise."

Jamie nods and kisses me on the cheek before turning to head back inside.

"You need to go on a date with someone else, El." His hand is on the door handle, and he says it as if the idea of me dating people has only just occurred to him.

"I did! I do."

"No, you don't. And not a couple. Not for a stupid challenge. A proper date."

"I know. I know. You're right," I say.

"She's not that special, you know." Jamie smiles. "I love her. But she's just Ray. There are thousands of them out there. The world is full of Rays."

I nod. But I don't agree with him. There's only one Ray. That's the problem.

When I get home, I can hear Amelia and her boring boyfriend giggling in her room. I get a glass of water from the kitchen as quickly as I can, just in case they emerge, then go straight to my room and close the door. I pull out my phone and start systematically working my way through all the dating apps I've got neglected accounts with. I half-heartedly scroll through profiles "liking" anyone that makes me feel anything other than entirely depressed or disgusted. I send a couple of *hellos* and feel the self-loathing to my very core. When I'm done, my eyes swimming with filtered photos of people holding dogs that don't belong to them, I put my phone facedown on my bedside table, grab my laptop, and settle in for a night of watching the rest of the hair-burglar documentary.

I feel myself relaxing during the reenactment, my shoulders loosening slightly as the woman puts her hands to her hairless head and screams into oblivion.

CHAPTER SEVEN

It all happens surprisingly quickly once we've made the decision to buy the house. Will and Ray kick everything into gear, filling out endless forms and spending a lot of time on the phone chasing people who don't seem to do anything. I see Ray at work, pacing up and down the corridors, frowning into her phone. The dreary admin of it all makes the whole process feel distinctly unwild, but I don't mention that to Ray because I think she might genuinely be on the verge of a nervous breakdown.

When Will told Melissa he was buying the house, she was furious but couldn't really give him a clear explanation as to why. Perhaps she had just expected him to mope about, waiting for her to take him back. Perhaps she had not considered that a dead grandmother might mean an unexpected windfall. Either way, despite some initial upset, it seems to have empowered Will. Spurred him on to believe that he's made the right decision. That this move now belongs to him—well, to us.

When I told Rob and Polly about the move, they were supportive, although I'm not sure that they entirely understand it.

"Wait so, you're not actually buying the house?" Rob asks. "Your name won't be on the deeds?"

"Not technically, no," I say. "But everything I pay into the mortgage I'll get back and any profit we make on the house we'll split. Will had it all officially drawn up. I'll be paying into something I'll get back rather than into Amelia's parents' mortgage. It's a solid investment."

I say *investment* confidently, and I feel like it works to convince them. They both nod as if simply the act of knowing the word counts for something.

"Have you told Mum and Dad?" Rob asks.

"I texted them saying I was moving out to the countryside, but I'm not sure if they really got it."

"Why? What did they say?"

"Mum just sent back a load of farm animal emojis and a selfie of them sunbathing giving me a thumbs-up."

"Well, that's quite nice," Rob says. He smiles tightly. As much as we're our own team I know there's a lot he doesn't say to me about them. He's my big brother, he wants to protect me from it. I'm sure he saves his biggest rants for Polly.

"It is," I say. "And you know, it's evidence that they're alive and well, wherever they are."

I want to savor the moment when I tell Amelia that I'll be moving out at the end of the month. I've been fantasizing about it for a long time, so it needs to be just right. I send her an email from my bedroom while she's in the kitchen. It's petty, but I take a great deal of satisfaction from hearing her say "Oh, for fuck's sake" and then stomping toward my room.

"Come in!" I say sweetly, when she raps on the door. Three short, sharp knocks.

Amelia waves her phone at me, her eyes wide, burning with rage.

"Are you being serious?"

I smile at her as if I haven't noticed that she's furious.

"Deadly serious, I'm afraid, Amelia. You see, I've bought a house."

I mean, it's not technically a lie. There is a house being bought, and I am moving into it.

"*You?* No, you haven't," she scoffs.

"I have. Out in the countryside. Four bedrooms."

I swear her jaw actually drops. It's really quite brilliant. While I'm waiting for her to be able to speak, the upstairs neighbors crank up the power ballads. I like this one, it has about six key changes. I've decided it's the Lithuanian equivalent of "Flying Without Wings."

I point upward. "Won't miss this," I say, smiling serenely.

"This is very fucking inconvenient," Amelia says, and stalks out of my room, slamming the door behind her so hard that it bounces back open.

It is such a wonderful moment that I wish I could do it all over again. Instead I pack up my room with my door open, singing along loudly in my best attempt at Lithuanian. It doesn't take long to pack. I don't have many things. I don't even own my own bed—it was already here when I moved in. I'm going to be sleeping on a yoga mat for the time being, but it doesn't matter, because it will be *my* yoga mat, in my own room.

We have one final night out planned before we move to the new house. It feels like a big goodbye even though we will be coming into London five days a week for work. Still, it's the end of an era. It's also Ray's birthday, which we didn't want to get lost in all the preparations for the move. Well, Ray didn't want it to get lost. She goes big for her birthday every year. Perhaps it's something to do with being an only child. She has come to expect a lot of fuss. But we're moving in the morning and have promised ourselves that we'll be on our best behavior tonight.

We're going to the Royal Vauxhall Tavern. It's one of our favorite, nostalgic nights out and the first queer space that Ray, Jamie, and I went to when we became friends. Ray has been coming to nights here since she was a teenager, since she looked old enough to get in. I think about it sometimes, what she was up to while I was sitting in my room dreaming in the suburbs.

Will can't make it because he's at a straight wedding reception at a posh hotel, but as well as Jamie and me, Ray has invited Kirsty and a few people she went to university with. We drink at Jamie's flat first because he lives in Kennington, closest to the RVT. Kirsty has made a birthday cake. She tries to wave it off as nothing, but it's clear a great deal of care has gone into it. She brings it out of the kitchen shyly, covered in lit candles, and when Jamie switches out all the lights we sing. Ray perches on the arm of the sofa, reveling in the attention, and once she's blown out the candles, she kisses Kirsty and whispers something in her ear. I look away. I'm not sure that chocolate cake is the best pairing for the cheap sauvignon blanc that I'm drinking, but I take a slice anyway. When Jamie's yelling at us to hurry up, as we're getting our shoes on, I tell Kirsty it was delicious. She beams at me, squeezes my arm gently as if I've said something important, something else entirely.

We're already pretty drunk by the time we arrive at the RVT but still someone orders a round of tequila shots. I plan to sip mine, aware of the chocolate cake sitting heavily in my stomach, but Jamie is standing next to me and won't allow it.

"El, do it properly, have some respect," he says, shaking his hand, getting rid of the excess salt.

I roll my eyes but do as he says. The tequila is warm in the back of my throat. I avoid the salt and the lime—the taste of my teenage-drinking disasters.

The small room is filled with so many bodies that it's impossible to move without brushing past someone. It could be claustrophobic, but tonight it feels glorious, a pleasure to be nothing but a part of this heaving, sweaty mass. Every song is the right song, everyone is happy and singing and laughing. Ray's friends have pills, but I refuse and so do Jamie and Ray. We think of Will. We promised, we say, we promised we'd be on top form tomorrow.

After a while we all dutifully head out to the smoking area so that Ray can have her annual birthday cigarette. She used to properly smoke but now just treats herself once a year—well, twice if you count the New Year's Eve cigarette, which we don't. It is actually an entire packet of birthday cigarettes, resulting in a bout of intense self-loathing the next day, but she still refers to it in the singular, and no one ever corrects her.

One of Ray's friends from university offers me the packet, and I take one. I'm not a very good smoker but I've had enough to drink that it feels like it might be a good idea. I take one drag and immediately remember why I don't do this. I'm wip-

ing my streaming eyes with the back of my free hand when I
hear someone saying my name.

"Eleanor?"

I squint, blinking tears away, and see that Rozália is standing in front of me, smoke unfurling from her nose, her cigarette
held loosely in her hand. She breathes it as easily as fresh air.

"Oh," I say, "hi." I wave with my free hand, aware of the single tear making its way down my cheek.

"Why are *you* here?" Rozália says, not waving back.

She looks deeply concerned, as though I'm her grandmother
and she's found me wandering the streets dazed and confused.

"For my friend's birthday."

I point to Ray, who is standing behind me, and Ray briefly
turns her head from her conversation to nod at Rozália.

"But why are you crying?" Rozália says, frowning.

I stub the cigarette out on the wall behind me and then wave
it at her by way of explanation.

Rozália rolls her eyes. She looks around her, as if to check
no one has seen us together.

"Why are *you* here?" I ask. It's just not the kind of place I'd
expect to see her at for some reason. I can't imagine her dancing
to pop music. Maybe she's here ironically.

Rozália shrugs. "My friend works here."

"I see."

"Behind the bar."

I'm about to ask about this friend and whether I've heard
about them before but she gets in there first.

"Hang on," Rozália says quietly. Her eyes widen, and she
points at Ray in what I think is meant to be a subtle way, but
subtlety is not really one of Rozália's strengths. "Is that her?"

"Who?" I say.

She rolls her eyes at me again.

"Ray."

I nod. I give her a look that I hope conveys that I want her to be cool and to shut up but also that I have no idea what she's even insinuating.

"Interesting," Rozália says, nodding slowly.

"No, it's not," I say. "It's not interesting."

"Very interesting indeed," Rozália says, taking one final drag on her cigarette and then stubbing it out.

"Stop it," I say. "Go back to your friends. Or go to bed. You're only twelve."

Rozália smiles and taps her glass to mine before she leaves.

"You would look good together," she says to me, loudly enough that Ray turns around.

"What was that?" she says as Rozália walks away.

"Nothing," I say. "She's very drunk; she doesn't know what she's saying, poor thing. She's been through so much."

Ray gives me a funny look but thankfully doesn't press me on it. She's too drunk or perhaps she simply doesn't care.

I spend the rest of the night dancing and trying to avoid Rozália. At some point, Kirsty leaves because she has to work in the morning. She and Ray have a brief, fraught conversation in the middle of the dance floor. I wonder if at some point Ray had said she'd go home with her or promised that the night would wrap up early. On her way out, Kirsty gives me a tight smile and lifts her hand slightly in lieu of a goodbye. My heart sinks, but I'm not sure why.

Jamie, who always magically knows the exact right time to go home, comes to find me just before 1:00 a.m. to tell me he's leaving and that I should leave too as "the night is about to die."

He's presumably told Ray the same thing, because she

comes up to me moments later and says into my ear, "I'm coming home with you, El."

I pull back and look at her blankly, frowning slightly, trying to take in what she's saying.

"I, um." I can't quite figure out how to respond. I feel sure that I've misheard her.

She leans forward again.

"I've left my keys at home, and Will's not back yet. I could ask Thea for hers, but she's miles away in Shepherd's Bush."

She looks at me, her face close to mine. She frowns slightly.

"That is OK, isn't it?" she says. "I can stay at someone else's if it's not . . ."

"No, no," I say, "it's fine. Of course it's fine."

She smiles, relieved. I can't believe she thinks there's a chance I might not want her to stay. I would have her move into my tiny room on a permanent basis in a heartbeat.

"Shall we leave now?" she says. "Jamie just told me the night is completely done. That it's only going downhill from here."

"He's not usually wrong," I say. "Yes, let's go."

We leave Ray's friends to it. I hug them goodbye. They wish us luck with the move, their eyes glassy, and suddenly it feels real. We're moving tomorrow—today! But first, Ray is sleeping over.

In the car on the way back to mine, the Uber driver has nineties dance anthems blaring out of the speakers in the headrests, which means we can't really talk, but it does give me the opportunity to try to remember exactly what kind of state I've left my room in. Are there clothes all over the floor? Is there half-eaten cheese on my bedside table? Have I got the *Frozen* duvet cover on the bed that I was sent by accident and just kept instead of returning? I can't definitively say no to any of these questions.

I'm relieved when we arrive home to find that the flat is empty. Amelia is obviously staying at her boyfriend's house tonight. I pour Ray and myself glasses from Amelia's jug of filtered water that I'm not meant to use. We stand and drink them in the dark before filling them up again immediately.

"It is funny to think that I've only been here a couple of times," Ray says, walking up the hall toward my bedroom before I can stop her. I was hoping to find an excuse to go and inspect it before she went in there.

"This one's your room, right?" She nods toward my closed bedroom door.

"Um, yep. Listen, sorry if it's a bit of a mess. I wasn't expecting . . ."

Ray rolls her eyes and opens my door. She flicks on the light, and she smiles in delight at the sight of my room. There are indeed clothes all over the floor, spilling out of boxes and bags. And there is indeed a snowman on my duvet cover.

"Very festive," Ray says, sitting on the edge of the bed and running her hand over Olaf's carrot nose.

"Yes," I say, trying to avoid catching her eye. "Thank you. It's a family heirloom, my grandmother's, it's very special to me."

I switch the main light off and turn a lamp on instead, the soft light somehow making my messy room look less atrocious. I walk over to my suitcase, surreptitiously kicking the clothes on the floor under the bed as I go. I sniff, trying to figure out if my room smells like the unlit fresh-linen-scented candle on my bedside table or of the sweet chili crisps I was eating before I left the house this evening.

"Do you want, um . . ." I root through the pile of pajamas I packed earlier, trying to find something to give Ray that isn't too humiliating. I land on blue cotton shorts and a white T-shirt that I once borrowed from Rob and never gave back. "These?"

"Thanks," she says, catching them as I throw them to her. I kneel on the floor next to my open suitcase and watch as she lies back on my bed, making no moves to get changed. She lifts her arm up to her face and covers her eyes with it briefly. I wonder if she can feel the room spinning.

"So," she says, "I guess this will be the first and last time I'll sleep at your house."

"Well, technically," I say, "soon you'll always be sleeping at my house."

A smile spreads across Ray's face. She sits up slightly.

"Huh, you're right. God, I'm so stupid. I can't believe I left my keys behind."

"I can," I say.

"It always works out though, doesn't it?" she says. "Now instead of spending the last night in London by myself, I get to spend it with you."

I don't know what to say to that. I concentrate on zipping my suitcase back up.

"What happened with Kirsty tonight? It looked pretty intense." I keep my eyes firmly fixed on the task at hand.

Ray sighs.

"She wanted me to leave with her, I think because it's my last night here. She felt I should."

"I get that," I say.

"But I wasn't ready to go."

I nod. I don't want to push it. I don't know why I asked or what I was hoping to hear.

Ray swings her legs back over the bed and pulls her T-shirt over her head, swapping it for the one I just passed her. She's always been like this. Uninhibited. Like she doesn't even notice I'm there, or she does and she doesn't mind me seeing her.

I head into the bathroom to get changed. I pull on an oversize T-shirt that comes down to my knees and watch myself brushing my teeth, my eyes bloodshot and wild, trying to implore myself to get it together. I splash cold water on my face and shiver.

When I get back to my room, Ray is already in bed. She covers her face and groans when I apologize for not having a spare toothbrush and ask if she wants to borrow mine.

"Will you think I'm disgusting if I don't brush my teeth?" she asks, her voice muffled, just her eyes peeking out from under the covers.

"Quite disgusting," I say, just because it seems like the right answer.

"In that case, I will. For you."

"Thank you," I say.

I crawl into bed once she's gone and lie there with my heart hammering. I rearrange myself a few times before she comes back in, trying to decide what might be the most flattering position. An arm flung above my head, on my side, my head resting on my hand. When she comes back, I am simply flat on my back, staring at the ceiling.

"Are you OK?" she says, climbing in beside me. "You look like you're having an existential crisis."

"Oh, you know," I say. "Just the usual."

When Ray's settled, I reach over her and switch off the lamp. There's a knack to it. In the dark she turns to face me, and I take a deep breath. She smells like cigarette smoke and toothpaste.

"El," Ray whispers.

"Yes," I whisper back.

"I can't believe you have a *Frozen* duvet cover."

"Fuck off."

I smile, despite myself. I feel my cheeks redden.

"I can't believe they even make them for double beds. I mean, was it intended for adults?"

"I don't know, Ray. I didn't buy it. It came by accident."

She's quiet for a moment.

"But you kept it."

"I kept it," I say. "I didn't think anyone else would see it."

Those words hang in the air for a moment. I close my eyes, momentarily floored by my loneliness. Sometimes buried so deep that I almost don't feel it at all. Sometimes right on the surface, I guess.

"I'm not bringing it with me," I say eventually.

Ray rolls onto her back so she's looking up at the ceiling too.

"New start, new snowman," Ray says.

I can't help but smile.

"New start, *no* snowman," I say.

"Right," Ray says. I can tell she's smiling too.

I fall asleep quickly after that, but I'm aware in the early morning, in a brief moment somewhere between waking and sleeping, of us facing each other, of Ray's arm flung out, my knees curled up to my chest, her hand brushing across my bare thigh. Perhaps I dreamed it, because in the morning she's far away on the other side of the bed wrapped up in the duvet, and I'm cold, trying to warm myself up with what's left.

CHAPTER EIGHT

Ray orders an Uber at seven thirty after several panicked phone calls from Will, who went into her room this morning to wake her up, only to find her bed unslept in and half her room still not packed up.

"Will, relax," she says, placing her phone down on my bedside table and putting it on speaker as she gets dressed. "I'm literally getting in an Uber as we speak, the movers aren't coming until ten. We've got too much time, if anything. We're going to be ready early. OK?"

"Ray," he says, his voice slightly hoarse. I picture him putting his fingers to his temples, counting to ten. "Please. Promise me you'll be ready on time. I really just need everything to go smoothly today." Perhaps he's also hungover.

"Trust me, Will," she says, lifting a dark blue hoodie of mine from the top of a box and holding it up to ask if she can wear it; I nod, and she pulls it on. "Everything's going to be just fine."

"Do you want anything?" I say, watching her try to locate her shoes. "Water? Tea?"

She shakes her head.

"No, I'm fine thanks, El." She glances at her phone. "The car is literally here anyway."

There's a loud beep of a car horn from outside as if the driver heard her.

She looks up at me from tying the laces on her sneakers.

"Plus I don't want you to get out of bed," she says. "You look too cozy."

She leans over the mattress to kiss me on the cheek.

"See you later," she says, and then pauses in the doorway. The horn blares from outside again, but it's as though Ray can't hear it. She doesn't even blink.

"Bloody hell, El. I can't believe it's really happening."

I shake my head. "Me neither."

"See you at home," she says, raising a hand and then running down the hall. I hear her answer the phone just before she pulls the front door open.

"Yes, Will! I'm around the corner, I'll be thirty seconds, max."

The morning goes by in a blur. Not too long after Ray leaves, Rob pulls up in a van he's hired. I thank him profusely, but he insists this is a fun day for him. I believe him. He loves driving things and lifting things. I'll never understand it.

"You look exhausted," I say, watching as he picks up the first box. "Why are you so pale?"

"Long week," Rob says. He doesn't look at me, focused on the job at hand. "Come on, let's get going."

Loading my belongings into the van doesn't take long. There isn't much. I strip the bed while Rob is carrying out two huge Sainsbury's bags full of books. I roll the *Frozen* duvet cover up and throw it in the bin before I leave.

"Didn't you want to say goodbye to Amelia?" Rob asks, as I pull the front door closed for the final time.

"No," I say. "I mean, I literally can't. She's not here."

Rob laughs. "Charming."

I've already said a goodbye of sorts. After I made my cup of tea this morning, I left her a note on the fridge saying, *I think you're out of milk:)*.

We drive south to pick up Jamie in Kennington. When we arrive, he is sitting on the doorstep outside his flat surrounded by cardboard boxes and suitcases. He stands and waves frantically as we pull up, as if we somehow might miss him.

"Robert," Jamie says, kissing Rob on both cheeks, "our hero."

"My pleasure. Although I seem to remember that I was promised pastries in exchange for removal services," Rob says, grabbing a couple of Jamie's suitcases and throwing them in the back of the van.

"Have I ever let you down?" Jamie says, leaning nonchalantly against a cardboard box. And then, "Listen, be right back."

Before we even know what's happening Jamie darts off down the street, presumably to procure the pastries he's forgotten about. Rob and I spend the next ten minutes loading all of Jamie's belongings into the van, putting the last box in just as he strolls around the corner, carrying a tray of coffees in one hand and an enormous paper bag in the other.

"Told you I wouldn't let you down," Jamie says. "Wow"—he looks at the empty pavement—"that was fast work."

"Would have been much faster with three of us," I say.

"Shhh," Jamie says, holding out the tray of coffees to me. I begrudgingly take one. "Don't be a grump on moving day."

We all climb into the front of the van, Jamie wedged into the seat between Rob and me. We drink our flat whites and take bites out of all the different pastries, passing them round so we get to try each one.

"So how was last night?" Rob says. "You both look pretty shattered."

"Um," Jamie says, "I actually look very refreshed and well rested, thank you."

"Why are you wearing sunglasses inside, then?" I ask.

"Fair point," Jamie says, his mouth full of pain au chocolat.

"It was good," I say. "It felt like a nice way to say goodbye."

"Yeah, what time did you leave? Did Ray stay until the bitter end?" Jamie asks.

"Um, well. Ray actually forgot her keys, so she ended up staying at mine."

Jamie turns very slowly to look at me. I'm glad I can't see his eyes through his sunglasses. I can see his raised eyebrows though. He takes a sip of his coffee.

"Did she now?"

I glance at Rob, who is completely focused on his croissant, oblivious to Jamie's reaction.

"Yes," I say.

"Well," Jamie says, "isn't that nice. A lovely birthday treat for Ray."

I dig my elbow into his side, and he yelps. I can't help but laugh. Giddy all of a sudden with the prospect of the move, about being wedged into a van eating croissants with two of my favorite people, about having spent the night with Ray.

The giddiness subsides gradually throughout the journey as we hit traffic and as we finally leave London and drive on quieter roads, past fields and trees. At one point we get stuck behind an actual tractor, and I worry that Rob is getting so stressed that he'll have an aneurysm.

"Rob," Jamie says. "You need to relax. This is just country life. We will probably have to stop to let some ducklings cross soon."

When we arrive, Will and Ray rush out of the front door. They both have a totally wild look in their eyes. Like it's finally hit home what we're doing.

"The removal guys just left," Ray says by way of greeting, as we get out of the van. "They're gone. All our stuff is in there."

She shakes her head a little, like she can't really believe what she's saying.

"All right, Rob," Will says, stepping forward and holding out his hand.

"All right, mate," Rob says. "Traffic not too bad?"

"Yes, mate," Will says. "You know how it is. Saturday morning."

"Got stuck behind a tractor," Rob says.

That seems to be enough chat for them. Without discussing it they both move to the back of the van and start moving boxes.

It doesn't take long for us to get all our things inside. The five of us stand in the kitchen, leaning against unfamiliar surfaces. I run my finger along the sideboard behind me, and when I lift it up, it's gray with dirt.

Ray gestures to a white bakery box on the counter.

"Help yourself to cookies," she says.

Rob, Jamie, and I each take one. Ray and Will have obviously already been eating them, but I can see that they once spelled out *New Home*; they're surrounded by cookies in the shape of front doors.

"These are amazing," I say. "Who are they from?"

"Kirsty," Ray says, picking up a front door and running her finger through the red icing. She licks it off before biting into it. "I think she arranged to have them sent here a while ago. Or maybe I'm forgiven."

"Who's Kirsty?" Rob asks, dusting crumbs from the *N* cookie off his shirt.

"Ray's girlfriend," Jamie answers for Ray, while her mouth is full.

"Oh!" Rob says, his head snapping up from inspecting his shirt. He glances at me, frowning slightly, and my stomach flips. Perhaps he's not so oblivious after all. I feel some shame at his surprise. Have I really never mentioned Kirsty?

I don't quite meet Rob's eyes, busying myself instead with taking everyone's various water bottles and filling them up. The water from the tap either comes out in a drizzle or a dramatic spurt. No in-between.

Fortunately no one else seems to register Rob's reaction to learning about Kirsty. I know my brother well enough to be sure that he won't ask any more questions. He won't make me talk if I don't want to.

Once the others have said their goodbyes and sent him off with a front-door cookie to see him through his journey back to London, I walk him out to the van.

"Thank you," I say, wrapping my arms around his waist and hugging him. "I don't know what I'd do without you."

He puts one arm around my shoulders and holds me for a moment. He lifts the front door to his mouth and takes a bite, and then he brushes my hair slightly. Presumably I am covered in crumbs.

"Anytime," he says, as I pull away.

"Get home safe," I call, as he walks around to the driver's side. When he's opened the van door he stops, his hand resting on the top. He drums it with his fingers.

"You will be OK here, won't you?" he says. He's biting the inside of his cheek, just like I do when I'm uncomfortable.

"Yes," I say quickly. I laugh. "Obviously, I'll be OK. I'll be better than OK. Great!"

He looks at me for a moment longer, and I nod. An acknowledgment that I know what he's getting at. I desperately don't want him to say it.

"I'm fine," I say. "It's not . . ."

I can't say it's not what you think.

"It's not a problem," I say.

"OK," he says. And then he smiles, a proper smile, like he's relieved. He believes me. "I'm happy for you. We'll come and see you soon."

"Be careful driving home," I say. "You really do look awful, Rob. Maybe you're coming down with something."

"Maybe," he says, smiling grimly. "I'll be fine."

I wave until his car is gone from the driveway, until he's at the bottom of the hill, until he's just a speck in the distance.

Back inside the house I find the others have left the kitchen and are standing in our new living room, which is piled high with boxes and random bits of furniture that we've found on Facebook Marketplace in the past few weeks. Now that Rob has left and we're alone, it suddenly feels very quiet here. Silent in fact. The four of us stand and look at each other. For a long time, no one says anything.

"Well," Ray says eventually, her hands on her hips. "Fuck."

Will laughs and then sits down on top of a box marked "Stuff." Definitely one of Ray's.

He rubs his eyes and looks blearily up at the rest of us. He looks even skinnier than usual. The stress of these past few weeks has clearly taken its toll on him.

"This is surreal," he says, shaking his head. "It wasn't too long ago that it was meant to be me and Mel sitting here."

Ray moves to stand next to him and squeezes his shoulder.

"Oh, Will. I'm sorry," she says.

"No, no," he says, "it's OK. It's good. This feels right. It does feel right, doesn't it?"

I nod. Weirdly it does feel right. I mean, it feels insane but it feels right. I can see how one day, this could be our home. Maybe once I've got a bed. That will be a start.

"Will," Jamie says, nudging him so that he shifts over and Jamie can perch on the box next to him, "it's been a mad day. It's OK to feel weird. This is weird."

Will nods. He wraps an arm around Jamie's shoulders, partly affectionately but mostly because now he doesn't have enough room to sit down and he needs the support.

"Good weird though," he says.

"Good weird," we all agree.

We choose bedrooms like we're kids on holiday. We let Will have the first pick, which seems only fair as he not only paid for the house but is also clearly on the verge of some sort of crisis. The rest of us fight it out. At one point Jamie is scream-ing while Ray tries to pick him up and move him out of the big bedroom overlooking the garden. She wins that particular fight. I end up with the slightly smaller room. The walls are lilac and have a band of floral wallpaper around the middle. I think

I actually chose a similar color for my bedroom when I was ten years old. Ray and Jamie say it makes sense for me to have the smaller room because I "don't even have a bed"; they don't listen when I tell them that's obviously only temporary. I'm happy enough though, really. This bedroom overlooks the garden too, and it's next door to Ray's room. I roll my yoga mat out right next to the adjoining wall and then tell myself off for being a creep. I don't move it though.

We don't unpack any of the useful stuff. None of us can find a phone charger. We don't know where the kettle is. Ray has, however, packed a hammer and some picture hooks in her backpack so she can go around the entire house hanging up all our various prints and photographs. When you've been renting for ten years there's something deeply satisfying about taking a nail to a wall and hammering it in. A tiny demolition that says, *This is mine to destroy, should I want to.*

Over the course of the day several neighbors pop by to welcome us to the village. Well, they claim it's to welcome us to the village. I think most of them are probably very concerned about four young people moving into a village full of identikit families. We don't really fit the mold. And I'm sure they paid a lot of money to live in a place where people fit the mold.

One of the neighbors, an elderly woman, brings us a cake. We see her wobbling up the hill, struggling with her walking stick and her Tupperware box. Ray runs out to meet her. They arrive at our front door, the woman's arm linked through Ray's, both giggling at something. Up close, the woman is absolutely tiny: she can't even be five foot tall.

"This is Sally," Ray says, "she's made us a cake, isn't that amazing?"

"Oh," Sally says, blushing, "it's just a lemon drizzle, it's nothing."

Will and Jamie appear in the hallway too, and we all gush over the cake, and Sally takes the four of us in. You can practically see the cogs in her brain whirring. She frowns.

"So, the four of you? Are you . . . are you?" She pushes her glasses up her nose. "Married or . . . ?"

Will laughs easily, puts his arm around Jamie's shoulders and squeezes.

"No, Sally. We're all just good friends."

Will is regularly mistaken for Jamie's boyfriend given how much time they spend together, and every time it happens, he just says, "I should be so lucky." I love Will.

"I see," Sally says.

I watch her take in Jamie's outfit. The shorts are extra short today. His T-shirt is slightly cropped. Sally's eyes widen suddenly, and my heart sinks. I stiffen. Preparing myself for whatever she's about to say.

"Have you met the other ones?" Sally asks. She points down the hill with her walking stick.

"Sorry?" I say.

"The other ones, you know . . . Rafe and Jim, they're called. Lovely boys. They live in the blue house just off the high street. They've got spaniels. Always do a lovely sponge for the fete."

Jamie glances at me, his eyes wide, and I look away, afraid I might giggle.

"We haven't yet, Sally," Ray says, grinning. "But we'll look out for boys and their spaniels."

"Do you want to come in?" Will says, "I'm afraid we've not really got anywhere to sit at the moment. . . ."

"No, no," Sally says, "I just came to say hello. Maybe another time though."

She peers into the house behind us, clearly very keen to have a look around.

"Definitely another time," Will says, and Sally beams. Ray's not the only old lady charmer among us.

Ray ends up walking Sally all the way home, which is just to the bottom of the hill and a couple of houses down.

"I can't believe you've met someone already," Jamie says when she gets back.

"What can I say?" Ray says. "I'm irresistible."

"I think I might still be in with a chance," Will says.

"So there *are* gays in the village," Jamie says triumphantly.

"Aren't you glad you've got the bedroom at the front now?" Ray says. "Now you can sit on the windowsill looking out for anyone walking a spaniel carrying a sponge cake."

We spend the afternoon half-heartedly unpacking but mostly running around the house trying to find the spots with good phone reception. Will had the good sense to get the Wi-Fi set up last week so we can walk around on FaceTime to various family members giving them tours of the house, bumping into each other in the hallway and waving to whoever's on the screen.

"Say hi to Yai," Jamie says, shoving his phone in my face. All I see is the top of his grandmother's head. She has her phone pointed at the ceiling.

"Hi, Yai!" I say, dutifully, absolutely certain she has no idea who I am.

A rapid burst of Thai comes out of Jamie's phone, and he screws up his face, trying to pick out some key phrases. Despite describing himself as bilingual (usually with a wink), from what I can tell, his Thai isn't great, although he manages to have an extremely close relationship with his grandmother anyway. He FaceTimes her at least once a week, and she's on Whats-App. He loves to send her photos of his outfits every day so she can tell him how handsome he is. He covers the phone with his hand and looks at me conspiratorially.

"So I told her that I bought the house myself because I'm doing so well," he says. "I think she thinks you're one of the movers."

He takes his hand away from the phone screen and beams at Yai and then looks back up at me with a patronizing smile.

"Good job!" he says to me, and then moves their tour along to the kitchen.

I head into my bedroom, and on a whim, call Mum. I don't expect for a second that she'll answer, but almost immediately her tanned face pops up on the screen, pixelated, her long, dark hair blowing in her face. I wince and turn the volume down; all I can hear is the wind.

"Mum?"

"Hi, honey!" Mum yells.

"Are you on the . . ."

"We're on the ship! We're up on the deck sunbathing although it's a little windy today. I keep losing my hat, Daddy has to run off and get it for me."

I close my eyes briefly. I really can't cope with her calling him "Daddy."

"Oh, great," I say, squinting at the phone, "listen, I'm ringing because today I moved into the—"

"Say hi to your dad, honey!" Mum trills. "What do you think of his new trunks?"

The camera pans down to my dad's near-naked body on a

sun lounger. He is wearing the smallest swimming trunks I've ever seen. Once again, I squeeze my eyes shut.

"Oh my god, Mum! No! Is he wearing a thong?"

She chuckles delightedly.

"We're on holiday, darling, we thought they were fun."

Dad says something inaudible, and Mum giggles and slaps him. I wonder what time it is on the boat; I'm guessing on international waters it is always cocktail hour.

"Anyway," I raise my voice over the sound of the wind, "this morning we moved into the—"

"Are you on the farm?" my mum says. "Are you all moved in OK?"

"Yes! Do you want a tour, I could—"

"We do, honey," Mum says, "but we've got yoga in ten minutes. Your dad can nearly do a headstand, can you believe it?"

"I hope he puts some trousers on first."

"What's that?"

"Nothing," I say, "you guys have fun."

"Listen, honey. Send us some photos. We want to see what you're up to down there on the farm. What an adventure you're going to have!"

She beams down the phone at me, and I see how thrilled she is that I'm doing something exciting for a change. Or that I spontaneously called her. Both. I can't help but smile back at her. She's right. It is an adventure.

Mum turns the phone to Dad again—thankfully just his face. He waves, and I hear Mum yelling, "Love to you darling, from me and Daddy and Bernard Bear!"

"You're not even with Bernard, he's at the dog—"

Before I can even finish my sentence, she's gone. Off to do obscene boat yoga with my naked father.

Late in the afternoon, just as we're all starting to flag, Will rounds us up and takes us outside. We all grumble as he herds us out the front door.

"It'll only take a minute," he promises, "then we can sit down and have a drink."

We line up in front of the house and look at him. He clears his throat. I notice that he's standing weirdly, one hand behind his back like a butler.

"Are you about to make a speech?" Ray says. "Should I be filming this?"

"No, I'm not going to . . ." Will's cheeks redden slightly. "I'm not making a speech. I just wanted to . . . So when Melissa and I were going to move here she always said we should call the house Meadow View—"

"Why?" Jamie interrupts, frowning. "You can't see a meadow from here."

He spins around to check and then nods, confirmed—no meadow.

"What even is a meadow?" Ray says.

"Exactly," says Jamie.

"Right," Will says. "I never liked it either. But I was thinking this house really should have a name. And when we came here all together for the first time, we stood out here and even though the inside was pretty rotten . . ."

"Is pretty rotten," Ray says, and I elbow her in the side.

"Let him finish," I whisper. I nod at Will, encouraging him to continue.

"Yes, true. It is pretty rotten. But what I remember is the lavender. The smell of the lavender."

He gestures to all the bushes surrounding us, and I reach out a hand to touch one, rubbing a flower between my fingers.

"And that was such a happy day, and I thought maybe that's the perfect name, so . . ."

He pulls out a slate sign from behind his back. Written in white letters on the front is *Lavender House*.

"Wilma!" Jamie exclaims, reaching forward to take the sign from him, to get a better look.

"I love it," I say.

"Yeah," Ray says, squeezing his arm, "a thousand times better than Meadow View."

"Really? Are you sure? Because we can change it if . . . put it to a vote or something. . . . It was just . . ."

Will is smiling broadly, his face totally flushed now—I think half-embarrassed, half-thrilled by our reaction.

"No," Jamie says. "It's perfect."

"I think we might need someone to come and put it up for us, but for now . . ."

Will takes the sign back from Jamie and leans it up against the wall on our porch.

"Welcome to Lavender House," he says.

We're all quiet for a moment, taking it in.

"Come on," Ray says after a minute, clapping her hands together decisively. "Let's go and get a drink."

We gather around Ray's nan's old dining room table on some chairs we picked up last week from a girl who was clearly selling everything that belonged to her ex-boyfriend. They're vintage and beautifully restored and quite obviously cost more than the £50 for all six that we paid for them. We haven't unpacked any glasses, so we're drinking champagne out of mugs. Weirdly, when you buy a house, which in and of itself is a huge celebration, people buy you bottles of champagne on top of that. I really needed this champagne when I was living in Amelia's box room trying to decide if I could afford to buy a pizza from Tesco Express for my dinner ahead of payday. No one buys you champagne to cheer you up, though.

After a couple of mugs of champagne, I feel the adrenaline from the day start to wear off and a sleepy contentment washes over me. Will orders pizza from the one pizza place in the nearest town that delivers to the village. We'd had a small moment of horror when we realize there is no Deliveroo and no Uber here, but it's quickly forgotten when the pizza arrives, and we decide we'll just eat pizza all the time. And cook. We'll probably all just become incredible cooks. We eat as though it's our first meal in months. I can't remember ever having done so much manual labor. I tentatively press my arm to see if it's developed a muscle—nothing yet.

We "retire to the living room," in Ray's words, for our final bottle of champagne and Sally's lemon drizzle cake, which is sharp and moist and delicious. We don't know where the plates are, so we just pick it up out of the box with our hands. It has been presliced as if she instinctively knew we wouldn't be the kind of people able to locate a knife.

There's nothing to sit on yet, since we insisted the disgusting sofa be removed from the house before we moved in, and so we sit on the tatty red carpet and lean our backs against boxes. Ray is next to me, and when she crosses her legs, her knee rests on my outstretched thigh. I don't move, and neither does she, and so we sit like that eating cake and drinking champagne in our home, and I think, if I died right now, I'd die happy. I'm too drunk and sleepy to chastise myself for being melodramatic.

"We should have a housewarming," Jamie says, crawling around on the carpet, topping up everyone's mugs.

"Yes!" Ray says. "When? A couple of weeks? A month? We can get the house in decent shape by then, can't we?"

Will nods.

"Yeah," he says. "Maybe a few weeks to get ourselves sorted, although I do think the trick is to do the housewarming before you make the house *too* nice."

"We'll organize it," Ray says. "Well," she says, looking at me and grinning.

"I'll organize it," I say, "*obviously*." I always pretend to be slightly put-upon but actually I do love to organize stuff like this. I am already mentally planning a guest list, a signature cocktail, the perfect name for the WhatsApp group.

"Do you think we should invite people from the village?" Will asks. "We probably should, shouldn't we?"

Jamie nods.

"We've obviously got to invite the boys and their spaniels."

"And Sally," I add.

"And your friend," Ray says.

"Who's my friend?"

"From the pub."

"Oh, Rachel," I say. "Yeah, I hadn't thought of that."

"It'll be good to get to know everyone," Ray says. "And for them to get to know us. To know that this is a good commune, not the kind of commune that tries to recruit people and take all their money."

"Well," Will says, "we'll see how much the renovations are, and then we'll see about that."

"True," Ray says. "Needs must."

That night I lie on my yoga mat, wrapped in my duvet, scrolling through my phone, trying to find a bed frame that I can make Will go and collect in his car next week. I wince at the price of mattresses. I don't understand how they can cost so much. As I roll over on the hard floor, a nail sticking up from the floorboards bruises my back. I concede that this may be a cost that I am going to have to somehow suck up.

I am getting used to the earthy smell of the house now. I think another accurate word to describe it would be *damp*. Or *dank*. When I was brushing my teeth, I am certain I saw a mushroom sprouting from the bricks surrounding the rotten windowpane.

I reach for my journal and read May's entry where I wrote *Made a decision to move out of London (bye Amelia!) and into a commune in the countryside.* I pick up my pen and next to *June* I write *actually left London and moved into a dilapidated commune in the countryside. With Ray. Maybe the wildest thing yet.*

Tomorrow is July. At the moment the page is blank, and I truly cannot imagine what wild thing might fill it. Six months ago I thought I'd be trapped in Amelia's flat forever, and look at me now—with a floor to call my own. I suspect I'll have traveled to the moon or similar by Christmas. There's no way Ray can accuse me of anything other than being the boldest, most adventurous woman she knows now.

In the darkness I listen to the new noises. No power ballads. Just creaking floorboards, the rustle of trees in the breeze, something slightly alarming happening in the pipes. There's Ray climbing into bed in the room next to mine. I lie with my hand tucked under my pillow, facing the wall between us.

Before we went to bed, Ray and I stood at the back door and stared into the darkness of the garden. Just shapes and smells and unfamiliar noises, all my senses heightened at the touch of Ray's arm, her fingers brushing against mine.

"It feels magical out there, doesn't it, El?" she'd said, her eyes looking right into mine, straight through me. It was one of those moments where I felt she could read my mind, all the thoughts I've ever had.

"Yes," I whispered. She held my gaze for a second, and then she smiled at me, squeezed my hand, and walked away, leaving me alone, staring out into the dark.

CHAPTER NINE

We've all taken two weeks of annual leave in order to start work on the house. Jamie has set up an Instagram account called @TheVillagePeople69, which attracts several thousand followers in just a few days. I think this is partly due to the novelty of a bunch of queers (and our generous straight benefactor) setting up camp in the countryside but mostly because Jamie keeps posting photos of himself shirtless holding drills with hashtags like #DaddysHome. We spend a week unpacking boxes, ripping up carpets, sanding floorboards (Ray is in her element, and we were wrong—she does know what she's doing), and bleaching everything in sight. The earthy smell begins to fade. It starts to smell like paint and cleaning supplies and the meals we're cooking. It starts to smell like home.

On the Monday morning after we moved in Will drove me

to a house two villages over, where we picked up a white metal bed frame and a mattress from a very nice lady who insisted it was "barely used." I don't like the frame, but it's cheap, and actually, once it's set up in my room, it looks fine. Certainly much better than the yoga mat that I slept on all weekend despite Ray's pleas to just sleep in her bed. I don't know why I didn't give in. It would be too painful maybe. Or a slippery slope. Or maybe I'm just a martyr, which is the accusation she and the others rudely leveled at me.

I take it upon myself to tackle the garden, and so every morning I get up early, before the others, and start clipping and trimming and clearing. I make lists of things we need to buy from garden centers and hardware stores. I turn soil and inspect plants for signs of life. I find raspberries and strawberries and gooseberries thriving. *We can live off the land,* I say to the others in the evenings, feverish with excitement as I eat tiny, sharp, potentially poisonous berries and google *how to grow carrots.* Right at the end of the garden there's a wall with ivy growing up it and some slightly moldy decking. I make plans for a terrace, a little corner of the garden with festoon lights and comfy seats and maybe even a firepit. It feels like a dream. But it's real. I can bend down and touch the ground and run the soil between my fingers, dig my nails into it and make my mark.

Ray promises that on Saturday morning she'll take me to the garden center and we'll get everything we need. We take Will's car and my shopping list and choose paving stones and trellises and outdoor lights and soil. We wince at the price and put it on my credit card. *It's an investment,* we say to each other over and over again. We drive into the town nearby and buy coffee and posh bacon sandwiches (even though we both consider ourselves to be vegetarians) and sit on a bench overlooking the park.

"This is all very quaint, isn't it?" Ray says, taking a bite of her sandwich.

We watch as a group of teenage boys drinking cans of energy drink take turns kicking a swing.

"It's charming," I say.

"Well, not this necessarily," she says, "but I mean going to the fucking garden center on a Saturday morning. What are we going to do later?" She puts on a high-pitched posh-lady voice. "Go to the village pub? Tell stories by the fire?"

I look at her.

"I mean, probably. We are going to go to the pub, and then I'd imagine we'll come home and gossip about everything."

"That sounds really nice actually," Ray says. "I do want to do that."

"Are you missing London?" I ask, nudging her knee gently with mine.

"Well, yeah," Ray says. "It's home isn't it?"

If I was Ray I'd be missing home too. Home for her was never her damp shared house with Will, it's her mum's house, and her nan's flat. Her huge, close-knit family who fight constantly and scream with laughter and have raucous parties and love each other loudly and fiercely. When I first met them at a birthday party Ray's mum was throwing the year after I'd met her, I immediately felt that I knew her better. That I understood why she is the way she is—confident and free-spirited and carefree. Ray claims her mum drives her mad, but I know she talks to her every day. She has the kind of family that I longed for when I was growing up. That I know Rob and Polly will have one day. That I hope I will too.

"It's been a weird few days," I say. "You won't be missing it when we're commuting next week."

"True," she says, and smiles. "I'm not complaining, you know."

"You're allowed to complain."

"I'm not," she says. "I'm bloody lucky. I have nothing to complain about."

I wait a couple of beats. Take a sip of my coffee. I wipe my finger around the inside of my paper bag to pick up any stray crumbs.

"Are you missing Kirsty?"

"Yeah," Ray says. And then, "No. I don't know. I think I miss having the option to see her. I miss knowing she's there."

I nod. "You'll see her next week."

"I know. And she might come and stay soon too. Once we're a bit more settled."

I force a smile, biting the inside of my cheek.

"Lovely."

"Come on, you," Ray says, grabbing my knee and squeezing before hopping up from the bench. She reaches her hand out. For a split second I think she means for me to take it, but I realize she wants me to pass her my paper bag for her to put in the bin.

"Let's go and build your beautiful garden."

When we arrive home, Will opens the front door before we're even out of the car. For a moment I find myself wondering if we might be in trouble, as if he's my dad.

"You're going to want to see this," Will says by way of greeting, walking around to the trunk to grab a bag of soil.

"See what?"

"Just go round the back," Will says.

"Should I be nervous?" I ask.

Will just shakes his head. He's trying his best to look exasperated, but I notice that despite himself, there's a flicker of a smile.

We walk through to the garden via the side gate and see that Jamie is sitting cross-legged in the grass with his arms wrapped around a chicken. There is another chicken lurking near a bush and another making her way through the open back door.

"Meet the girls!" Jamie says, thrilled. He gives the chicken's head a little pat as though she were a dog. It is immediately clear that he has absolutely no idea what he's doing.

"Oh, I love them!" Ray says, throwing down the trellis she's holding and striding toward the back door to collect the wayward chicken.

"Um, Jamie. Where did they come from?" I ask.

"Well," Jamie says, putting his chicken down and brushing off his shirt. "I got talking to Rafe and Jim."

"Oh god, were you really watching for them out your window?" I ask, walking around the edge of the garden, trying to sheepdog one of them away from the hedges, worried she'll escape.

"No! They just happened to be walking their dog as I happened to be taking in the view."

"So he ran downstairs and collared them," Will says.

"We bumped into each other in the street, and I introduced myself! They're really very nice. And excited to have us here. This place has been vacant for ages, and they've been keeping an eye out for who would end up taking it on. *Anyway,* long story short. They were on their way to meet a friend who rescues chickens and wanted to know if we were interested, and we've *always* said we wanted hens."

"We have literally never said that," Ray says.

"It was implied," Jamie says, "but then I said that we didn't have a coop, so they said we could have their old one because they've recently upgraded. They dropped it round here and then gave me a lift to collect the hens and voilà, our new babies!"

"Jamie, do you like chickens?" I ask, jumping back as one of them pecks at my sneakers.

"I like rescuing vulnerable animals, Eleanor," he says seriously. "I like changing lives."

"Right," I say dubiously.

"So you're going to be responsible for them?" Will says. "You have to feed them, put them in the coop every evening and make sure it's completely secure. Or foxes will get them."

"No!" Jamie says, as if this is the first he's heard of foxes. "No! I'll protect them from danger! These are going to be the happiest chickens in the world. I've already named them—Edward, Jacob, and Bella."

Ray groans.

"Please tell me these are not Twilight chickens," she says.

"Sorry," Jamie says, "but they are my daughters, and those are their names."

We sit awhile in the grass and watch them get used to their new surroundings. We put down some of the chicken feed the rescue lady gave us, and it's oddly satisfying watching them eat it. The closer we look, the sadder they seem. Patches of missing feathers, skinny where you'd expect them to be round.

"The chicken lady said once they're happier they might lay eggs," Jamie says, picking Edward up as she waddles past and stroking her gently under his arm. "But they might not. And that would be OK too," he says, addressing the chicken. "Edward, you're just here to enjoy yourself."

We spend the afternoon in the garden with the chickens. Ray and I make great progress with what we decide to call "the nook": we attach the trellis to the wall and clean the decking the best we can. We drag plant pots up there and make plans for furniture, a firepit, lights.

"It'll look a bit like where they go to do the recouplings in *Love Island*," Ray says when I've finished describing my plans in detail.

"Exactly," I say.

We investigate the ancient shed and find that behind it there are short stumpy logs, clearly intended to be split for firewood. Inside, among a lot of other junk, there are some rusty, old tools and an ax.

Ray's eyes light up.

"Ray," I say, "no. You don't know what you're doing."

"It's not hard," she says. "I'll just stand them up somewhere flat and chop."

"We don't need any firewood," I say. "It's boiling hot."

"Stores for the winter," she says quietly, transfixed as she picks up the ax, testing the weight of it.

I can see that I'm fighting a losing battle.

Ray takes the ax outside to show the boys and then insists we help her carry the logs onto the patio, where she can stand them up on the paving stones. We gather around as if she's about to put on a show. We're all quiet while she watches a YouTube tutorial on her phone, biting her lip in concentration.

"OK, got it," she says after a couple of minutes. "Easy."

She takes off the shirt she was wearing so she's just in her tank top. As she picks up the ax, Jamie cries out.

"Stop!"

"What? Why? What's the matter?"

"Pose with it for a sec," Jamie says, getting to his feet and aiming his camera at her.

Ray rolls her eyes, but she obliges. I know she's secretly loving the attention.

"Get some action shots, J," she says.

"Obviously," he says. "This is great content. You look hot."

She does. Ray raises the ax above her head, and I cover my eyes, watching through my fingers as she brings it down and splinters the wood. After the first few times when it's clear she isn't going to lose control of the ax or chop off her hands, I relax and settle into just watching her. After only a few minutes she's pouring with sweat and Will passes her a bottle of water. She swigs from it and wipes her mouth. She grins at me when she catches me staring.

"You want a go, El?"

I shake my head. "Definitely not."

"She's happy just watching," Jamie says to Ray, and then quietly, just to me, "you pervert."

When the sun goes down and we're exhausted, covered in soil and can't face any more weeding, we give the chickens some more pellets and feed them a couple of homegrown strawberries straight from the plant, which they seem to enjoy. We make Jamie come downstairs to round them up and put them away for the night, which is one of the funniest things I've ever seen. Nothing in recent memory has made me howl with laughter as much as watching Jamie jogging around the garden trying to catch three chickens. Every time he gets one, another escapes. In the end, Will rescues him. Ray and I can't help, as we have sunk to the ground, hysterical. The chicken coop looks a bit like a playhouse and once Will and Jamie have battened down the hatches, we do a lap of the perimeter, inspecting it for possible fox entryways.

"Should we get a security camera?" Jamie says, biting his lip.

"For the chickens?" asks Ray. "No."

"Ray," he says, "they're my *children*."

We get to the pub by seven and happily, it's livelier than when we came before. Not busy necessarily, but there's a gentle background hum of conversation, the sound of glasses clinking. There's faint music playing in the background, so quiet that I can barely make out what it is. I very nearly remark on how nice it is not to have to shout over the music to hear each other but stop myself when I remember that I am not one hundred years old.

Rachel is behind the bar along with her dad, and when we walk in, she looks up and smiles. She's serving a customer but mouths to us, "Be with you in a minute."

It feels good to see a familiar face. I realize that aside from Sally and the neighbors who popped round on day one, I haven't spoken to anyone in person apart from Ray, Jamie, and Will since we arrived.

We sit outside to make the most of the balmy evening. All the other tables are occupied, mostly by families. Nearly all of them have dogs. It's actually not a dissimilar scene to some of the pubs I used to go to in Leyton, which seem to double up as crèches on weekends.

"So, how are you all getting on? All settled in?" Rachel has a notepad and pen poised as if she might jot down our answer.

"Um," I say, looking around the group, "I'd say we're getting there. I mean, it's clean now. I would say it's safe to live in, what do you think?"

"Oh yeah," the rest of the group echoes, "safe to live in now."

"Well that's something," Rachel says. "And you're enjoying village life?"

"Absolutely," Ray says. "Sally made us a cake on our first day here, which was very kind. Everyone's been so welcoming."

"We got given some free chickens today," Jamie says. "Live ones."

Rachel laughs.

"Oh, wow, cake and chickens. The full welcome package!"

"We're going to have a housewarming in a few weeks," Will says. "Show off our handiwork. It would be nice to get to know everyone. Do you think it would be the kind of thing people would want to come to?"

"Are you kidding?" Rachel says. "A chance to snoop around someone else's house and drink? You'll be turning people away at the door. It will probably make the parish news."

We order a couple of bottles of wine and fish and chips, which Rachel says is the best thing on the menu. She's right. It's delicious. Everything is fresh. The chips even have little bits of their skins left on them—rendering them, in my eyes, a vegetable.

I hold a chip up as if inspecting it in the light.

"We could grow these, you know."

"Chips?" Jamie says. He is not paying attention because he's trying to find his light for a selfie, no doubt for @TheVillagePeople69. He has huge sunglasses on and is raising his glass of rosé, cheersing the air.

"Potatoes," I say. "Then we could make our own chips. Farm to table."

Ray laughs. "I had no idea you were so into gardening, El. Our very own Charlie Dimmock."

"What are you talking about? I've always been into gardening! I grew those herbs on my windowsill once."

They'd died. But still.

"So the housewarming," Ray says. "Let's pick a date. Let's sort a theme."

"Is the theme not just . . . housewarming?" Will says.

"Oh, Will." Ray looks at him kindly. "Do we really want all our new village friends to think we're sad and boring?"

Jamie shakes his head at Will in disappointment.

"Do we want Sally to think we don't know how to throw a party?" Ray continues. "Do we want the parish news write-up to say 'a quiet but pleasant affair'?"

Will holds up his hands in defeat.

"Fine. Fine. Sorry. Of course. A theme."

"Right, so," Ray says, "I think, and Jamie agrees with me, that the theme should be—festival."

She looks at Jamie, and he nods. This feels rehearsed.

"Exactly." I almost expect Jamie to say, *Thanks, Ray,* as if they're taking it in turns to present a news segment. "So that means music, lights, the garden looking *stunning,* which," he says, pointing at me, "is already well on its way."

He looks to Ray, and she continues.

"And everyone has to dress like they're going to Glastonbury, and we thought we'd put a bell tent up in the garden and serve local beers and cider, and someone can do face paint and . . ."

"Do we have a bell tent?" Will asks.

"Not at the moment," Ray says, "but I mean, worst-case scenario we can just stick Rob's tent up, can't we, El?"

"Erm," I start to protest, but the presentation is not over yet.

"And as Jamie says, we'll string up a load of lights, and we can put loads of camping chairs and blankets out so people can sit down, and we were thinking this theme means other than to use the loo, it keeps people strictly outside so we don't have to worry about the house."

Ray looks at Will, and he breaks out into a smile.

"OK, sold," he says. "It sounds like fun."

"El?"

"I'm in," I say. I'm excited to have a chance to show off the garden. "Wait though," I add. "How are we going to invite everyone? Like . . . am I going to have to print paper invitations?"

Jamie shakes his head and waves his phone at me.

"I'll invite them in the group. Just tell me what to say."

I frown.

"What group?"

"The village WhatsApp group."

"What?"

I look at Ray and Will, who also seem to have no idea what he's talking about.

"Yeah, Rafe and Jim told me about it. It's good actually, people are often giving stuff away on there, mostly zucchini to be honest. And complaining about stuff. Litter, where people are parking, that sort of thing."

"Well, will the older people be on there? What about Sally?"

"She's the group admin. She actually just changed the photo to that Italian one from *Strictly Come Dancing*. There's been a bit of drama about it. She really should have put it to a vote to be fair. Wait," Jamie says, "do you want me to add you guys?"

"No," we all say at once.

"No, absolutely not," I say again. "More than happy for you to be our representative, Jamie. Thank you."

"So when are we doing this thing?" Will asks. "I want to invite everyone in good time."

I wonder if he's going to invite Melissa. I don't want to put him on the spot by asking.

"Bank holiday weekend?" Ray says.

"Sounds good." I say. "That's a lot of time to get everything sorted."

"Jamie?" Ray says.

"Hmm?" Jamie looks up from his phone. "Sorry, just catching up on the goss. Someone blocked someone else's car in at the church plant sale yesterday. How bad is that?"

He doesn't wait for any of us to answer.

"Oh, also they're doing a karaoke night at the village hall to raise money for blind dogs, so I think we should go. It's next weekend."

"Blind dogs?" I say.

"Yeah," he says, looking back at his phone.

"Not guide dogs for blind people?"

"Possibly," he says. "Shall I tell them we're in?"

"I mean, I've got nothing else on."

"I'm in," Will says, "so long as I don't have to sing."

"Ray?" Jamie says.

"Um." She taps her fingers on the table. "Potentially. I might be busy. It depends."

"Shut up," Jamie says. "I'm putting you down as a strong yes."

When we get home we light the fire with Ray's carefully cut firewood. It's the first time we've done it since we moved in, and despite assurances from the estate agent that the chimney's been thoroughly swept, I brace myself for a cascade of pigeons or squirrels or whatever thing crawled up in there and died a hundred years ago. Thankfully, nothing appears, and we gather around marveling at the fire. We've been itching to light it ever since we got here. None of us have ever had an open fireplace before, and it feels Dickensian almost. Like one of us should sing a song or read a poem. Perhaps toast something on it.

We only have it properly going for a few minutes, the flames licking the grate dramatically, before we decide we need to put it out because it's July and we're absolutely roasting. Still, though, it's the experience that counts.

"Good to test it before the winter," Will says, wiping sweat from his forehead.

I'm just getting into bed, settling down on top of the covers to read my book about the Golden State Killer, ensuring I spend the night waking up every time I hear a mouse scuttle under the floorboards. I pick up my phone and see that someone's sent me a message on Hinge. This is actually a miracle because I can't remember the last time I bothered to scroll through people's profiles, let alone interact with anyone.

It's a woman called Sabine. I remember her because in her photo she was at the restaurant in Broadway Market that Rob and Polly took me to. I'm just about to reply to her when there's a faint knock on my door.

"El," Ray whispers, "are you asleep?"

"No," I say, "come in." I put my phone facedown on the bed.

I always want to see her even when I am wearing some of my worst pajamas. In this case, a pair of pink satin shorts and a matching strappy top with *squad goals* embroidered on it. My mum and dad sent them to me in the post for my last birthday. It was a nice thought. Well, it was a thought, and that was something, at least.

Ray pushes the door open and grins when she sees me cross-legged on the bed.

"You planning to scare yourself to sleep?" she says, sitting on the edge of my bed and picking up the book.

"I am, yes."

Ray smells like smoke from the fire. She'd insisted on being the one to get it going even though she doesn't know what she's doing. If it was anyone else, I'd be telling her to get away from my bed.

"So this came for you." Ray passes me a card. "I found it just now underneath a pile of junk and bills."

I take it from her and immediately recognize the handwriting. Inside the envelope is a card with a tanned woman wearing a bikini, holding a cocktail on the front of it. It looks like something from a slightly porny eighties calendar.

Eleanor!

We're having a fabulous time! We're docked in Aruba and daddy's been scuba diving!
Speak soon!

xxx
P.S. Hope you're enjoying life on the farm!!!!!

I laugh and pass it to Ray to read.

"Life on the farm!"

"I know," I say. "Actually I'm amazed they retained that I'd moved. I didn't think they were listening at all when I told them, but they must have saved the address. So that's nice."

"It's almost a housewarming card, isn't it?" Ray says. She closes the card and then holds it up against my wall. "And if you frame it, it's a housewarming present as well."

"Almost *too* thoughtful," I say.

Everyone else's parents have sent normal housewarming gifts—food and wine and gift vouchers for John Lewis. Rob and Polly sent champagne and flowers, which I was furious about because they'd already helped so much with the move, but they also gave me an extra gift: they'd given me a bike. They insisted they'd got it secondhand and they'd paid basically nothing for it, but I'm not sure I believe them. It looks in perfect condition to me. It's mint green and I'm going to buy a basket to attach to the front of it; I'm going to be the most confident and proficient cyclist in the village.

They also bought me a matching helmet, but not, as Jamie rudely suggested I might need, knee and elbow pads or indeed, stabilizers.

I expect Ray to get up and head to bed but she doesn't. She lies back instead, her head resting on my pillow. It is going to smell like I'm sleeping in a bonfire.

I turn around to face her, leaning against the wall, my knees pulled up to my chest.

"This bed is pretty comfy," she says, wriggling slightly, making it bounce.

"Yeah, the lady said that it's only been slept in a handful of times."

Ray makes a face, wrinkling up her nose.

"What?"

"Did someone die in it, do you think?"

"Ray!"

"What?"

"Probably," I say.

She grins. "I like living with you already," she says.

I feel my cheeks flushing, the red creeping up my face and over my ears. I put my hand on my chest, hoping it's not spreading there, scarlet against the pink.

"It's been a fun week," I say. "Like being on holiday."

"El, this isn't a holiday, this is our life now." Ray puts her hands behind her head, and my instinct is to lie down beside her, to put my head on her shoulder. I fold my arms against my chest instead. The tips of my toes are touching the denim on the side of her thighs.

"I feel very lucky," she says.

"So do I," I say, watching as she adjusts herself in my bed, her head against my pillows.

CHAPTER TEN

The first day of the commute into London is actually quite fun. Will works from home on Mondays, so he waves us off at the door in his dressing gown, and Ray, Jamie, and I cycle to the station together in the sunshine. It feels as though we're on a very wholesome family holiday. I'm wearing a deeply impractical floral tea dress because Ray once said there was nothing hotter to her than women riding bikes in dresses. I am very concerned it's going to get trapped in the wheels or possibly ride up around my waist. I think I pull it off though, and actually, with my work bag in my basket, I feel very chic. Possibly like I am in a French film about an enchanting woman who never gets helmet hair. I catch Ray watching me when I get off my bike at the station and kneel down to try to figure out the overly complicated lock. I've decided to believe it was because she was checking me out and not because she was concerned I was going to make us miss our train.

I work a nine-to-five working day, but Ray and Jamie work shifts; this week they're both starting at 8:00 a.m., so I decided to go in with them—the first time I will ever have been early to work. We're toward the end of the train line, so we manage to find seats together and spend the journey chatting about jobs we need to do around the house and how extortionate the train is. The train is so expensive that I am virtually spending the same amount of money as I was when I was living at Amelia's flat in Leyton. Jamie googles how long it would take us to cycle into London, and we all briefly get very excited about becoming Olympic-standard cyclists and saving hundreds of pounds a month. The excitement quickly dissipates when we discover it's an eight-hour round trip, potentially involving a motorway.

I'm surprised when a couple of people at work, who I would normally only describe as "nodders"—as in, our only interactions are that we nod at each other when we're making a cup of tea—come up to me and ask about the house. It takes me a while to work out how on earth they all know about it, but when one woman gushes at me that she "just adores chickens" and that "Jamie seems like a total natural," I quickly realize that it's because they're all following his renovations Instagram account. Last night he posted a photo that he made Will take of him, lying topless in the grass, surrounded by the chickens with the caption "Earth Mother," which seems to have been extremely popular.

"Are you meant to be biting your lip in this?" Will had said, frowning at the phone screen, "or do you want me to take a normal one?"

Jamie sighed loudly.

"Everything I do is deliberate, Wilma!" he said, allowing himself a moment to breathe and untense his abs, "be a good Insta-boyfriend and just do as you're told."

"Yes," I say to the woman as I accept a chocolate chip cookie from the packet she's offering me, something that has never happened before, "he's a total natural. Very good at . . . it all."

An image of Jamie screaming hysterically when he accidentally switched on the drill he was holding for one of his photoshoots pops into my mind.

"Well," she says, "I can't wait to see how you all get on. See you later. It's Emma, isn't it?"

She doesn't hang around long enough for me to correct her, just speeds away back down the corridor with her mug of tea. It's fine. I can be Emma once in a while for chocolate chip cookies.

I meet Rozália after work as usual. She's done a lunchtime shift at the restaurant and has brought us both a takeaway carton filled with lobster mac and cheese, so instead of going to the coffee shop we go and sit on the green opposite to eat our picnic.

I am supremely grateful to be fed. I realize that I don't have any food at home unless one of the vampire chickens has laid an egg. There's no shop in the village, so we keep having to try to remember to buy things while we're in London or we have to cycle out after work or send Will in the car. We're planning to start doing a weekly big shop, which will hopefully mean I won't be eating cereal every night for dinner for much longer. Plus, soon we'll obviously be living off the land. It's only a matter of time before we're entirely self-sufficient.

"So," Rozália says, spearing a piece of macaroni with an expensive-looking silver fork, which she has clearly stolen from work, "you moved."

"Yep," I say. The mac and cheese is delicious. I'm sure it probably costs about forty pounds in the restaurant, so it tastes all the better for being free. "I moved. I'm a country girl now. I'm even raising chickens."

Rozália smirks, her version of bursting out laughing.

"No, I'm not joking. We have literal chickens."

She looks horrified.

"So you're a farmer now?" she says.

"No, I wouldn't say that."

Rozália looks at me and frowns.

"A chicken farmer," she says, as if to clarify her question.

"No, I don't farm them. I rescued them. We adopted them from a lady who saves them from battery farms."

Rozália spoons macaroni into her mouth and smirks again.

"What?" I say.

"So, you are rescuing chickens by day and lesbians by night."

I laugh then.

"It's my calling, Rozália. What can I say? So how are things? I missed you last week."

Rozália rolls her eyes, but I know she's secretly pleased to hear it.

"Yeah, fine. Just worked a lot. Met up with my brother."

I stop, my fork midway to my mouth, a piece of lobster balancing precariously.

"You met up with your brother," I repeat.

"Yeah."

"You're just going to drop that in like it's nothing."

She shrugs and takes another mouthful. Chewing slowly, deliberately to delay her answer.

"So?" I say, once it's clear she's not going to give me anything.

"So what?"

"So how did it go?"

"We went for breakfast. I had this croissant, and it was the best croissant I've ever had in my life. It had almonds and chocolate in it. It was in Victoria Park. Have you had the croissants from the café there?"

"Yes. How did it go with your brother, I mean? Not with the croissants."

"Oh, fine. We went for a walk around the park."

She looks across the green instead of at me, weighing up what she wants to say. I let her take a moment while I try to decide whether to make myself uncomfortably full now or whether to be smart and save the rest of the mac and cheese for lunch tomorrow. I shovel another forkful in while I think.

"It was good to hear about his life. He's moved out too. He's living with friends. I think that's why he felt able to get in touch, because Mum and Dad won't know that he's seeing me. When we said goodbye he said, 'You're the same.'"

"The same as what?"

"Yeah, that's what I said," she says, looking at the grass instead of me, "and he said 'the same as before.' I think he was surprised. I feel like maybe he'd been told some horror stories about what my life looked like now."

I nod.

"It's good to know I haven't changed," she says quietly.

"Do you feel like you've changed?" I ask.

"No," Rozália says, "I've always been the same."

She pauses to think for a moment. She puts the lid back on her plastic food container and I reluctantly do the same.

"Perhaps," she says, "I am a bit tougher now than I used to be."

I bite the inside of my cheek. I want to reach out and hold her hand, but I'd probably find myself in a headlock before I knew what was happening.

"You've had to be," I say. And she nods, just slightly.

"You know you're handling everything really well," I say, "but it would be OK if you weren't. You don't have to have your shit together all the time."

"I do," she says simply. "Because if I don't, and everything falls apart, I don't have any backup."

"There's Lisa," I say, who I know for a fact would have every single person she works with come and live with her in her two-bedroom flat if they needed to. She'd give you the shirt off her back in a heartbeat but in a sort of terrifying, aggressive way.

"And me, of course," I say.

A tiny smile plays on Rozália's lips.

"What are you going to do?" she says, "have me come and live with you, put me to work on your chicken farm?"

I smile at the idea of anyone attempting to put Rozália to work on a farm.

"Maybe. And listen, I'm on your side. Always. You know that, right? Me and Lisa. In your corner. So don't ever feel like it's just you, because you're wedged in between us. Forever. Sorry."

"Ugh," Rozália says, "wedged in between you."

"Yeah I know, sorry. I could have put that better. You get what I'm saying though. We're *family.*"

I say it like Lisa says it, which is exactly like how Phil Mitchell from *EastEnders* says it.

Rozália smiles then, a proper smile.

"God," she says. "I guess you really can't choose your family, then."

I laugh.

"No, in your case, unfortunately, you can't even call it your 'chosen family,' you just got stuck with us."

She's quiet for a moment. She gets out a pouch of tobacco and starts rolling a cigarette.

"The family who chose me," she says, without looking up.

I nod, watching her. Hoping that she can somehow feel my fondness for her radiating off me.

"Exactly," I say.

By Wednesday the novelty of the commute is already well and truly over. It no longer feels like a wholesome family holiday or an adventure. It feels like a slog. This is mainly because it's been pouring rain ever since Monday evening and cycling up the country lane in torrential downpours on a bicycle meant for fannying around a French farmers market is no fun. Jamie and Ray are much more confident and always whizz off ahead, however much they insist we're all riding together. Every time a car goes past or one of my feet slips off the pedal, I feel sure I am going to die.

She died as she lived, frantically trying to keep up with Ray.

Mercifully, by the time we arrive at the office the rain has stopped, and when the notification pops up on my screen to tell me it's time for the Thursday audit meeting, the sun is actually shining.

Jamie can't come with us today because he has a real meeting. His yearly appraisal where his manager pretends to know who he is and what he does. Jamie was meant to fill out a form about his achievements and failures and goals for the future. His biggest achievement was writing a headline that went viral on Twitter, his biggest failure is that he still does not know how to use commas correctly. His goal is to google *how to use commas*.

I am obviously secretly thrilled that it's just Ray and me at the meeting today. Well, it's only a secret to Ray; Jamie messaged me this morning saying, *Enjoy your sexy little audit meeting, you cheeky little monkey, why don't you put BEING IN LOVE WITH YOU on the agenda?! Don't have too much fun without me. I want the full minutes later.*

I have not justified it with a response but because I don't have anything else to do, I will, in all likelihood, email him a full report this afternoon.

At the Swedish coffee shop, I order my usual—a giant cinnamon bun and a disgusting coffee. I turn to Ray.

"And you'll have the same, yeah?"

"Um," she says, hesitating, frowning at the counter in front of her as if we haven't seen what's on offer a thousand times before.

"Actually I'll have a green tea. And a bit of the chocolate one."

She points at something called a Kladdkaka.

The scowling Swedish woman behind the counter rolls her eyes as though Ray not wanting exactly the same as me has deeply inconvenienced her.

"Are you OK?" I say, as we sit down.

"Yeah, why?"

"Just, the chocolate one? We never get that."

Ray laughs. "I just fancied a change. Maybe I'm having a wild year too. This is *my* wild thing."

"Hmm," I say, unconvinced. "OK."

"So what's new with you?" Ray asks, as the plates of cake get thrown down on our table.

"Well," I say. "Actually there *is* something new with me."

Ray raises her eyebrows and takes a bite of her cake.

"I'm going for a drink with someone after work."

My adventures on Hinge, after Jamie's talking-to about there being plenty of Rays in the sea, have finally paid off.

Ray raises her eyebrows even farther and widens her eyes in faux shock. Or maybe it's actual shock—this is a very rare occurrence after all.

"A drink? Like, a date?"

"Not *like* a date, Ray, an actual date."

Ray nods and puts down her fork. She sits back in her chair and looks at me. She smiles in a way that releases a thousand butterflies into my stomach.

"Well, who is this person? Are they good enough to be taking you out?"

"Her name is Sabine. I don't know much about her other than she has been very nice, and she asked me out for a drink pretty much straightaway instead of faffing around chatting for weeks."

"Quite forward," Ray says.

"That's what you would do," I say.

"Exactly," she says.

"Anyway, I'm excited. It'll be good for me. I haven't been on a date with anyone since the night I didn't have a threesome."

I don't know if it's strictly true that I'm excited. I mainly feel sick about it and a sort of deep sense of dread. I feel with absolute certainty that tonight is going to be one of the worst nights of my life. But I think that's normal before a date.

"So what are you doing tonight?" I ask.

Ray sighs and picks up her fork. She doesn't eat any cake though, just taps the prongs gently against the plate.

"I'm staying at Kirsty's, I think."

I nod and take a bite of my cinnamon bun.

"You sound really happy about it," I say, covering my mouth to stop crumbs escaping.

Ray squashes a bit of cake under her fork so that it oozes through the prongs.

"Yeah. I think I'm going to break up with her."

I stare at her, my eyes wide. I put my bun back down on my plate.

"I thought you weren't even technically together," I say.

Ray nods. "I know, but we are, aren't we, really? Like for all intents and purposes we are, and I just don't think that it's fair to her."

Ray rubs her eyes and looks up at me. She looks tired. I try not to read meaning into Ray's decision. She isn't saying that she doesn't think it's fair to Kirsty because she's madly in love with me. That is just my brain saying that. Wishing it.

"Why isn't it fair?" I say, swallowing a mouthful of vile coffee, as if I need any help making my heart race faster right now.

She sighs again, dragging the tea bag around in her cup by its string. It's dark now, pond colored. It's going to taste bitter.

"I think we feel differently about each other. No, I know we do. She wouldn't ever say it, but I know she was hurt about the house and me moving out of London. But honestly, El, it didn't even occur to me to talk to her about it first. It didn't even cross my mind. And it really should have done, right?"

I nod.

"Plus, I just . . . with the new house and everything being

fresh I just sort of want a new start. All change, you know? Being with Kirsty sometimes feels like always keeping one foot in a door to the past. I need to move forward."

"I get that," I say. I really do. No one understands the need to move forward like I do. "I'm sorry though, Ray. Breaking up is always horrible."

"Thanks, mate," she says.

God, I hate it when she calls me mate.

"I'm happy for you though," she continues, "at least one of us will be having fun tonight."

I smile and squash a piece of bun in between my fingers.

I wonder if you know, I think, *I wonder if you know that I'd cancel it in a heartbeat to be with you. Not even to go on a date with you. Just to sit in the same room as you.*

I have to believe she doesn't know. Because the alternative is too painful to bear.

When we get back to work, I log in to the instant messenger and see that Jamie is online.

Eleanor: *how did the appraisal go?*

Jamie: *fine, he agrees it's a good idea to learn commas and he bought me a cup of tea*

Eleanor: *nice*

Jamie: *how was the audit meeting? what's the goss?*

Eleanor: *you probably already know about ray and kirsty*

Jamie: *yeah, time for you to make your move, el*

Eleanor: *shut up! i'm actually going on a date tonight*

Jamie: *no way*

Eleanor: *yes way*

Jamie: *who? woman? man? neither?*

Eleanor: *woman, i feel sick about it to be honest, j*

Jamie: *yeah, i mean dating is hideous, isn't it? what a waste of time.*

Eleanor: *ok thanks good talk*

I'm early to meet Sabine, so I just walk up and down the opposite side of the street, listening to music to try to make myself feel like a strong, confident woman. I think of possible topics of conversation in case we run out of things to say. I know that she also likes to watch grisly true-crime dramas and reads terrifying books that keep her up at night sleepless and sweaty. I rack my brain for anything I know about current affairs. There is a chance she might expect me to know about the news based on my job. I know a politician is in trouble today for ... something. It's to do with a committee for sure. Surely she won't want to talk about disgraced politicians. Or is that what people like to talk about on dates now? I curse myself for being so out of the game and quickly google *politician bad* so that I am up to speed.

When I finally cross the road and get to the wine bar she's

chosen, Sabine is already there. She's sitting in a seat at the window facing out. She looks exactly like she does in her photos. Shoulder-length dark hair, dark eyes, tall. We notice immediately that we are dressed identically. Black jeans, white T-shirt, stonewashed denim jacket, Vans.

"Ah," she says, smiling as I approach, "you came in uniform."

I laugh.

"Yeah, I came straight from the meeting."

We pore over the menu, eventually selecting an orange wine created by an entirely female-run and -owned vineyard. When they bring the wine to our table, we swill it around in our glasses and take tiny sips, tasting the flavor profile.

"This," Sabine says, "is definitely a wine."

"Oh, without a doubt," I say. "This is wine. Orange in hue."

"Orange in hue, and," she says, taking another sip and closing her eyes briefly, "interestingly, not at all orange in flavor."

"Fascinating," I say. "Not even a hint of Fanta?"

"Not in this year's vintage."

It is surprisingly easy to talk to Sabine. We don't even have to rehash our true-crime conversations. She tells me about her job at a bank where she predicts the future (this is my basic understanding of what she does) and how she finally moved into a place by herself this year.

"Oh god," I say, moving onto a glass of chilled red that tastes exactly the same as the chilled orange, "it must be amazing to live by yourself."

"It is," Sabine says, "in many ways it's amazing. It has its ups and downs. Like anything."

I find myself telling her about the house, then. She raises her eyebrows.

"So it's still a house share but just sort of . . . out in the sticks."

"It's not a house share, Sabine," I say, smiling, kindly. "It's communal living. The future."

"Right," she says.

"We've got chickens."

"Oh," she says, "sorry! I didn't realize there were chickens there. That's a commune for sure."

"That's right. We're considering a duck. Maybe even, one day, a goat. We're going to live off the land."

"Sounds fabulous."

"It is. Well, it will be. Ray and I have built the most amazing nook in the garden. The whole garden is beautiful actually, we've been working on it together. It's coming along surprisingly quickly. But then she does work fast."

Sabine takes a sip of wine and stabs an olive with a cocktail stick.

"And Ray is?"

"My best friend. She lives in the house too."

Sabine raises her eyebrows as she chews.

"Does Ray have a boyfriend or . . ."

My honk of laughter answers the question for her.

"Sorry," I say. "I just . . . I can't imagine Ray with a boyfriend, that's all."

"So she has a girlfriend, then?"

"No." I put down my wineglass, swirling around the dregs at the bottom. "Well, sort of. It's on/off. It won't last. They might even be breaking up tonight actually. As we speak."

"I see. And are you . . . hoping it won't last?"

She's smiling at me, but I can see it's a genuine question. Am I that transparent even to a stranger?

"Of course I want it to last! She's my friend; she's my best friend! I want her to be happy."

My voice is about three octaves higher than usual. Famously a sure sign that everything is absolutely fine.

Thankfully we quickly move on from talking about Ray. We talk about Sabine's ex-girlfriend, who moved to Dubai last year, posts nothing but photos of her eating brunch in tiny bikinis and now has seventy thousand followers on Instagram. I tell her about Greg. How it feels weird to have spent so much time with someone and now not to speak to them at all. And weirder still how much that doesn't upset me. How I sort of don't really believe he even exists anymore now that I don't know him.

"It's mad because if I had to cut a friend out of my life it would kill me," I say.

"Mm, like Ray for example," Sabine says.

"Well, yeah," I say into my glass of wine, "or, you know, any friend."

It's things like this that make me worry that I have little images of Ray flashing in my eyes whenever I think about her. So, all the time.

When I tell her about my Wild Year, Sabine bursts out laughing, covering her face with her hands.

"Don't laugh at me!" I say, unable to help myself from laughing too. "I honestly think it's helped me come out of my shell a bit. It started off as this challenge because . . ."

I find that I don't want to tell her it's because of Ray: once I start pulling at that thread, I worry that it will become horrifyingly clear, that of course it is. Everything is because of Ray.

"It started off as this stupid challenge, but honestly, I have this compulsion now to keep going. To see what I'm capable of."

I haven't said that out loud before, but it's true. I do feel that.

I have always felt a certain freedom within the rules. Now that I am contractually obliged to live outside my comfort zone, I feel much more able to do it. To enjoy it even.

"Sorry, no. I'm not laughing at you. I'm just laughing at the concept, I think it's brilliant. A lot of people could probably stand to make an effort to push themselves like that, to be less inhibited. I could probably do with a year in the wild."

"I recommend it," I say, and then because I have had a couple of glasses of wine and she's gorgeous and smiling at me at a candlelit table, I add, "I still need something for this month."

"Noted," she says, smiling. "I'll get thinking."

We stay until closing time, eating tiny bowls of food with our fingers and drinking increasingly expensive wines by the glass. Sabine is very graciously paying for most of everything, which seems fair enough given by my estimations she earns about ten times more than me. I really should have got into hedge funds instead of news. I make a mental note to find out what they are.

We stand on the street outside, each with our phones in our hand, neither of us making a move to go home. It's quiet. Most people have already hopped in their Ubers or made their way toward the overground.

"So the last train back to the commune is pretty soon," I say, glancing at the time on my phone.

"That's a long way to go at this time," Sabine says.

"Oh, you know, it's not that bad. It's just the overground and then a quick sprint to the train and then it's forty-five minutes and then a cycle. Ninety minutes door to door, tops."

Sabine smiles, cocks her head to one side and repeats, "That's a long way to go at this time."

My eyes widen, understanding.

"Yes, it is such a long way. Very far. A treacherous journey as well. All that cycling in the dark. I'll never make it."

It turns out we can walk back to Sabine's from the wine bar, which makes the fact that she chose it for our date highly suspicious in my eyes.

"I see," I say as we set off.

"What? It's a nice bar!"

"Highly convenient, isn't it? *Oh, my flat just* happens *to be moments away!*"

She laughs.

"It worked though."

"It worked," I agree. "Is it where you take all your dates?"

She just smiles and points toward the top of the road.

"It's just up there."

Sabine's flat is on the top floor of a converted house. In the living room there are two huge windows with shutters overlooking the leafy street below. I peer down the hall and deduce that there must be at least two bedrooms. Maybe even three.

"Fucking hell," I say as I'm taking my shoes off in the hallway. "This must have cost a fortune! Sorry. That's so rude of me. It must have done though. Wait. Sorry, no. That's rude."

I wonder if there might be an opportunity for me to take my phone out and do a video tour to send to the group.

Sabine just laughs; she must be used to people being impressed with this place.

"Do you want another drink?" she asks as I follow her into the kitchen.

"Yes, please," I say. I run my finger along the wallpaper in the hallway as I follow her, a William Morris print.

I lean on her breakfast bar and watch as she opens the cream-colored Smeg fridge. When we had to buy a fridge for the new house, we all thought we were going to treat ourselves to a Smeg as a moving-in present to ourselves and then we saw the price and screamed.

Sabine has rows of different drinks stacked on the shelves like it's a hotel minibar. She has an entire shelf dedicated to Diet Coke. Another to sparkling water.

"Whoa," I say. "Wait though, where's your food?"

"Well," she says, "I tend to work pretty mad hours, so I'm never really here to eat. I just order stuff in."

She pulls out a bottle of white wine and shows it to me.

"Is this OK?"

I nod. She could have shown me anything and I'd have nodded.

We sit down on her sofa, and she puts on some music. Something inoffensive and folky that I vaguely recognize. She has what looks like a record player, and maybe it is, but I realize she's just connected her phone to it and is playing music through it like it's a regular Bluetooth speaker. I find that, for some reason, unreasonably disappointing.

I take a sip of the cold wine, and while it's delicious, I find that actually, I don't want anything else to drink. My mouth feels fuzzy, and really I want a glass of water or a cup of tea. I hold on to my glass because I'm nervous and worry that if I put it down, I'll forget what I normally do with my hands. I can feel the shine rapidly fading off the evening even though I desperately don't want it to. I want to cling on to it. I can't help but feel that I'm in the wrong place, that I'm not meant to be sitting in this perfect flat with the perfect fridge. My mind keeps flicking to Ray, whether she's breaking up with Kirsty, what they're doing right now. How much I want to pick up my phone and text her. I'm aware of the feeling that I'm always somewhat split in half. Whatever my body is doing, my mind is always with Ray.

"Everything OK?" Sabine asks.

"Yes!" I say, fixing a smile on my face. "Perfect."

Sabine looks at me.

"Eleanor. You look like you're sitting in a doctor's waiting room."

I suddenly become aware that I'm tapping my foot and stop it.

I sigh, closing my eyes briefly.

"Sorry." I lean forward and put my glass down on the table. "I'm not very good at this."

"At?" Sabine says, also putting her glass down.

"This." I gesture around the room, at her. "I know everyone says this, but I don't actually do this very often. Or, you know, ever."

Sabine nods.

"Nor do I," she says. "I know you think I do, but I don't. Not really."

"Right," I say.

"But this is your wild year," she says. "You must have done some pretty crazy stuff? Crazier than sitting in my flat drinking a glass of wine?"

"Well, in April I tried to have a threesome, but they did it without me. And I was really quite happy about it."

Sabine bursts out laughing, and I laugh too. It feels like a relief.

"You tried," she says, "and that's the important thing, I think."

I nod.

"I can still go home," I say, looking up at the clock on the wall in front of us.

"You can't," she says, "there's no way the trains are running this late."

"No," I concede, "but I can go and stay at my brother's house. He loves it when he wakes up and I'm drinking his coffee at his kitchen table."

She laughs.

"I don't want you to go anywhere," she says. "Unless you want to leave."

I shake my head. Surprised to find that it's true. I don't want to leave.

We end up staying up until it's light outside. It's easy to talk to her, in the way that it sometimes is easy to talk to a stranger in the middle of the night. Where time doesn't feel real, words don't feel as though they have consequences. We talk about parents, siblings, where we want to be in ten years' time. She tells me about how afraid she is that she's wasted so many years climbing a career ladder that she isn't even sure she wants to be on. I tell her I'm afraid I've done the opposite, wasted years hanging on to the bottom rung. I tell her about Ray. Properly tell her about Ray. How painful it is. How I know I need to move on but that I can't quite bring myself to do it. That the closeness of her as a friend is enough some days and so lacking on others that I can hardly stand it.

We drink a cup of tea together and watch the sun rise from Sabine's beautiful windows. She tells me she's never done that before. How she's lived here for almost six months and has always missed the sun. By 5:00 a.m. it is light enough outside that I decide that it's as good a time as any to leave. It's just over an hour's walk from here to Rob and Polly's, where I can have a shower and borrow some of Polly's clothes, and 6:00 a.m. doesn't feel like a totally unreasonable time to turn up. I might even be able to pop into a shop to buy them something for breakfast to apologize for being such a pain.

Sabine walks me down to the street and kisses me goodbye in the doorway. A proper kiss. Gentle and firm. A proper goodbye too. I know we'll never see each other again.

I set off slowly down the road, squinting in the sunlight, delirious with tiredness, typing out a message to Ray.

I'm in Hackney, just heading to Rob's. I'll be early to work today if you want to get a coffee. Hope things went OK with Kirsty.

I don't expect her to see it for another couple of hours at least, but she reads it straightaway. My heart leaps when I see that she's typing.

Want to go to Polo Bar? I could be there in 30 mins.

Polo Bar is a twenty-four-hour café opposite Liverpool Street station. It is quite literally never closed—not even on Christmas Day. It's been there forever and is an institution for anyone who doesn't keep regular hours in London. We used to go there all the time when we were on night shifts during our internship. It's where we went with Jamie after the holiday party where I had told Ray how I felt about her. We haven't been in a long time.

OK, I'll get an Uber now. Hope you're OK.

I forget the need for a shower or sleep or clean clothes immediately. As though all my basic needs can be met by Ray.

When I arrive, Ray is already there sitting in a booth at the back of the café. Only a few of the other tables are occupied. A couple of men in suits who don't look like they've been home. A paramedic sleepily making his way through a plate of pancakes. It feels like time stops in this café. It could be midday; it could be midnight.

I order a cappuccino, an orange juice, and a cannoli, a meal that feels like it encompasses most of the major food groups and should go some way toward rejuvenating me. On the Uber ride over, a headache set in, pulsing behind my right eye, and now as I walk over to the table, I realize that it is not just my head but in fact every single part of my body that is aching. I am too old to stay up all night baring my soul to strangers. I feel completely depleted.

"What a pair," Ray says, as I sit down, wiping yesterday's mascara away from under my eyes. Ray looks as though she hasn't slept at all either. She's wearing the same gray sweatshirt she was wearing yesterday. She has a huge vanilla milkshake in front of her, and she pushes it toward me. I take a sip, and the sugar hit feels restorative. When the waitress comes to drop off my drinks, I ask for a milkshake too.

"I feel like the cure for any hangover is just one of every single kind of drink. And then, when you've made your way through all the drinks, you're fine again," I say.

Ray nods and smiles. "I know. You say this to me every time we're hungover."

"It's true though."

"This isn't really a hangover though," Ray says, picking the straw out of her milkshake and licking cream off it. "This is just severe sleep deprivation."

I grimace.

"How did things go with Kirsty?"

Ray shakes her head.

"It was horrible. She was really upset. And she gave me a really hard time, which I totally deserved. I know that. But it doesn't make it easier to take."

The waitress comes over and places my milkshake down on the table. I line it up next to my orange juice and my coffee like it's a beer flight and I'm taste testing them. I don't even know where to begin.

"What did she say?" I ask, and then quickly add, "You don't have to tell me if you don't want to go over it, obviously."

"Well," Ray says, picking up my cannoli and taking a bite. She pauses to wipe chocolate cream from her lip. "Where do I even start? She said I'm inconsistent, unreliable. I don't know what I want. I've used her like she's a convenience and dropped her when I've found better offers. She says I've got her hopes up and shot them down so many times she never has any idea where she is with me."

I bite the inside of my cheek. Poor Kirsty. I thought I'd feel happy that they'd broken up, but I don't. It's hard to decipher exactly what I feel underneath all my aching bones and my cloak of exhaustion but it's nowhere close to happiness, nowhere close to hope.

"Oh god, Ray. I'm sorry. You're not . . . I mean maybe you have been all of those things to Kirsty at some point or another but . . ."

"No, I have, I have," she says, holding her hand up to stop me. "It's OK. You don't need to make excuses for me. I know what I've been like to her. I don't know why I've done it. I think she's right. I've always had my eye out for something better. And I don't even know what it is I'm looking for, you know? It's just that something isn't quite right. It never quite clicked. But that wasn't her fault. That's me. I just can't help but feel that whatever we had, even when it was great, it was never the greatest. Does that make sense? Like I just know there's someone out there for me where it would be the greatest. But she's right. I shouldn't have kept her hanging on. That was wrong."

She sighs and leans back in her chair, closing her eyes briefly.

"I should have let her go a long time ago."

I don't know what to say. I just take a sip of my orange juice. And then my coffee. And then my milkshake. I wait for them to start working their magic.

"Anyway," Ray says, "I haven't even asked you why it is that you're up and about at five in the morning, sitting in a twenty-four-hour café in yesterday's clothes."

"Ugh," I groan, putting my head in my hands. "Well, I stayed at Sabine's house. The girl I went on a date with last night."

"I feel like usually that would be a good thing and we should be excited about it," Ray says, "but I'm sensing not in this case?"

I shake my head.

"She was lovely," I say. "Completely lovely. But I got really weird when we went back to hers. And then we just stayed up all night talking like it was our last night on earth. I feel like I told her everything I've ever thought. A total purge."

"God," Ray says, "I almost feel jealous. It's so intimate. I don't know that I've ever done that with someone. Do I know everything you've ever thought?"

I can't even stop myself from laughing, I'm too tired.

"No." I say. "Absolutely not. No one does."

"Well, now Sabine does," Ray says.

"Maybe I'm just not meant to date," I say. "Maybe I'm just not that kind of person. I just need to be content with staying at home with the chickens on the commune. Maybe I'll rescue something else. A cat. A donkey maybe."

"You can do both," Ray says. "Not the cat and the donkey. I mean dating and life on the commune. You just haven't met the right person for you yet. It will happen, and it'll just make sense. That's what everyone says. You'll just know."

I nod and watch her as she finishes off my cannoli and grins at me, asking permission and apologizing all at once.

"You're right," I say. "I'll just know."

We're quiet for a moment. I watch a disheveled man in a pin-striped suit with bloodshot eyes stuff three forkfuls of pancakes in his mouth, check his phone, and then bury his head in his hands.

"Quite wild to stay up all night and end up back here, isn't it?" I say, immediately aware of how pointing out the wild thing automatically diminishes it. My fingers are twitching to get my notebook out of my bag so I can write about the events of the past twelve hours before I forget anything.

Ray runs a hand through her hair and sits back, studying me.

"El, you know I really don't give a shit about that, right?"

I take my hand out of my bag beside me, where I've been reaching around for my journal, and pick up my milkshake instead.

"Like, you really don't have to prove yourself to me. I hope you don't think I want you to do that."

I force what I intend to be the casual laugh of a very chilled person, but it sounds hysterical. The man in the pin-striped suit snaps his head up and glares at me.

"I don't, obviously. It's just, um, you said, on New Year's Eve . . ."

"I know, but it was just a joke, El." Ray looks exhausted all of a sudden.

I bite the inside of my cheek. It feels like she's on the verge of snapping at me. "Right, I know."

"Are you enjoying it?" She taps my foot under the table with hers, and I breathe a sigh of relief: she's not irritated.

"Yes," I say. "Sometimes no, obviously, but mostly yes. I don't feel stuck anymore. I feel, well, I feel a bit mad at the moment to be honest, but definitely not in a rut."

I used to wake up in the night seized with fear about my life going nowhere, and now when I wake up, it is because of the ancient pipes rattling or the families of mice living in our walls throwing midnight parties. An improvement I think.

"Good," Ray says, "if you're happy, I'm happy." She pauses and leans forward again, giving me a dazzling smile, and I find myself leaning forward too, mirroring her. "But you know, El, I love you wild and I love you cautious, right? I love you whatever."

My eyes widen, and all the blood in my body goes to my head. Is it possible to faint while sitting down?

"We all do!" she says, and picks up her phone and starts scrolling.

I deflate. The blood floods back to where it's meant to be. I dig my fingernails into my palms; I've got pins and needles in my hands.

"Oh," I say. "Thanks!" I smile at her weakly.

"Come on, let's go," Ray says. "We've got to get through the entire day somehow. I'm going to need a lot of coffee."

She gets up first and gives me her hand to pull me up. I hesitate for a second, and then I reach out and let her. My fingers tingle as she squeezes them, bringing them back to life.

Fortunately Mona must be spending the day haunting somewhere else, which means that I manage to sit at my desk with my eyes glazed over until around midday when I slope off to Pret and buy two jambon-buerres and a love bar and sit down to eat on the wall outside, unable to take another step. I barely taste the food, as though my body is deciding what is absolutely necessary to keep pushing through the tiredness—my taste buds didn't make the cut. As I unwrap my second jambonbuerre and take a bite, I think that this must be what it's like when you're out in the wilderness, when food is simply fuel to survive. Ray hasn't seen my message about coming out for lunch, which means she's either swimming or dead. Either way, I go upstairs and put the love bar on her desk with a note saying, *Hope you are alive.*—E. Jamie is working from home today, otherwise I wouldn't have dared. I haven't replied to his message in the group calling Ray and me dirty stop-outs. I'll deal with him later.

I spend the afternoon in the copier room napping in the corner. I'd like to say that it was a low point, but actually it's the best part of my day. I get a solid two hours of sleep and feel significantly better when I come to. At quarter to five I head back up to my desk with a notebook and a highlighter clutched to my chest. I don't know what I think I look like I've been doing, revising for my high school exams maybe. At five on the dot, I pack up my things and head downstairs. Ray was meant to finish work at four, so I'd assumed she'd have just headed home, but I'm thrilled to see her sitting in reception, her nose buried in a book that she's nodding off into.

"What are you still doing here?" I ask. She looks up at me bleary-eyed; she's wearing her glasses instead of her contact lenses, which means she really must be tired. Maybe because I'm delirious with exhaustion or maybe because I just want to, I reach out and touch her hair, pushing it back slightly. It's too intimate a gesture to pass off as a friendly ruffling, too gentle. Ray smiles at me and briefly leans her head into my hand before getting up.

"I'm waiting for you," she says. "And reading a book someone got me for Christmas."

She waves it at me. I'd bought Ray a terrifying book that I
had loved: it's part psychological thriller, part horror, set in a
small town in rural America. Ray's not really a reader, but she
has been dutifully carrying it around in her tote bag for the best
part of eight months.

"Enjoying it?" I say as we head toward the doors, waving at
Reggie, the security guard, as we go.

"Only a sadist would enjoy this, El."

"Ah, yes," I say, brushing past her as she opens the door for
me, "that's me."

On the journey home there is a signal failure and our train stops
just outside our station for nearly an hour. During that time,
Ray and I go through all the stages of grief in rapid succession.
We are stuck on anger for a long time. It is indescribably irritating to be able to see the platform from the window but not be
able to get out. Ray stands up a number of times, insisting she
is just going to "walk along the tracks." A few people in the carriage nod and murmur encouragement as if they're going to follow her, but she lets me talk her down every time. Just as we're
lifting ourselves out of depression (scrolling through pictures
of the chickens on our phones, stroking their feathers with our
fingers, wondering if we'll ever see them again) and moving
into acceptance (rooting through our bags for sustenance and
deciding we can live on a half-eaten family-size bag of chocolate buttons for at least a week), the train starts moving again.

It means that by the time we get to our bikes, it's much

darker than we'd like it to be, especially when neither of us have had the foresight to attach lights yet. We cycle the entire way back with Ray in front holding her phone with the flashlight switched on. Every time a car comes past, I feel myself seizing up with fear, and Ray yells at me to "for god's sake keep your eyes open," which is fair.

We walk through the front door in grim silence and see that the entire hallway is lit by candles like a posh spa or as if someone is about to propose on a reality TV show.

Ray turns to me and frowns.

"Hello?" I call out. A few possible scenarios run through my mind, the first being that perhaps we have interrupted a very romantic burglar. I'm going to be the tragic subject of a successful podcast series, I can feel it.

Jamie appears at the living room door, clutching his phone. He shines the flashlight in our faces.

"Well, well. Look what we have here," he says, shaking his head.

"What's going on?" Ray says, kicking off her shoes and glaring at Jamie.

"I could ask you the same question, couldn't I? Not coming home for nearly forty-eight hours? Your father and I have been worried sick."

Will appears at the doorway behind Jamie and rolls his eyes.

"Power cut," he says. "Apparently the whole village is out."

"No," I say. I put my hand on the wall and rest my weary head against it. "But I'm so hungry."

I've been fantasizing about toast.

"How long has it been out?" Ray asks.

"A couple of hours now," Will says. He lifts his hand to show us that he's holding a tub of ice cream. "Hence us eating our way through the freezer."

We sit around the dining room table for the next hour eating half-defrosted pieces of cake and cookies from when we moved in. The whole room smells sickly sweet from all the scented candles we have burning. Artificial vanilla and fresh cotton and rhubarb sharp in the back of my throat. It is not the dinner I'd hoped for. I eat an apple too and then a banana and close to a liter of water—anything to make me feel slightly more human, although I know the only thing I really need is sleep.

Ray and I are both quieter than usual, giving monosyllabic answers to Jamie's incessant questions about our absences last night. While he's talking, I figure out that aside from my nap in the copier room, I've barely slept for more than forty hours. An all-time record, I think. At one point Ray looks as though she might drop off into her plate like a toddler, but then she whips her head up suddenly.

"Did anyone check in on Sally?"

Will nods.

"Yeah, I went straight round there, don't worry."

"I sent him down with a scented candle in case she didn't have any," Jamie says, as he scrapes at the bottom of a tub of ice cream.

"She was fine," Will says. "I asked if she wanted to come up here, but she insisted that she's used to it, apparently it happens fairly regularly."

"She's got a headlamp," Jamie says.

"Oh god," Ray says. She looks as though she might burst into tears. "That's too much. Was she wearing it?"

Will nods.

"She seemed quite excited about the whole thing, to be honest."

"I think she was just excited to see you, Will," Jamie says.

"Yeah, maybe," Will says. "Do you think I should have pushed harder for her to come up here? I could go and try again now."

"No, don't," Ray says. "It's late, we don't want to disturb her."

"We can invite her round soon," I say.

"We will," Jamie says. "Well, we'll be seeing her at karaoke on Saturday anyway. We can ask her then."

All three of us groan.

"I've confirmed that we'll all be there, and everyone's very excited about our inaugural village outing," Jamie says brightly. "So get over yourselves. We're going to have fun."

At the moment, I can't imagine even being alive on Saturday let alone having fun.

We all head up the stairs at the same time, holding our phone flashlights ahead of us, apart from Jamie, who is carrying a candle instead, like he's a Victorian in a haunted house. He is speaking in a low voice into his phone about feeling a "presence," and while the official line is that there's been a power outage, he "feels on a spiritual level" that it's something else. Just as his Insta Live has really got going, there's a faint click and we hear the hum of our various appliances start up again. In silence, I tentatively reach for the landing light, and when it switches on, a low, yellow light glows above our heads, we all breathe a sigh of relief.

"It heard me," Jamie whispers to his fans.

I wait until there's quiet on the landing, until I'm sure everyone's gone to bed, and then I head into the bathroom. I desperately want a shower, but I know it's likely that because of the power outage there'll hardly be any hot water. I decide it's worth the risk and stand shivering for a glorious thirty seconds under the trickle of warm water before it turns ice-cold. I wrap myself in my slightly damp towel and brush my teeth over the cracked sink, trying not to look too hard at my gray skin, the bags under my eyes, my damp hair hanging limply on my goose-pimpled shoulders. The bath mat is wet underneath my feet, and the carpet is wet underneath that. I think of Sabine's bathroom, gleaming and white like in a hotel. A walk-in shower that two people could fit in. How I sat on the edge of her bathtub, stared at myself in the huge mirror and thought only of Ray.

I pull the light cord and step out into the hallway, blinking as my eyes adjust to the darkness. I creep up the landing and just as I'm opening my bedroom door, Ray opens hers.

I turn around to look at her. She's changed into a vest top and shorts. She has her glasses on again. She smiles at me sleepily. I see her take me in: I'm conscious of standing in my towel, of my wet hair and blotchy skin. I shiver but I don't move to go into my room because I'm certain she's about to say something. I stay where I am, holding my breath.

She opens her mouth and then seems to catch herself. She shakes her head slightly as if coming to from a daydream.

"Good night, El," she says softly.

I exhale. It feels as though I'm deflating.

"Good night, Ray," I whisper.

When I get into bed, I open my diary to a blank page. My arms feel heavy, and my eyes are gritty and sore. I am deliriously tired.

I know Ray doesn't care that you're doing this anymore but don't stop. You might be exhausted all the time. And lovesick. But things are happening! You make things happen now. You are not stuck anymore.

I underline that last bit several times. I refuse to get stuck again. I won't.

CHAPTER ELEVEN

Karaoke starts at 7:00 p.m. sharp. As we suspected, it is actually an event to raise money for guide dogs, not as Jamie wrote in our joint calendar: *blind dogs:(.* We decide that we're going to be fashionably late, but as the clock strikes seven and we're sitting about with nothing to do, we realize that being fashionably late for an event at a village hall is even more tragic than turning up on time. We tuck the chickens in for the night and slope off down the hill.

Ray has been moping about ever since she broke up with Kirsty. I think it has less to do with missing her and more to do with hearing some hard truths about herself, which have clearly dented her pride. Another key factor in her mood change could be that we haven't had any hot water for the past couple of days. Not a drop since the power cut. The boiler stays fixed for about ten minutes after the plumber leaves and then dies again with an almighty clunk. This might have something to do with the fact that the boiler is so old it "could be in a museum," according to the plumber. We add *get a new boiler* to the ever-growing list of things we need to sort out. It goes right to the top, above *get rid of moldy bathroom carpet*. We've been avoiding tearing it out because we fear what lies beneath.

To try to cheer Ray up on Friday night, we ordered pizzas from the one pizza place that delivers to us and watched a film about ye olde lesbians walking quietly together on a beach, occasionally touching hands and stealing glances before returning to their husbands. Someone at work told Jamie that it was "amazing" and that we absolutely had to watch it, which is something a lot of straight people like to say about very mediocre but horribly tragic queer entertainment.

There is a sex scene so graphic and intense that it might have been quite hot had the actors had any chemistry and had Jamie not been doing a running commentary and screaming over the top of it. I glanced at Ray, who was sitting in the armchair by herself, but she wasn't even watching as one of the women started wailing like she was being murdered. She just looked down at her phone, biting her lip.

By the end, despite the fact that virtually nothing happened throughout the entire film, we were all crying.

"Fucking hell," Jamie said. "Does it all have to be so bleak? Is that what being a lesbian is all about?"

Ray laughed then, wiping her cheek with the sleeve of her jumper.

"Sometimes."

"Christ," Jamie said, "no wonder you're being such a downer, Ray."

This evening the hot water changed from lukewarm to freezing just as Ray stepped into the shower. We all heard her yowl. What followed was a tantrum so massive that she insisted that not only was she not coming to the karaoke for blind dogs but that she was never getting out of bed again. Jamie managed to turn it around by bringing her a glass of wine and climbing into bed with her to sing "My Heart Will Go On" (one of his top five karaoke songs) but with every other word changed to "Ray."

I stood in the doorway and watched as she squirmed and tried to shake him off while he spooned her and sang loudly in her ear. By the time he got to the second "once more, you OPEN the Ray," she was shrieking, partly in frustration, partly in hysterical laughter.

"Fine, fine! If you stop singing, then I'll come."

"Ray," Jamie said, squeezing her tightly around her wriggling waist, "I'll never stop."

"Oh," he called over his shoulder on his way out, "you should really call a plumber . . . the hot water isn't working."

He had to run to swerve the pillow thrown at his perfectly tousled hair.

Even though we're only a few minutes late, the village hall is packed. It's still very much light outside, but the shutters are down on all the windows and there are multicolored lights flashing on the walls, occasionally illuminating a fire-safety poster or a first aid kit. A massive disco ball is hanging from the ceiling, spinning slowly. A child in a sparkly dress is standing underneath it, watching it in awe. There are gold foil streamers hanging from every doorframe, so you have to push through them to get anywhere. I experience a wave of nostalgia almost like sickness. For school discos, for birthday parties, for Brownies on a Wednesday evening. This place feels like my childhood.

There's a hatch leading to a tiny kitchen where a bar has been set up, so Will and Ray go to get us some drinks. Jamie and I decide to do a lap of the room to see if we recognize anyone. We spot Sally immediately: she's holding an iPad and seems to be choosing a song with the help of a teenage boy who looks like he's being held hostage. His eyes keep darting about the room like someone might be secretly filming him or all his school friends are hiding behind a gold foil curtain. Sally looks up as we pass and smiles broadly and waves.

"Will you be singing tonight?" she calls out, raising her voice over the sound of the middle-aged man singing Justin Bieber's "What Do You Mean?" behind her.

"Try and stop me!" Jamie calls back just as I'm saying, "I don't think so."

We wave at Rafe and Jim across the room. They're deep in conversation with Rachel, who turns around to see who they're waving at and smiles. She beckons for us to come over and introduces me to Rafe and Jim, who I haven't actually met yet.

"You really came!" she says. "When I saw your reply to the group, Jamie, I couldn't tell if you were being serious or not."

"Of course!" Jamie says. "I never joke about karaoke."

"I'm so glad we did," I say, "it seems like the entire village is here. We'd have been missing out."

"Oh, the entire village *is* here," Rafe says. "I think there's only a handful of people who didn't come, and that's because they're away. Or maybe they've just switched their lights off and closed the curtains."

"We should have done that," Jim says.

Rafe slaps him on the arm. "He's joking," Rafe says. "We love these things, don't we?"

Jim smiles tightly and takes a large gulp of his drink.

Ray and Will walk over to us from the bar, and we adjust our little circle to let them in. They've bought us each a beer, which we accept gratefully. I drink at least half the bottle in one go.

"Now that I've got you all together," Rachel says, "I'm actually partly here on business, as well as pleasure, obviously."

She reaches into the tote bag she's carrying and pulls out a huge wad of raffle tickets. She's met with a series of groans.

"I know, I know," she says. "Sorry. I promised I'd do it though. My dad's really involved in these things, and he ropes everyone in."

"I don't have any cash," Will says, patting himself down.

Rachel reaches into the tote bag again and pulls out a tiny card reader, wincing slightly as she does it.

"It's um, it's a five-pound minimum. Honestly, I'm so sorry," she says.

Jamie is the first to pull out his card.

"If it helps even one blind dog, then it's worth it," he says.

Rachel frowns slightly but doesn't say anything, assuming perhaps that she's misheard him.

"What are the prizes?" Ray asks as she taps her phone to the reader.

"Well," Rachel says, handing over a reel of green tickets. "There's a whole table of them in the corridor. Some of them are genuinely quite good. There's a magnum of champagne, Eurostar tickets to Paris, that kind of thing. There's also like ... bubble bath and a box of eggs. And I think someone knitted a scarf themselves, which is sweet but, you know, rubbish."

Ray nods and stuffs the tickets in her back pocket.

"Can you even believe this is your Saturday night?" Rachel says.

"I can't," Ray says, taking a sip of her beer. "But I'm happy to be here."

I donate £10, feeling a sudden wave of guilt, not able to recall the last time that I gave any money to charity, and Rachel gives me an extra raffle ticket for being so generous.

"I have a good feeling about this one," she says, peeling off a pink ticket and pressing it into my hand. "The champagne for sure."

We find a table to sit at, and after a couple more rounds of drinks the evening starts to feel much more fun. We get chatting to people, all of whom are interested in what we're doing to the house. A lot of them follow the renovations Instagram account and, from various people's drunken slipups, it transpires that a lot of them have also been looking at our personal Instagram accounts too. They all seem to know where we work and where we used to live. It is quite a nice feeling actually, like being a minor celebrity.

At one point we spot Will deep in conversation with a woman by the bar. She has lots of blond hair that she keeps flicking all over the place, which seems like a good sign, body language−wise.

When he comes back to the table with our drinks, he has a big smile plastered on his face.

"Who's that?" I say.

"Hmm? Who?" Will says, handing me a gin and tonic in a plastic cup.

"The woman at the bar with all the hair."

"That's Tess," Jamie answers for him. "She's very nice actually, she's on the WhatsApp group, but she doesn't get involved with any of the drama. She's always just offering wonky vegetables and duck eggs and stuff."

"She's a graphic designer, she said we might have seen some of her stuff on the tube. The one that says not to push people on the escalators or swear at them or something," Will says. "Anyway, she moved here last year."

"By herself?"

"Well, she actually moved here with her husband," Jamie says before Will can answer, "but he left her. And now he lives in *Germany*."

He raises his eyebrows as if that's the most scandalous thing he's ever heard.

"How on earth do you know that?" Will asks.

Jamie shrugs, and when we all continue to stare at him, waiting for an answer, he rolls his eyes.

"Fine. She was at the chicken lady's house when we picked up the girls. Rafe and Jim told me what happened on the way home. Apparently, the husband was a complete arsehole but really fit."

"She's gorgeous, Will," Ray says, ignoring Jamie. "You should ask her out."

Will laughs. "OK. Sure."

"You should!" I say. "Or at least ask her to come to the housewarming."

"Aren't we inviting the whole village to the housewarming?" Will says.

"Yes," I say. "But you should invite her personally, not just with the generic invitation to everyone. Mention it tonight. Then she'll know you really want her there."

He nods and glances back over at her.

"Maybe."

I think that he will. He looks happier than he has since we moved here.

At one point Jamie disappears and comes back to the table breathless and excitable—never a good sign.

"I've put our names down. We're on in about thirty minutes," he says to me, slapping my knee.

"Names down for what?"

He laughs as if I'm joking and then stops when he sees the look on my face.

"Singing, silly."

"I'm obviously not singing! Do it with one of them."

I point at Will, who is deep in conversation with Tess on the other side of the table pretending he can't hear us. Hoping that if he doesn't make eye contact, then perhaps Jamie will forget he's there. Ray, conveniently, is nowhere to be seen.

"Will won't do it, he's too boring. But you *have* to do it because you're wild this year. Remember?"

I narrow my eyes at him, trying to figure out if he's been chatting to Ray about me. He looks entirely serious. Perhaps she hasn't told him about our discussion at Polo Bar.

"Don't you dare use that against me. I have fulfilled my wild quota; I don't have to do anything wild until . . ."

I stop as I do my wild math and realize I am actually missing something for this month. Jamie looks gleeful.

"You need this," he says. "Or your sad, little notebook is going to be empty."

"No," I whisper. "No. I'll do something else. . . . I'll, I'll do a bungee jump, I'll . . . I'll dye my hair purple." I snap my fingers together. "I went on a date! I stayed out all night!"

Jamie shakes his head.

"No, El. Dating isn't wild. Dating is part of normal life. Now, what you are going to do is stand up on that stage and sing a song with me."

I feel my heart sink. He's right.

"I need a drink," I say to him. "I need thirty drinks. Do they serve shots here?"

"I'll sort some shots," Jamie says, leaping up from his chair, "I know Marjorie behind the bar."

Two shots of vodka later and I'm feeling slightly more able to face the music, literally. By the time it's our turn, everyone is as tipsy as we are and pretty much only paying attention to themselves, gearing up for their own performances. Will is chatting to Tess again; they look deep in conversation, and he keeps frowning and nodding very seriously. Perhaps they're talking about her fit husband who ran away to Germany. Ray disappeared to get some air a while ago and never returned, which I'm supremely grateful for. I don't think I'd ever recover from her seeing this.

"You're Britney, I'm Madonna," Jamie says to me as he hands me the microphone. And before I get a chance to think too much about it, the music starts and then I lose all feeling in my arms and legs for three minutes. I genuinely black out. I think my brain is trying to protect me from the trauma. I have a vague memory of Jamie doing a slut drop and me saying "Oh god, no" into the microphone when he gestured for me to do the same, but I only properly come to when the music stops and people are cheering and clapping.

I look up and see Will leaning against the back wall laughing his head off. Reassuring.

"Amazing," he mouths at me, and gives me a thumbs-up. Tess does the same, a double thumbs-up with a huge smile on her face. I immediately decide I like her a hundred times more than I ever liked Melissa.

A beaming Sally accosts us on our way to the bar. Her sequined top is sparkling under the lights.

"That was wonderful," she says. "Really it was. What a fun song."

"Thanks, Sal," Jamie says, as he leans down and kisses her on the cheek. "Love the outfit."

"Honestly," she says. She puts down her glass of wine on a nearby table and I see that her hands are trembling, just slightly. "It's lovely just to be out. I don't listen to music all that much anymore. I used to have it on all the time, I'd dance around the kitchen with my husband."

"I love a good kitchen dance," Jamie says.

"Do you?" Sally says.

"Love it. I will come and dance with you anytime. Just say the word."

Sally reaches out and takes his hand very briefly and squeezes it.

"I miss it," she says.

"The dancing?" I say.

"Oh dear," she says looking at me, her eyes shining, "everything."

Sally's name is called, then, and she shakes her head slightly and smiles at us both. She adjusts her top and stands up a little straighter, shoulders back, getting ready for her big performance.

"My turn," she says.

"You're going to smash it," Jamie says. "What are you drinking? Do you want a shot for your nerves? Are you a tequila girl?"

Sally throws her head back and laughs, delighted.

"I'd better not," she says. "I'll end up misbehaving."

"Oh good," Jamie says, "me too."

I find Ray standing outside, leaning against a railing at the back of the hall, just staring out at the fields. It's almost dark, although some pink and orange clouds remain in the inky-blue sky. There's a slight chill in the air now, and I shiver as I walk over to her. She smiles as I pass her a bottle of beer. She smiles even more when she sees that I am drinking a Smirnoff Ice. Marjorie had run out of tonic and suggested this as an alternative. I didn't argue.

"I haven't had one of those for years," Ray says, and holds out her hand for me to pass it to her. She grimaces when she takes a sip.

"I think all the enamel on my teeth just came off."

"It's nice though, isn't it?" I say, taking a sip, letting the sugar coat my tongue. "It tastes like being a teenager."

"Yeah," she says, "that's true. Like rotten teeth and being fifteen."

We're both quiet for a moment.

"I wish I'd known you then," I say.

"Yeah?" Ray asks. "I don't know. I was a bit of a nightmare."

"I don't believe it."

Ray looks at me and sees that I'm smiling, teasing her. She laughs.

"You'd have been too cool to speak to me," I say.

"Probably," Ray says, "which tells you how stupid I was, doesn't it?"

I take another sip of my drink and watch as the clouds move across the sky.

"So, you missed my big performance," I say, as nonchalantly as I can.

She turns to face me and takes a sip of her beer, trying to decide if I'm joking or not.

"You didn't," she says.

"I did."

"On your own?"

"With Jamie."

Ray breaks out into a grin and shakes her head at me in disbelief. Honestly sometimes she looks at me like I'm the best thing she's ever seen. This is one of those times and I can't help but break out into a huge grin too.

"Well, come on, then. Tell me all about it. What did you sing?"

"'Me Against the Music.'"

"Shut up."

"We did. Apparently Jamie really wanted to do Dane Bowers and Victoria Beckham but they didn't have it."

Ray laughs again. "I can't believe I missed it."

"I know," I say.

"I don't suppose you'd do it again?"

"No, never. It was a once-in-a-lifetime event."

Ray shakes her head. "I guess I'll just have to live with the regret forever."

We're quiet for a moment. I take another sip of my drink and shiver involuntarily. I wish I had my jumper. As if she's reading my mind, Ray hands me her beer and starts taking her denim jacket off.

"No, no," I say. "Then you'll be cold."

"I'm too hot," she says. "It's fine."

I know that can't be true, but I also know there's no point in arguing with her. I think she's going to pass me the jacket but instead she steps toward me and wraps it around my shoulders so that my arms are still free. She squeezes the tops of my arms briefly and then steps away again. I pass back her beer.

"Better?" she asks.

I nod. She turns back to the view, her elbows resting on the railing, and I mirror her.

"You know," I say after a few moments, "I think the last time I was standing outside a village hall like this, drinking an alcopop, I chipped my tooth."

I run my finger over the ridge on my front tooth.

"Oh yeah?"

"Yeah, it was someone's birthday party. I came outside with a girl. The only 'out' girl at my school. We were talking, and she made me laugh just as I was going to take a sip from my bottle, and I bashed it against my front tooth. It was such a shock. I don't remember anything else about that night now. I hoped we were going to kiss, but I spent the rest of the night with my hand over my mouth."

"I've never noticed it," Ray says, peering at me.

I dutifully open my mouth a little to show off the chip on my right front tooth. It's minor enough that I never got it fixed, noticeable enough that I see it every single time I look at my reflection.

"Huh," Ray says. She puts her hand on my chin and turns

my head slightly as if she's a dentist trying to find better light. She leaves her hand there, her thumb just under my bottom lip, just a beat too long. Or it might not be a beat too long. It might be a normal amount of time to inspect a tooth and it's just that time stands still for me every time Ray gets close to me. I'll never know which it is because at that exact moment the door to the hall flies open and Rachel comes outside.

"Oh," she says, as we spring apart. Or we don't. Ray just takes her hand away from my mouth. "Sorry, I just came out to get some fresh air. It's boiling in there."

She touches her hand to her forehead as if to take her temperature, to prove her point.

"Same," Ray says.

Rachel comes to stand next to me against the railings, and we all look out over the fields.

"So, Sally is really going for it," Rachel says after a few moments.

"What's she singing?" I ask.

"Dua Lipa."

I laugh. I'm sorry to be missing it.

Ray stands up straight and points into the distance.

"Is there a lake over there?"

Rachel squints, trying to figure out exactly what she's meant to be looking at.

"Um," she says, "I wouldn't say a lake as such, it's a big pond. People swim there sometimes. I used to swim there when I was little."

"Huh," Ray says, "I'd love to do that. Wouldn't you, El?"

"Erm," I say. I take a sip of my Smirnoff Ice to buy me some time. "I wouldn't *love* to do it."

I turn to Rachel.

"Is it, you know, absolutely disgusting?"

Rachel laughs, and I just know Ray is rolling her eyes at me.

"I promise it's not," she says. "It's lovely once you're in, if you can try not to think about what's lurking at the bottom."

"Right," I say, knowing I'll never think of anything else ever again. "It's just that I'm not really a pond person."

Ray frowns slightly, a smile playing on her lips.

I haven't ever told her this story, but when I was nine years old I fell into my next-door neighbor's pond. It was deep and murky, teeming with flies and gnats and ominous smells. He had gone inside to fetch us a drink, and I was leaning forward to get a better look at some frog spawn (sure, maybe I've always been a little wild and very, very cool) and I misjudged it, slipped, and fell. I was wearing dungarees and a jumper and my clothes felt immediately so heavy that I was sure I was being dragged down to the bottom. In the panic I swallowed some water and although my parents have since told me I am exaggerating or being dramatic, I remember feeling quite sure, as the pond water slid down my screaming throat, that I was going to die.

By the time my neighbor came back outside I had wrenched myself to the surface and was scrambling to get out, absolutely hysterical, which was compounded by the fact that I had actual frog spawn in my hair and horrifyingly, in my mouth. I was convinced that I had ingested some and that the butterflies I could feel in my stomach when I thought about it were actually tadpoles swimming about. My dad, ever sensitive, told me that we'd know for sure if when I sneezed, a frog came out of my nose. Well, let me tell you, I held in my sneezes for years, haunted by phantom frogs. I'm certain that's why I got so many sinus infections. It might sound silly all these years later, but the idea of voluntarily getting into a wildlife-filled body of water fills me with dread, like, to the point where I can't really feel my legs and my ears start ringing.

"We should go sometime," Rachel says. "I mean, if you want to."

"Sure," Ray says, answering for me, "we'll go, won't we? I'm sure you could be a pond person if you wanted to, El."

Obviously, Ray doesn't know about my near-death experience (yes, I am calling it that) and I want it to stay that way. I am already a near constant source of amusement to her and Jamie. The phrase *frog spawn in my mouth* is not one I want to be forever associated with.

She raises her eyebrows at me, a challenge. Maddening. The tadpoles in my stomach are doing overtime.

Before I can answer her the doors to the hall swing open and Jamie comes out. Before they slam shut again we're treated to a burst of Sally singing "Don't Start Now" in an impressively high key.

"What's going on out here?" Jamie asks, but then carries on talking before we can answer. "I've got such good content, honestly. The Village People account is popping off. I just got a DM from someone who wants to do a feature."

"A DM from someone at the parish news?" I say.

Jamie smiles at me sarcastically.

"No. Although, I was speaking to Gary, who does the parish news, and he said he's very keen to put something together. No, from someone at work on the features desk. You know Kyle."

"Gay Kyle?" Ray asks.

"No," Jamie says, "Mustache Kyle."

"Ah, OK," Ray says.

It's actually very confusing, because Mustache Kyle happens to be gay too.

"He wants to do something about queer people in the countryside or communal living or posting thirst traps with their chickens."

"Yeah, I bet he does," I say.

"What's that supposed to mean?" Jamie says.

"Mustache Kyle has always fancied you!"

"Sorry," Jamie says, "but no. This is about my art and my social media prowess, not about my body. Shame on you, Eleanor. Shame on you."

"Ooh," I say, ignoring him, "you should invite him to the housewarming. He can see us in all our glory."

"Yes!" Ray says. "Wait, does that mean we also have to invite Gay Kyle?"

"I guess," Jamie says. "Although not if I make it clear this is strictly a work thing."

"Yeah," I say, "tricky, because if we invite them we might have to invite Salmon Simon."

"Oh god," Jamie says, "good point."

"Sorry," Rachel says, "Salmon Simon? Does he eat a lot of fish?"

"No," Jamie says, "we once thought he said his name was Salmon in a meeting."

He says this like it is the most obvious thing in the world and that Rachel needs to try to keep up.

"OK, fine," I say. "Gay Kyle, Mustache Kyle, and Salmon Simon, and that's it from work."

"Wait," Jamie says, turning back to Rachel as if he's only just taking in the fact that she's there, "you're coming, aren't you? We've invited you?"

Rachel shakes her head.

"Oh no!" Jamie says. "How rude. I mean we're sending an invite later to the WhatsApp group, but you deserve an in-person invitation. It's Saturday in two weeks. Are you free?"

"Oh yes," Rachel says, "tragically free. I'm definitely in."

"Yes!" Jamie says. "Our first guest!"

We head back inside just in time to catch the raffle. Rachel was right, my extra ticket was lucky. The bubble bath is mine. I'm actually afraid to fill up our bath in case it disintegrates, but still, it's nice to win something. Tess wins the magnum of champagne and promises to bring it to the housewarming, further cementing her in my mind as superior to Melissa in every single way.

We walk home with Sally at around midnight but not before Jamie has performed a spine-tingling rendition of Mariah Carey's "Emotions." Perhaps spine-tingling isn't quite the right word. Maybe I mean ear-piercing or bloodcurdling. He's happy though, which is the main thing, and a total hit with everyone. I wouldn't be surprised if next week he is voted village mayor or something.

Sally (sensibly) declines Jamie's offer to come round ours and eat "a load of chicken nuggets" but she lets Ray take the teddy bear that she won in the raffle into the house for her. It's about twice Sally's size and wearing a bow tie. She asks Ray to put it in the window so it looks like it's keeping an eye on the street.

"You're very kind," she says to us at her front door as we're all saying good night. "I'm so glad you're here, that you moved here, I mean. And here right now to see me home. Here in general."

"We are too," we all say over the top of one another, laughing. And it's true, I realize. It's starting to feel like home.

After I climb into bed, still very much worse for wear, I take my notebook from my bedside table and write: *I sang in front of a room full of strangers (at karaoke, had not just lost my mind).*

I scroll through Instagram and see that Jamie has posted a video of the two of us singing together on the Instagram account. It's been viewed six thousand times already—the comments are just rows and rows of heart emojis. I didn't know anyone was filming us, but I should have known Jamie wouldn't have let the moment go undocumented. I brace myself for the feeling of wanting to die of embarrassment, but it doesn't come. The two of us singing together and giggling is actually just pure joy to watch. I look relaxed, happy even. At one point we hold hands and Jamie kisses mine and we look like total naturals, like we perform together all the time. I hesitate for a moment, deciding whether I want her to see it, and then send it to Ray.

You're in luck. Someone captured the magic tonight.

I just saw this! You're famous! I'm going to save it on my phone and whenever I'm sad I'll just watch this and feel immediately better. I love you both so much.

I've become very good over the years at not letting myself get carried away with even the most mundane of my Ray-based fantasies. But tonight I allow myself to get lost in them. I imagine what it would be like to walk into her room now. She would put down her phone and look at me quizzically; maybe she'd smile. I'd walk over to her and she'd put her hand up to my face, this time letting her finger brush over my bottom lip, and I'd kiss her. I'd just kiss her and it would be that simple. I let myself think that this could really happen. Because perhaps it could. Maybe I'm reading into things because they're really there. Maybe she really does feel it too.

I lie still in my bed, staring at the door. The version of myself that only exists in my head, the one who takes chances, steps out of my room and spends the night running wild.

CHAPTER TWELVE

Dear neighbors,

We're having a housewarming party to celebrate our new home in the village on Saturday on the August bank holiday weekend. The theme is FESTIVAL so come in your most outrageous outfits! It'll be seven till late, and there'll be food, drink, and potentially some live music (played from a phone). No need to RSVP just see you there!

Jamie, Ray, Will, and Eleanor
Follow us at @ TheVillagePeople69 to see what we're up to at Lavender House

Despite Jamie's stipulation that people need not RSVP, from the responses he receives on the group and the number of people we bump into on the street telling us they're looking forward to it, I think it's safe to assume the numbers for the party are going to be pretty huge. I feel a mixture of excitement and terror because every single day something else is going wrong with the house.

In the past week we've had a plumber and an electrician shake their heads grimly at us and tell us that whoever lived here before must have been "very into DIY" and "obviously not very good at it." Small jobs that we thought would be easy and, dare I say it, fun, turn out to be hugely expensive and time-consuming. We decide that while we're saving to eventually replace the entire kitchen, we'll paint the cupboards. We start off in high spirits, talking loudly about how the kitchen will be transformed by duck-egg-blue cabinets, how it will take no time at all with four of us doing it. How perhaps it's going to look so great that we won't even need to replace the whole thing after all; it'll be just like on *Queer Eye* after Bobby's worked his magic. How wrong we were. An hour and a half in and none of us are speaking. It becomes abundantly clear, the longer we spend painting, that the cabinets are going to look exactly the same but very badly painted blue. No matter how many coats we do we can't get rid of the obvious brush strokes, or the blue paint on the floor, or the fact that we're all total amateurs and don't know what we're doing.

When it comes to trying to reattach the cabinet doors, something that Ray insisted she could do and did not need assistance with, the tension reaches fever pitch, the rest of us standing in the doorway watching her as she whispers to herself something about it not making sense, before yelling in frustration, throwing the Allen key across the room, and taking herself outside for a pep talk. We watch her crouched outside the back door, her head in her hands, a broken woman.

Eventually the cupboard doors make it back onto the cabinets, but they don't really open like they did before, or close properly. None of us dare mention that to Ray. If you squint they look quite nice; if you get within a couple of feet it looks like a child chucked a can of paint at them. Around the edges, it's already starting to chip off.

In contrast to that particularly shoddy effort, Jamie does a beautiful job on the chicken coop. It's now bright blue and on one side he has painted the Progress Pride flag. It's perfectly done, neat and bright—it looks almost professional. He works on it for hours, his headphones in, traipsing in and out of the house to wash his brushes and gulp down water. While he's waiting for it to dry, he sits in the grass beside it, feeding the chickens carrot sticks. He seems to have infinite patience with it, doing second coats where he needs to, making the lines sharp and clear. It takes him three evenings after work. He's out there until dark every night.

When he's finally finished, he calls the rest of us outside, and we walk around it slowly, admiring it, congratulating him on doing such a great job.

"It's perfect, J," Will says. "Honestly, I had no idea you were such an artist. You'll have to paint a mural for us on the back wall."

"I don't think you can afford me, babes," Jamie says. "But I'll have a look at my schedule and see what I can do."

"It's amazing," Ray says, and sighs. "At least the chickens have somewhere nice to live."

"Oh no!" Jamie says, grabbing her by the waist and pulling her toward him, tickling her stomach as if she was a toddler. "Are we having another little tantrum about the kitchen cupboards?"

Ray wriggles away from him, laughing, holding out her hand to me to pull her away. I do, and she holds onto it for a second and then drops it, wrapping her arm loosely around my shoulder instead.

"No, I'm not. I honestly love it, Jamie. And I love the house. I do. I just hate when things don't go my way." She turns around to look at the house. "I love it even though it's hard to love at the moment."

"That's the best kind," Jamie says. "When it finally all comes together, it will be worth all the effort."

Rozália asks that instead of meeting on Monday at our usual spot, we meet later in the week at a bookshop on Marchmont Street. When I arrive she's leaning against the wall outside Gay's the Word, smoking. She's bought me a coffee. I know because she has already sent me a Monzo request for the entire bill, hers included. It is immediately clear from the grin on her face that she's seen the video of me doing karaoke on Saturday night.

"Don't," I say as I approach her and reach out my hand for my coffee. "Just don't."

"What?" she says, passing me the paper cup. She raises her eyebrows and stubs her cigarette out on the pavement under her shoe.

"You know what," I say, putting my backpack down on the floor by my feet and leaning beside her.

"I can't mention that I enjoyed your performance from the weekend? I didn't know you were a singer."

"I'm not a singer."

"Actually," Rozália says, "that's true."

I smile sarcastically at her, but she doesn't notice because she's looking at her phone, squinting at the screen in the sun.

"So why are we meeting here?" I say. "Bit out of the way for you, isn't it?"

"It's easier for you, no?" she says nonchalantly.

I shrug and take a sip of my coffee. I shudder involuntarily. I should have known. Rozália ordered it black, the only way she believes it should be served. "I don't believe that's why you chose to meet here—for my convenience."

She sighs.

"Fine. It is because I want to choose a book for someone, and I thought you could help me."

The way she says it is as if she is doing me a favor by giving me a job, like I'm a child. She glares at me impatiently, as if I'm holding her up by drinking the coffee she bought me.

"For who?" I say. I take another sip and grimace. Rozália rolls her eyes and holds out her hand. I give her the cup and she gulps down the rest before taking it to a bin across the road rather than answering my question.

"For who?" I repeat loudly when she gets back, so as to be heard over the sound of a man on an electric scooter yelling at her to "watch where she's fucking going."

Rozália sticks her middle finger up at him without missing a beat.

"It's for my friend who works behind the bar at the RVT. It's her birthday and she likes to read, so I want to buy her a book, OK?"

"OK," I say, holding my hands up. "No need to be so defensive about it."

She takes a deep breath, as if she's not able to deal with how irritating I'm being, and then gestures for me to follow her inside. I'm amazed to see her smile warmly at the woman sitting behind the till. Evidence that she can switch on the charm when she wants to.

We walk right to the back of the shop and start scanning the shelves although I don't know what kind of thing she's looking for.

I've been here before and every single time I come I vow to come more often, to spend my money in the right places, to expand my mind with the power of literature. Then I leave and promptly forget again.

"So, have you seen your brother again?" I say quietly, as though we're in a library.

"No," Rozália says at her normal volume, picking up a book from the shelf and reading the back cover.

"But have you spoken to him at least?"

She glares at me as if I'm interrupting her, as if she didn't invite me here herself.

"Yes!" she hisses. "We text all the time now, OK? Eleanor, please! I am trying to concentrate."

"Fine! Sorry."

I smile and go back to scanning the shelves. I pick up a book that promises to be horribly gruesome and darkly funny, not for the fainthearted. One of the quotes on the back reads, "I don't know that I'll ever be able to sleep again." My kind of thing.

"A present for Ray?" Rozália nods toward the book I'm holding.

"No. She'd hate it. It would be a good present for me though."
Rozália nods. "How are things with you two?"

"Fine," I say.

"Fine?"

We move to let someone pass us. I think about standing outside with Ray on Saturday night. Her jacket around my shoulders, her fingers grazing my bottom lip.

"Good," I say, letting myself enjoy the memory, unable to stop myself smiling.

"You're going to get together soon," Rozália says matter-of-factly. "I can feel it."

"Hmmm," I say, pretending that I'm concentrating on another book. But I don't jump to correct her like I normally would, tell her that she's being ridiculous. That I don't even feel that way. I'm quiet instead; I let myself allow for the possibility.

After checking my bank balance, I decide I really don't need to treat myself to a lifetime of nightmares today, so I wait for Rozália outside while she pays for the book she's chosen, a reissued classic with a beautiful cover. I hear her laughing with the bookseller, thanking her profusely, telling her to have a lovely day.

When she sees me waiting for her outside, she acts surprised, gives me a look that says "oh, you're still here then."

"Well, I hope your friend enjoys her present," I say, gesturing at the paper bag in her hand.

"Yeah, me too," Rozália says. "Thanks for meeting me here. Even though you were no help."

"A pleasure as always," I say, lifting my hand to wave goodbye to her. "See you next week."

"OK."

She turns and walks toward the bike rack at the other end

of the street and as I make my way toward the tube in the opposite direction I hear her yell, "Bye, Britney!"

A week after the karaoke night at the village hall, on Saturday morning, Rachel knocks on our front door. We have agreed to go swimming in the pond. Will managed to get out of it, saying he needs to stay in and wait for a tile paint delivery—our attempt to make the bathroom look less moldy without, you know, actually making it less moldy. I wish I'd had the good sense to organize something that meant I couldn't go. Although, realistically, and even though I loathe myself for it, if Ray was going swimming, then I was always going to go too. If Ray wanted to go swimming with bloodthirsty sharks, I'd no doubt be the first in the tank, sacrificing myself in case she briefly thought I was cool before they ate me. Jamie says he has to come because it'll be great content and he "wants to feel like a white woman finding herself" like he reads about every week in the supplements.

"I'm hoping it will cheer up," Rachel says, gesturing at the sky. She hovers in the doorway as we get our shoes on. There are big gray clouds although it's still uncomfortably warm outside. We only have to walk a few meters down the road before there are beads of sweat gathering on my upper lip and behind my knees.

It's nearly an hour-long walk across the fields to get to the pond. We walk most of it in single file to fit on the footpath, which means we either have to shout in order to hear each other or walk in silence. A slow march toward certain death. It gives me plenty of time to contemplate drowning. I have read that in the last moments of consciousness before your lungs succumb to the water, people experience a kind of euphoria. So at least there's that to look forward to.

Rachel leads the way with Ray behind her. Occasionally I hear a snippet of their conversation. A laugh carried on the wind, Rachel asking about the house, about the newspaper. I'm at the back of the group, watching Jamie stumble on the uneven path in front of me because he won't stop looking at his phone. I dread to think what I look like in the photos he keeps taking of us. I've got a black swimsuit on with baggy, black Adidas shorts over the top. I bought them once with the intention of running in them, but that never happened. I had to take off my gray T-shirt because I'm too hot and I was worried I looked like I was wearing a PE uniform, like the last girl to be picked to play football. I'm regretting wearing my knock-off Birkenstocks already. I can feel a blister forming at the top of my big toe.

The cumulative effect of my various maladies and the rising panic in my chest is a low-level nausea and a sort of drowsy light-headedness. I take some deep breaths and in doing so, inhale a fly. Perfect.

Although I've quietly worked myself up into quite the state by the time we arrive at the pond, I have to begrudgingly admit that it's very pretty, like something out of a fairy tale. The grass is tall and weeping willows line the banks, their branches grazing the surface of the water. A heron is sitting on the wooden jetty, which stretches out into the pond—an actual heron for goodness' sake. Apart from him, we're the only people here. I think about London Fields Lido on a warm Saturday morning, or Hampstead Ladies Pond. All those bodies in such a small space.

All those facilities, though. All those toilets and showers

and ice cream vans. I swat another fly away before it has the chance to crawl into my mouth.

We lay out the picnic blanket we brought with us close to the water and sit on it for a moment, taking in the view, recovering from our walk. I wipe my sticky forehead with the back of my hand.

"Right," Jamie says after a couple of minutes, "are we going to do this, then? I need someone to wait here for a second and get a video of me jumping in."

I hold out my hand to take his phone off him.

"It's going to be really cold," Rachel says. "Just to warn you."

"It's fine," Jamie says. "I'm boiling hot, it'll be nice to cool off."

I film Jamie as he walks up the jetty past the heron, which completely ignores him. He's wearing tiny black swimming trunks, and I can see from the way that he's walking that he's tensing his whole body for the camera. He does look great, to be fair. The followers who come for the DIY and stay for the thirst traps are going to love this.

Jamie looks at the camera, shoulders pushed back, abs taut, and yells "Three, two, one!" He jumps, pulling his knees up to his chest, and bombs into the water. When he comes up for air he gasps, pushing his hair out of his eyes.

"It's really fucking freezing," he yells at us, his voice a few octaves higher than before.

"Well done, J," Ray shouts back. "Best way to do it, just get straight in. You'll be fine in a minute."

"There's something touching my fucking foot," he screams as Ray stands up. "No, Ray. I'm not joking. There is literally a shark in here."

"That's it," I say. "I'm not getting in."

Ray ignores us both and carries on undressing, kicking her shorts off and leaving her clothes scattered around on the blanket.

"It's fine," Rachel says, coming to stand next to me. She's taken off her sundress and is wearing a navy-blue bikini with polka dots on it. Not for the first time it strikes me how weird it is that we would never strip down to our underwear say, at the pub, but because we're near a body of water it's fine. I am so self-conscious in my swimsuit that I may as well be standing here completely naked. In fact, I feel so awkward about it that it's a relief to have my focus shift away from the pond and onto my own thighs for a moment.

"It'll just be weeds that he can feel," she says. "Or maybe a tiny fish. Nothing scary though."

I nod and try to keep my face impassive as the words *maybe a tiny fish* create ripples of disgust deep in my stomach.

We watch Ray walk up the jetty and jump into the water with a splash. When she reappears above the surface, she makes a noise somewhere between a laugh and a howl, but she's grinning. She makes her way over to Jamie and jumps on his back. He tries to fling her off, screaming, "She's trying to drown me. It's a hate crime."

"Come on, El," Ray calls out, making her way back over to the jetty and hanging on to the side. She holds out a hand as if to help me in, even though I'm still standing far away, safe and dry on the picnic blanket.

"Follow me?" Rachel says. She starts heading off, and after a couple of beats I take a deep breath and go after her. Ray moves out of the way so that Rachel can jump in. I recoil as the water splashes me. It's clearer than I'd imagined but it smells very

much of pond, of weeds and moss and mud. Not like something I fancy dunking my body into.

I sit on the edge of the jetty and compromise by tentatively
dipping my feet in. The water is just as cold as Jamie's screaming suggested. Ray swims back over to me. Instead of holding
onto the side, she wraps her hands around my ankles and gently pulls. I squeal, clutching on to the jetty, kicking her away.
She laughs, totally unaware that she's just turned my legs to
jelly. If I tried to stand up now, I'd probably end up falling in.

"Don't you dare," I say, half-terrified, half-thrilled, wanting
her to touch me again.

"I won't," she says. "I won't if you get in now. If you keep
making a fuss, I will."

"I'm not making a fuss," I say, indignant. I look down at the
water below and shudder.

"You are a bit," she says, looking up at me. "You're being a
diva."

"Ray, we both read the article about that woman who got a
spider in her ear from a pond, and it gave birth to loads of other
spiders and now she has a head full of spiders."

I have to close my eyes briefly, it's a concerted effort not to
retch at the thought.

"OK, so don't let any spiders in your ears," Ray says. "Keep
them closed."

"Ray!"

"El, come on. That's not going to happen, is it? I'll inspect
your ears thoroughly when we get out. I promise."

I swallow and look down and, despite myself, despite so
badly wanting to be able to slide into the water next to Ray,
to feel her hands around my waist, for her to be proud of me

for being so brave, despite wanting to write about this in my journal later, for this to be another wild thing I've conquered, I know from the rising panic in my chest, the flutter of my heart, the lump forming in my throat, that I just can't do it.

I shake my head at Ray and find to my horror that my bottom lip is wobbling.

"All right," she says, "all right, fine. Don't get in."

She pushes herself off the side of the jetty, away from me, bored of coaxing and cajoling. I don't blame her.

I sit for a moment alone, watching Ray explain to the others that I'm not coming in.

"Boo, you whore!" Jamie yells at me.

I shrug, give them a weak smile and a wave and eventually make my way back over to our picnic blanket. I take a couple of sips of water and watch them splashing about, waiting for my heart rate to come down, for my disappointment in myself to subside. I quickly wipe away a tear, surprised at how cross with myself I am.

When the others get out of the water, they wrap themselves in towels and sit back down on the blanket next to me. Jamie shakes himself off next to me a bit like a dog would. He's been bitten on his ankle, and Rachel tells him it's probably a duck mite, which is horrifying and goes some way toward vindicating my cowardice.

I pull my knees up to my chest, shivering despite the glimpses of sun. Ray sits next to me and puts her hand on my shoulder, running her thumb over the spot where a new smattering of freckles has appeared.

"You're all pink, El."

I twist around, to inspect the spot where her fingers are.

"How can you burn in this weather?"

"It's my special skill," I say. I touch the back of my neck too. Ray watches me, waiting for my verdict.

"Burned," I confirm, as I feel the heat radiating off my skin with the back of my hand.

She shakes her head at me, smiling.

"Sorry for being pathetic," I say quietly as the others discuss the pros and cons of the various mites one can be eaten by in the pond.

"Don't say that," Ray says, looking up at me, surprised. "Ever, OK? You're not pathetic."

"OK," I say. I can't help but feel a thrill at provoking such a strong reaction from her, although "not pathetic" is a pretty low bar for a compliment, isn't it? "Just not wild, then." I pull my T-shirt back on before the sunburn gets any worse, and when I look back at Ray, she's watching me.

"Pretty wild to let a spider just hang out right there on your . . ."

Ray taps gently on her own earlobe, and I leap up, shrieking, throwing my hand up to my ear. Ray bursts out laughing. Of course there's no spider.

"I hate you," I say, shuddering involuntarily. I rub my ear against my shoulder as I sit back down, just in case. Phantom insects crawl all over my body.

"I don't think so," Ray says, still grinning at me.

Rachel offers us homemade chocolate chip cookies from a Tupperware box she's brought with her, and we apologetically unpack a family-size bag of salt-and-vinegar crisps, our only offering. Rachel politely claims they're exactly what she wants.

"These are amazing," Ray says, biting into a cookie, holding her hand underneath it as a plate.

"It's nothing," Rachel says. "When we swam here when I was

little, we always used to bake something to eat afterward, so it's just a tradition I can't shake. It feels wrong to swim without a treat afterward."

I think about when my dad would take Rob and me swimming, usually on a weekend when Mum was busy in the shop. He'd never get into the pool, but he'd watch. And he really did watch, or at least I think he did. It certainly felt like every time we turned to him wanting his attention—showing off our handstands or how fast we were going—he'd already be looking. When we left, he would play a game where he'd pretend we weren't allowed sweets from the vending machine after our swim. He'd let us get to the car, by which point we'd be hysterically laughing and pleading and then he'd put on a big show of relenting, hand over some coins, and we'd race back inside. I haven't thought about that in a long time. I think sometimes I'm guilty of that—forgetting the fun. I realize with a sharp pang of guilt that I haven't thanked them for the card yet.

We're all quiet for a minute, concentrating on eating. I didn't realize how hungry I'd got after the long walk and the panic. I watch Ray as she eats. She's abandoned her towel and is instead just sitting cross-legged in her black bikini, completely uninhibited. The opposite of me, clutching my dry towel around me, trying to cover up every inch of skin. She catches my eye as she's asking Rachel a question about other local swimming spots and smiles. I blush, embarrassed to have been caught looking at her. I shuffle up to Jamie and lean over his shoulder as he scrolls through all the photos he's taken today, and we select the best ones for his post. We choose some photos of flowers, some of the pond, some of us walking. The first photo is of Jamie pulling himself up out of the water. "You've got to give the people what they want," he says. We workshop captions and eventually settle on "Wild Things."

"I'm obsessed with that account," Rachel says. "I can't believe how many followers you've got."

Jamie grins.

"Are you on Instagram?" he asks.

Rachel nods, her mouth full of cookie.

"Tell me your name, I'll find you."

"Rachel Lewis," she says, putting the rest of her cookie down and brushing crumbs off her hands over the grass. "There'll be a thousand of them, so if you just search—"

"Got you," Jamie says. He looks up at her and smiles. "I'm going to have a stalk in front of you, sorry!"

She laughs and waves her hand.

"Go ahead, it's not very interesting."

"OK, so let's see, let's see . . . what can we find out about Rachel Lewis. She used to live in . . . Vauxhall?"

"Close, Stockwell."

"Damn it, thrown off by the city farm."

"Sorry."

"OK."

Jamie carries on scrolling.

"She loves to take photos of her breakfast. I'm seeing pancakes, I'm seeing French toast. She's got a sweet tooth."

"Spot-on," she says.

Ray points to the cookies, silently asking if she can have another one, and Rachel pushes the box toward her.

"Is this your boyfriend?" Jamie says, turning his phone around. We all lean in to look at a photo of Rachel standing next to a tall man with a bit too much beard. They look like they're at a wedding, all dressed up and posing in front of a flower arch.

"Yes," Rachel says. "I mean, no. Not at the moment. I don't really know."

"Jamie!" I say. "Enough stalking now."

"No, no," Rachel says, "it's fine."

She sighs. None of us say anything, even though we all obviously want to hear the story.

"So basically," Rachel says, "he cheated on me."

"Oh god," I say, "I'm sorry."

"Well," she says, grimacing slightly, "he kissed someone else."

We're all quiet for a moment, not quite sure what we're meant to say.

"It was someone at work," she carries on. "He's a lawyer and they were working on something for months, it was all very intense, lots of late nights, and then they had a huge setback, this massive blow, and they got very drunk, it was very late and they ended up kissing."

"How did you find out?" Jamie says.

"He told me," she says, picking up her cookie and taking a bite.

"Well, I guess that counts for something," I say tentatively. Not sure if it really does or not.

"No, it does. It does," she says. "I forgive him for that. We've all done stupid things. It was one time. It just threw up a lot of other stuff in our relationship that we'd been ignoring. Highlighted other problems that we should have been dealing with."

"So you moved back here?" Ray says. "And he's still in Stockwell?"

"Yeah," she says, "we live in a one-bedroom flat, so we can't really get any space from each other if we're both there. His parents are in Scotland, so it made sense for me to be the one to leave, for now."

"Well, I hope you can work it out," I say. "If that's what you want."

"Thanks," Rachel says, smiling at me. "You know, I really don't know what I want."

We walk back slowly, but it somehow doesn't seem to take any time at all. Halfway home I abandon my shoes, preferring to step on the rough path barefoot than keep antagonizing my blister. The ground is warm, the sun is shining. It feels surprisingly good, like I'm slotting into place in the outdoors rather than fighting against it.

"How's the party prep coming on?" Rachel says from the front of the group.

"Well," Ray says, "we've just been trying to focus on getting the house socially acceptable."

"Getting there?" Rachel says.

"Yes," Jamie answers for Ray, "we are. I think it's coming along great."

"I do too," I say. "I think we'll be in good shape for the party."

"You are coming, aren't you?" Jamie says to Rachel.

"Yes," she says. "Definitely. And by the sounds of it, so is absolutely everyone else in a two-mile radius. Do I need to bring anything?"

"Just yourself," I say.

"And maybe," Jamie adds, "some food."

"Oh yeah," I say. "Bring some cookies!"

Rachel laughs.

"OK, if that's what you want."

We part ways near our house, at the bottom of the hill. Rachel's parents' house is another ten minutes up the road, but she's got her bike here, locked to a railing.

"This is technically not allowed," she says as she crouches down to unlock it, "so I'm sure there'll be a passive-aggressive notice about it on the WhatsApp group already."

Jamie and Ray thank her for being their swimming guide, and I mumble something about "maybe next time" and she's kind enough to say, "Yes, definitely!" We watch her as she cycles off, her dress flapping slightly in the breeze. She's confident, straight into the middle of the road, no helmet.

When I get home, I make a beeline for the bathroom and scrub my skin harder than I've ever scrubbed it before. Despite not having gotten in the pond, I can feel it all over me. The potential for stray spawn. I take the showerhead and spray water directly into my ears and then sit in my room carefully sticking cotton buds as far as I can inside them until I'm entirely satisfied they're spider-free. Even then I spend the evening intermittently touching them, phantom legs tickling my ear canal, sending shivers down my spine.

"There aren't any spiders in there, El," Ray says without even looking up from her phone, "unless they crawled up through your feet."

We're all sitting in the living room, deciding whether to watch a film.

I shudder. I hadn't even thought of that. I get my phone out and start typing *foot spider pond death* into Google.

"Stop googling it," she says, still looking down at her phone. "It was a joke."

"I'm not," I say. I put my phone away but not before I've seen the words *fatal water spider bite*. Shit. Jamie momentarily stops scrolling through Netflix to hold his iPhone up to the side of my head. He shines the flashlight directly into my ear. He studies it very carefully.

"No spiders," he says after a while. "A fish, some worms, a little duckling, but no spiders."

"Very reassuring," I say. "Thank you."

Ray smiles listening to us but still doesn't look up from her phone.

We decide to let Will choose a film, and he selects something extremely long about the First World War. We all pretend we've been wanting to see it for ages because we never let Will pick anything and if he wants to watch a very long, dull film, then that's what he gets to do.

"Powerful," Jamie whispers intermittently and we all murmur in agreement. Will smiles; he obviously knows we're only watching it for him.

I zone out during most of the film, my mind flipping back to the afternoon. I let myself take a break from lamenting my imminent death and instead think about sitting on the edge of the jetty, my legs dangling over the side, Ray's hands gripped tightly around my ankles.

CHAPTER THIRTEEN

At work over the next couple of days, people who I've previously barely spoken to continue to come up to me and chat as if we're good friends. This is because Jamie is no longer viewed simply as a diversity hire doing well for them but as an in-house celebrity. His Instagram account has close to a hundred thousand followers now. His in-box is filled with brands trying to get him to advertise their products. He is in talks with a rescue charity about being their chicken ambassador or something equally ridiculous. And because I'm featured in his posts framed as, essentially, one of his assistants, I am now famous by proxy.

"Eleanor!"

A wide-eyed blond woman accosts me as I come out of the stall in the toilets and start washing my hands. I look up to catch her eye in the mirror, and she beams. I smile back tentatively, trying to place her. She's neither heading into the toilets nor washing her hands, and I wonder if she came in here just to see me.

"How are you doing, lovely?" she says.

"Um," I say, shaking my wet hands over the sink; I'm not sure I can put them under the dryer now, it feels rude somehow to make a lot of noise while this stranger is trying to talk to me. "Fine. How are you?"

"Oh, you know how it is," she says, and laughs.

I literally don't know how it is—I have no idea *who* she is. I laugh a little with her, trying to think where I might have seen her before.

"So," she says decisively, as if we've been chatting for ages and she's really got to get on, "I was talking to the lovely Kyle, and he was telling me about your fabulous house."

"Ah," I say, "yes."

"And I'm just obsessed with your account," she says, nodding at me encouragingly.

"Right," I say, "well, it's Jamie's account."

"Yes, of course," she says, "gorgeous Jamie! I never see him around though."

That's because you're not able to follow him into the toilets, I think.

"So the lovely Kyle was telling me about your fabulous house, and it just so happens that I literally live like one village over."

"Oh, really?"

"Well," she says, waving her hand dismissively, "like five villages over. Like a ten-minute drive." She pauses. "Like a ten-to forty-five-minute drive."

"Wow," I say. "Well, it's a lovely part of the world. We're really enjoying being there."

I pat my damp fingers on the front of my jeans and step back, a slight move toward leaving in the hope she might follow my lead. She stays firmly where she is.

"So obviously Kyle is going to your little soiree on Saturday." The smile on her face doesn't waver for a second. I didn't think it was possible for her eyes to open any wider, but they do. She looks at me expectantly. Damn it, Mustache Kyle. We're not meant to be talking about the party at work; Jamie has deliberately kept it a secret so we don't have to invite "all the losers" (his words). It's meant to be just Mustache Kyle and then Gay Kyle to keep him company. Salmon Simon was invited too but can't attend because it's his birthday, which all of us had entirely forgotten. He's actually quite annoyed at us for poaching the Kyles from his birthday drinks.

"Yes, he's writing a feature," I say. "On us, well, on the house. Listen." I point to the door. "I've got to get back."

I grimace slightly as if I have a mountain of work waiting for me and not just a coffee that I don't want to get cold.

"Of course, of course," she says. Her disappointment is palpable. She follows me out of the toilets, and I hold my hand up to wave goodbye.

"Good to see you," I say limply.

"Amazing to see you," she says. "We're going to see so much of each other now that we're practically neighbors, I'm sure."

I watch her walk off, trying desperately to remember her name.

When I get back to my desk, I open up my instant messaging group with Jamie and Ray.

Eleanor: *so, a blond woman just accosted me in the toilets*

Jamie: *OI OI*

Eleanor: *she's a fan of yours, j. she clearly wanted an invite to the party.*

Ray: *who was it? what did you say?*

Eleanor: *no idea. i just pretended like i didn't know what she was getting at and escaped.*

Jamie: *well done, babes, i've been getting it all week. i don't even know how people found out other than that kyle can't keep his mouth shut.*

Ray: *are we accidentally having the party of the year except we've only invited pensioners and like . . . the local pta?*

Eleanor: *i think so*

Jamie: *i love it, it makes it even more exclusive and ridiculous*

Eleanor: *j, you should have got a sponsor for the party*

Ray: *ha, sponsored by chicken pellets and mold remover*

I snort and immediately Mona is beside me. I sense her before I see her, a dark shadow looming.

"What is funny?"

"Oh," I say, "um, I read something that made me laugh."

I quickly close the chat box.

"A joke?"

"Yes."

"What is it?"

"Um, I don't remember."

Mona tuts.

"Sorry," I say.

"I love jokes," she says.

"Right," I say, "well . . . next time."

I wait for her to disappear into her puff of smoke and open the chat box again.

Eleanor: *sorry, got Mona-ed*

Jamie: *oh god, she's actually a menace to society, she shouldn't be allowed, it's like . . . when she looks at me i go ice cold*

Ray: *is it bad that i quite fancy her?*

Jamie: *yes*

Eleanor: *yes*

Ray: *i think it's the combination of the boots, her frenchness and her cold, cold heart*

Jamie: *get help*

Ray: *don't shame me, the heart wants what it wants*

Jamie: *this isn't about your heart, you pervert*

Ray: *ok let's delete this now or we're going to end up in hr or something*

Eleanor: *i'll delete, are we meeting for lunch in 5?*

Jamie: *yes, i'm starving and i want to do last-minute party planning*

Ray: *yes, i'm sick of hearing jamie talking about how he's wasting away but no party planning there's nothing else to plan*

Jamie: *a party is never really fully planned*

Eleanor: *ok see you both downstairs*

I delete our conversation, and once I've checked the coast is clear of Mona, I head to meet them. All the way down the stairs I lament my lack of heavyweight boots, my unexciting Englishness, and my warm, aching heart.

On the Friday evening before the house party, just as we're washing up after dinner, Jamie suddenly freezes and then drops the cutlery he's holding on to the table with an almighty clatter. We all spin around to glare at him.

"There's a fox in the garden," he says.

"How do you . . . ," Ray starts to say but she doesn't get a chance to finish because Jamie bolts out of the back door and starts yelling. We all go after him and watch as he runs barefoot down the garden shouting "Fuck off" at the top of his lungs.

I'm just about to laugh when I see that he's right: a streak of red out of the corner of my eye as a fox darts under a hedge and out of sight.

"Oh my god." Jamie runs back to us, his eyes wide with panic. "Where are they? We need to find them. Did he eat them? Did he eat them already? Oh my god, we're late to put them to bed. Oh god, I'm going to be sick."

"It's OK, it's OK," I say. "They'll just be pottering around, I bet you got to the fox before they even knew it was there."

My heart is hammering in my chest as I walk slowly around the perimeter of the garden, trying not to look at anything too closely, lest I see a dead chicken and have to break Jamie's heart.

"I've got one!" Ray yells after a couple of minutes.

"Which one?" Jamie says, running toward her.

"How the fuck would I know, Jamie?"

"Oh, it's Bella!" Jamie says, as he gets to them. He takes Bella from Ray and cradles her under his arm.

"OK," Will says, emerging from under a hedge with another chicken clutched under his arm. "I've got Edward."

"How are you telling them apart?" Ray says, shaking her head at Will.

"They all look totally different," he says, "plus, you know, their personalities."

We lock Edward and Bella up in the coop and then spend another twenty minutes inspecting the garden for any trace of Jacob. I find myself calling for her like she's a dog. Ray walks around shaking a bag of chicken feed. There's no sign. Just as it's getting properly dark and I'm wondering how best to suggest that perhaps we need to accept that Jacob's not coming back, Jamie yells from the back of the garden and we all run toward him.

I see him from a distance in the nook, he's on his knees bending over something. My heart sinks, but when we get closer, he turns around and grins at us.

"She was hiding," he says, pointing under the decking, "she's so clever. The cleverest chicken in the world."

"Oh, thank god," I say, lifting my hand to my chest. My racing heart begins to slow, relieved for Jacob and relieved that our beautiful garden nook isn't going to be associated with heartbreak forever.

We lure Jacob out from underneath the decking with strawberries and then once she's safely shut away with her sisters, we triple-check the locks as if a fox might come back with a credit card or a hairpin to try and break in. Jamie promises the chickens he'll come out to check on them before he goes to bed.

We need a nightcap to calm down after all the excitement. We have some whiskey, which none of us like but which Will gets given every year for Christmas from his granddad. He now has several bottles of it, and we choose one at random. It is supposed to taste of "peat and fruit," but instead it just burns satisfyingly at the back of my throat. Calming in a medicinal way. We raise a glass to the chickens being safe and to Jamie and his sixth sense.

"A mother always knows," he says solemnly.

When we go to bed, I hear him talking in hushed tones in his bedroom, and I just know he's doing an Insta Story about it.

The day of the housewarming flies by. We wake up early to glorious sunshine and drink coffee together on the back step, smugly talking about the beautiful weather as if it was our doing, as if we'll personally be providing sunshine for our guests.

As I'm rinsing out our coffee cups in the kitchen sink, Ray comes up behind me and puts her arms around my waist. She hugs me gently.

"It's going to be fun tonight, isn't it, El?" she says, her chin resting on my shoulder, her breath on my ear. I carry on washing up as if all my insides haven't just liquefied.

"It is," I say. "I think it will make us feel even more at home here."

"I think you're right," she says, moving her hands to my hips and squeezing gently before letting go. "We've got a lot of work to do first though."

She disappears out of the room and I stare out of the kitchen window blankly, washing the same cup over and over.

We clean the downstairs of the house meticulously, as if it's going to be inspected. Will ties some balloons to the front door which makes it look a bit like a five-year-old is having a birthday party, but he seems so excited about his contribution that none of us have the heart to say anything.

"Love it," Jamie says, standing in front of the house, admiring them, "so fun, Wilma."

Will beams. He's glued to his phone for most of the day, grinning at it every time a message comes through.

"Tess is definitely coming, then?" I say.

"Yeah," he says, blushing slightly. "She's asking what to wear. I mean I'm just wearing normal clothes. Can I just say normal clothes?"

"No!" Jamie says, gliding past carrying an armful of tangled-up fairy lights. "Tell her to wear something outrageous, I did actually specify that on the invitation."

"Whatever she wants," I say quietly, once Jamie has disappeared into the garden, and Will nods gratefully. I might be a novice at dating, but even I know that texting a woman you barely know and telling her to wear something outrageous isn't really done.

We carry every single chair we own out into the garden and arrange them in various places on the patio and on the lawn. We do the same with all our blankets and throws, and by the time we're finished, the garden is transformed—it looks better than we could have hoped. Jamie has procured a bell tent from a brand that contacted him on Instagram, and it's mercifully easy to put up. It's mustard yellow, big enough for at least ten people to sit inside. We hang rainbow bunting from it and fill it with all the cushions from our living room.

The garden looks inviting enough that hopefully people will want to sit outside and not just congregate in the kitchen. This is partly for health and safety reasons as well as wanting people to enjoy the garden—although our carbon monoxide detector says otherwise, we're pretty sure there are at least three appliances leaking gas in there.

Will and Ray drive to the big supermarket and come back with enough booze for about a thousand people. Will says he'll tell us how much it all cost tomorrow, that we should just enjoy today. I check my account balance and grimace. I wonder if he'll let me set up a payment plan.

In the late afternoon we carry out a huge plastic bucket with handles that we found in the shed and fill it with ice and as much beer and wine as we possibly can. Will and Ray bought crisps and dips and bread and olives at the shop, and we have decided that we can rely on our neighbors to provide the rest of the food. We're certain that none of them will turn up empty-handed. As a finishing touch, once Jamie's managed to untangle them, Ray and I string lights across as much of the garden as possible. Across the patio, in the hedges, up the trellis in the nook, through the trees.

We've barely sat down all day, and all of a sudden, it's two hours until everyone is meant to arrive and none of us are showered or dressed. As we run up the stairs, Ray shouts, reminding us of the strict three-minute washing policy because of the hot water situation.

When I get out of the shower (cool, but not yet freezing), there's a glass of white wine waiting for me on top of my chest of drawers.

"Thanks, Ray," I yell through the wall. I don't think she hears me over the sound of her music blaring. I can't remember the last time I got ready for a party without the soundtrack of Lithuanian power ballads. I almost miss them.

I've been struggling with what to wear tonight, but I've decided that since we've chosen such a basic theme, I'm fine to go with a basic outfit. I've got a white summer dress that nips in at the waist and ties up at the back just under my shoulder blades, leaving most of my back bare. It reaches halfway down my shins, showing off what couldn't quite be described as a tan on my legs, but they're certainly not as translucent as they used to be.

I leave my hair down, and it does exactly what I want it to, it's the perfect amount of wavy without me even having to do anything to it. It hangs down past my shoulders now. It hasn't been this long in a while, but haircuts have taken a back seat recently, so I can pay for things like sandpaper and polyfilla. It's lighter than usual from spending so much time in the sun, the strawberry blond side of auburn. I wear my usual tiny gold hoops, and I place a floral headband on my head studded with tiny yellow and white flowers. It sits on top of my hair like a cheap plastic halo. I take a sip of wine and study myself in the mirror. I look OK, I decide. Perhaps a little bit like I'm about to be sacrificed during a summer solstice ceremony but, like, in a sexy way.

Will and I are the first ones downstairs. We sit on the patio with Jamie's twenty-seven-hour-long playlist already blasting out of the speakers. Will is essentially wearing what he was wearing earlier, a plaid shirt and jeans, and when she comes downstairs, so is Ray. High-waisted Levi's with a white T-shirt tucked in and the sleeves rolled up.

"Whoa," she says, when she sees me. "Look at you."

"I know," I say, blushing and reaching up to my head, "the flowers are stupid."

"No," Ray says, smiling, "they look perfect. Wow."

I lift my hand to my chest, checking to see that my heart is still beating and hasn't actually exploded. I'll probably be replaying that "wow" all night. "So what part of this look is 'festival'?" I say as she sits down next to me.

Ray smiles and holds a finger up, while she reaches into her pocket. She produces some tiny nineties-style sunglasses with pink-tinted lenses and puts them on.

"Of course," I say. "Makes total sense now."

"They complete the look," she says, taking them off again and placing them on the table in front of her.

She picks up her wine and looks at me again. I smile back at her, my cheeks warming.

"How are you feeling, Will?" I ask, pressing my wineglass to my cheek, trying to cool down.

"Yeah," he says, surprised, as if he's never been asked the question before, "good. OK. Fine."

"Surreal, isn't it?" Ray says. "Having this party in our own actual house."

"It is, yeah," Will says. "You know, sometimes I still can't believe Melissa isn't . . . that this isn't . . . not that I'm complaining, I just don't think my brain has caught up with what's happened sometimes. Mostly I'm there but some days I'm still processing."

Ray rests her head on his shoulder.

"You're doing great, Will," she says quietly.

He nods.

"And Tess is coming," I say. "For you."

"Oh, well," Will says, immediately blushing furiously, "for the party."

"For you," Ray repeats, lifting her head up and adjusting his shirt where she's creased it. "And isn't she lucky?"

Will's ears turn pink.

Jamie has kept his outfit a secret, so we've been speculating about all kinds of wild costumes he might have gone for. When he finally comes downstairs he looks unbelievably handsome and, surprisingly, somewhat understated. Well, understated for Jamie. He's wearing a matching shirt and shorts that could definitely be pajamas and are a bright floral print, all pinks and reds. He's got the same sunglasses as Ray, but they're tinted blue, and a bucket hat that would make me look like a ten-year-old but looks perfect on him.

"The big question," he says, once we've all finished gushing over how good he looks, "is can I wear my rainbow Crocs in front of people?"

"What people?" Ray says. "Specifically?"

Jamie pauses, chewing the inside of his cheek.

"Mustache Kyle," he says eventually.

"Oh my god!" I say. "So you actually care about what Mustache Kyle thinks? I thought we'd just invited him on a very professional basis. Work only."

"All right, Midsommar," he says, looking me up and down. "Fine. I do care a bit. Plus he'll be taking photos for the feature, won't he. So, Crocs or no Crocs?"

We decide that Jamie really can pull them off and that wearing Crocs is all about your state of mind. If you believe in the Crocs, then other people will believe in the Crocs. Jamie rounds up the chickens and before we lock them away so they don't get spooked by party guests, we put Jamie's phone on a timer and get a photo of us all together. Ray, Will, and I hold the chickens, and Jamie lies down in the grass in front of us. We just take one because we don't have time to do a full shoot, but the one we do take is perfect. We're all laughing hysterically because Edward flaps her wings just as the photo is taken. Ray is midscream.

Guests start arriving at seven on the dot, and for the next hour there's a steady stream of people knocking on the door, which means the four of us are kept busy showing people around, fetching drinks and impressing upon them how important it is that they don't approach the speakers or deviate from Jamie's carefully curated playlist.

We were right to trust the villagers to provide us with food. Nearly everyone arrives clutching something homemade. Our patio table is heaving with fresh bread and cakes and huge bowls of elaborate salads that look straight out of the pages of a Sunday food supplement. I mean, I do literally recognize some of them from last week's magazine. The Waitrose in the nearest town must now be fully sold out of figs.

Rob and Polly are among the first to arrive. They need to leave early because they have to make an appearance at a friend's birthday party back in London. I can't believe they even came at all, but they insist it's their pleasure, that coming here means that they don't have to spend as long at a party that they don't want to go to, that I'm helping them out if anything. It's all nonsense, and it's so kind that I could cry. Their contribution to the heaving table of food is a cheese board and a bottle of wine far too fancy for the occasion. I immediately hide it at the back of the fridge.

"This is fantastic, El," Rob says as I give them a tour of the downstairs of the house. "It's transformed from when I dropped you off. You're doing a great job."

They politely ignore the various upsetting smells, the chipped paint, the crack in the bathroom window sealed up with tape. They focus instead on the garden and the freshly sanded floorboards. They gush over the fireplace.

"Imagine it at Christmas," Polly says, reaching up and touching the exposed brick, "with all the stockings hanging up."

"Maybe you can come to me this year," I say. The idea hadn't even occurred to me until now, and I am flooded with pleasure at the prospect of being able to host them for once. Polly nods, but she doesn't say anything, instead focusing on trying to wipe some soot from the fireplace off her hands.

I'm about to show them my bedroom when Ray comes out of hers, pulling the door closed behind her.

"Hello!" she says, beaming. "Getting the grand tour?"

She hugs Rob and Polly.

"I'm so sad that you can't stay," Ray says. "El was saying you need to get back early? You'll come back though soon? We'll have a dinner party or something."

"Definitely," Polly says. "I'd love that."

When Ray goes back downstairs, and I lead them into my room, Polly remarks on how lovely she is, how it would be nice to see more of her.

"She is lovely," I say. I hardly dare look at Rob, although when I do look up he's pretending that he's examining my rotting window frame.

Rob and Polly honk with laughter when I show them the soft-porn housewarming card from Mum and Dad taped to my wall.

"It's actually perfect, isn't it?" I say.

"Perfect," Rob says. "I'm quite jealous. We've not had any correspondence yet, have we, Pol?"

She shakes her head.

"Just from Bernard," she says.

"Poor Bernard," I say.

Once Rob and Polly have left to head back to London, I pour myself a glass of white wine and walk a lap of the garden introducing myself to all the people I haven't met yet. Some people have brought their children with them and the bell tent is proving to be a big hit. When I look inside, I see that it is packed with ten-year-olds. I pass Jamie telling a group of rapt people about the fox incident last night, except the way he tells it the fox was the size of a Great Dane and he had to wrestle the chickens from its jaws.

I find Rachel by the food, placing a platter of cookies down. A platter is not an exaggeration. I think there are enough there to feed the entire party.

"Hey!" I say, and she spins round from the table and smiles.

"Hello," she says, and after a brief hesitation, steps forward and hugs me. I reach around her with one arm, aware of not wanting to spill any wine down my white dress.

"You look great," I say. She's wearing the sundress with sunflowers on it that she was wearing the first time we met at the pub. She's also gone for flowers in her hair, although instead of a crown like mine she has her hair pulled back with a single yellow flower in the tie at the nape of her neck. Presumably as a nod to the festival theme, she is wearing Hunter wellies.

"Oh, thank you," she says, looking down at her outfit as if she's forgotten what she's wearing. "So do you. It looks like everyone made a real effort."

"Thank you for bringing those," I say, gesturing at the cookies. "Honestly if everyone hadn't stepped up, we'd all be getting way too drunk. We'd bought, like, a jar of olives for one hundred people."

Rachel laughs, her cheeks reddening slightly.

"It's nothing compared to some of this stuff," she says. "Everyone's gone all out. They're excited that you're here. We're all excited that you're here."

Rachel waves at someone behind my head. It's a woman I recognize from karaoke night but whose name I don't remember. I know she works in London too because I sometimes see her in the mornings at the station. If we acknowledge each other at all, it's with a grim smile—commuter etiquette. You can't start talking to people in the mornings, no one wants it. I turn around and see the woman gesturing for Rachel to come over and join her.

"You go," I say. "I'm going to eat something and check on everyone inside."

"I'll see you later though," Rachel says, holding up her finger to the woman to indicate she'll be a minute.

"Definitely," I say. "Have fun!"

I stand and eat figs and pieces of cheese out of the various salads for a while, watching the party around me, greeting people as they come to get food, chatting with them about the garden, how I'm enjoying the village, the glorious weather. I'm not usually confident at parties or with strangers, but I feel different here, in my own home. More assured.

Of course people are gathered in the dining room and the kitchen despite our requests that people stay outside. I find Rafe and Jim chatting with Ray and a woman who is introduced to me as the person who gave us the chickens. The kitchen is already a mess. Plates stacked precariously, empty bottles, cupboards ransacked for glasses despite the hundreds of compostable cups we've put outside next to the drinks bucket.

"We were just heading back outside," Ray says, holding her hands up to me in surrender, as if I am the only one who cares about enforcing the outside rule. As if we are not all worried about potentially poisoning our guests. "Are you coming?"

"Yes," I say. "In a sec. Just nipping to the loo."

"Come and find me in a bit," Ray says as she walks past me, squeezing my arm. "Don't stress about people being in here, it's fine, OK? We've all survived the past few weeks. And we'll clear it all up tomorrow."

"OK," I say to the back of her head as she disappears out of the kitchen. "I'll come and find you."

I run upstairs to use the bathroom that our guests are not allowed to use. Perhaps the only VIP bathroom in the world with slugs living in it. On my way back I head into my room, grab my phone, and take a photo out of my bedroom window of the party below. I sit on my bed for a moment, a brief respite from the exertion of being around so many people. Jamie's playlist is blaring; at the moment it's Robyn, "Dancing on My Own." I'm sure people must be able to hear it for miles—perhaps even the blond woman from the toilets at work is standing in her own garden, five villages over, listening.

After a couple of minutes, once I've checked my eyeliner hasn't smudged and spritzed myself with perfume again, I head back downstairs. The kitchen is empty now, so I take the opportunity to pour myself a glass of the secret nice wine that Rob and Polly brought with them. I walk out into the garden and stand for a moment by the back door to take it all in. Jamie comes to stand next to me and puts his arm around my shoulders.

"It's going well, I think," he says.

"Definitely," I say. We watch Will and Tess sitting next to each other on a picnic blanket, just outside the bell tent. She laughs at something he says and leans forward to touch his knee. She leaves her hand there.

"She must really like him," Jamie says, "because Will isn't really very funny, is he?"

"Jamie!" I say, looking at him and frowning.

"What, do you think Will's funny?"

"No," I say.

"Exactly, I'm saying it's a good thing. She obviously finds him funny. So that's nice."

"Have you done your interview with Mustache Kyle?" I say, taking a sip of my wine. It is much nicer than what we're serving the guests.

"We've had a good chat, yeah," Jamie says. He's trying to be casual, but he's smiling.

"Oh my god, Jamie, do you *like* him?"

"No!"

"You do!"

"Well, maybe," he says. "You know there's more to him than just a mustache."

"I would hope so."

"He's very sweet actually. We were talking about dating in London, and he's sick of it too. He's had some bad experiences recently. I said he should date a country boy instead."

"And what did he say?"

Jamie grins.

"He said that's exactly what he's trying to do."

I squeal and wrap my arms around Jamie's waist, hugging him tightly.

"Make sure he's a really good boy, Jamie. The best, OK?"

"I will," he says, and kisses me on the top of my head.

I pull away and readjust my flower crown.

"So, is there anyone here for you tonight?" he says, a glint in his eye.

"Oh, you know," I say. "No one in particular."

"El," he says. "You are ridiculous."

"I know. I feel ridiculous all the time. You don't have to tell me."

He takes a sip of his wine. He's drinking a very pale rosé with ice cubes clinking about in it. He does this to "rehydrate on the go" and claims it means he can drink three bottles and not get a hangover.

"I think you should go and say something to her."

"Obviously not," I say, smiling as someone whose name I've forgotten walks past and mouths "great party" at us.

"Why? Why should you obviously not do that?" Jamie says.

"Because, Jamie. I know she doesn't feel the same."

Jamie sighs, exasperated.

"You don't know that. You once said something a million years ago when you had a boyfriend. You have no idea how she feels now. She broke up with Kirsty because she felt like something was missing, that she's looking for the real thing. Well, what if the real thing is you? It's been sitting under her nose this whole time and she's just waiting to discover it."

I'm quiet for a moment. He really is very good at motivational speaking.

"If she doesn't feel the same way, Jamie, it will ruin everything. I feel like I'll just die."

"El, what you have now isn't real though. You're not best friends. You don't want to be her best friend. You're living this sort of half-life where you live on scraps from her and hope, and you just wait for something to change but you don't actually do anything about it. And you won't die. If she doesn't feel the same, you can be heartbroken and then you can move on. That's got to be better than what you feel now, hasn't it? It will be real at least."

"What? You think I should just go and say something? Just go up there"—I point vaguely at the garden, not actually knowing where Ray is—"and say, what? *I'm in love with you. I've been in love with you since the day I met you. I go to sleep thinking of you and I dream of you and you're all I want the moment I wake up?"*

I'm trying to sound sarcastic, but I hear the sincerity cutting through. I realize that a part of me is desperate to say something. That I want Jamie to push me.

Jamie takes another sip of his drink, his eyes wide. He nods slightly, taking it all in.

"Um, I might not say exactly those words," he says. "Maybe just like, *Hey, you know I've always had a crush on you, right? And now you're single I just wanted to put it out there."*

"Oh yeah, that's good, that's really good," I say, wondering if it's too weird to write down what I'm going to say first.

"It's less terrifying than what you just said, I think," he says.

"What if she says she doesn't like me like that though?" I say quietly.

"But, El," Jamie says, "what if she says she does?"

I nod. I know he's right, and buoyed by the wine and Jamie's life coaching I feel the fantasy version of me who tells Ray how I feel rising to the surface, breaking through into reality. I can do this. I'm going to do this. I feel sick at the prospect but it's thrilling too. Jamie's right. What if she feels the same way?

"OK," I say to Jamie.

"OK?"

"Yes. I'm going to do it. Wish me luck."

"Good luck, El," Jamie says. "I'm rooting for you. Come and get me in a bit if you're not too busy snogging each other's faces off."

I laugh, the idea too absurd and wonderful to even entertain.

I walk a lap of the garden scanning the crowd for Ray but can't see her anywhere. I'm briefly waylaid by Sally, who is sitting on a camping chair, drinking bottles of Peroni and telling a group of people, including Rafe and Jim who are nodding politely, about the time she lived in Greece for six months and it was "just like *Mamma Mia*."

I look down the garden, away from where the bulk of the people are, and realize that Ray must be in the nook. It's perfect. We'll be able to talk in private up there, out of the way of the rest of the party. I walk up the path carefully, the paving stones still slightly uneven. This bit of the garden is darker, away from the multicolored bulbs we strung up on the patio. The terrace glows ahead of me, a beacon in the darkness. It looks magical, the fairy lights twinkling against the night sky. I still can't quite believe Ray and I built it ourselves. I feel as though my whole body is singing with excitement about the night, about the fact this is my home, about the prospect of drinking a glass of wine with Ray in the dark and finally telling her how I feel.

When I'm only a few wobbly paving stones away, I look up to call out to Ray and freeze. I'm right. Ray is in the nook, but she's not alone. I don't let myself believe it for a second. They're talking. Ray's just talking to someone. I hear a giggle, and my stomach turns. Ray's hand reaches around the back of Rachel's head, drawing her closer. I close my eyes briefly, so tight that I see stars behind my eyelids. I take a deep breath and open them again. I know I need to look.

I've seen Ray kiss people before, but just a peck on the lips, a hello, a goodbye. I've never seen her kiss someone like this.

I have an overwhelming urge to run, but when I turn, the stone beneath my feet tilts and the wineglass in my hand falls and shatters. The noise is unreasonably loud, as if it's amplified by the darkness.

"Hello?" I hear Ray's voice. "Everything all right?"

I drop to my hands and knees to try to pick up the glass, my back turned to them. I start sweeping shards with my bare hands, tiny crystals lodging themselves into my palms. I know I should stop, but I just feel that if I can clear it up quickly, I can get rid of any evidence that I was ever here. I can disappear.

"El," Ray says, her voice much closer now. Right behind me. "Fuck, El. Stop it."

She drops down so she's kneeling beside me. She grabs my hand, and when she does, a shard of glass slices through my thumb. I yelp and snatch my hand away from her.

"What are you doing?" she says, trying to take my hand back to inspect the damage. I resist her, keeping it clutched to my chest. When I look down there is blood streaked on my white dress.

"Nothing," I say, not meeting her eyes. And then, quietly, "I dropped a glass."

I don't want to look at her. I know she thinks I'm being mad. But if I look at her, I'll cry.

"Just let me go inside and get a broom," she says, and then as I go to pick up another shard of glass, she raises her voice.

"Stop fucking touching it, El. You're going to hurt yourself. You *have* hurt yourself."

I turn to look at her then. We're both quiet for a moment. She's staring at me, her eyes wide, not understanding what's wrong with me.

"I have hurt myself," I echo eventually.

She nods slowly.

"Yes. That's what I'm saying. So let's go and get you cleaned up. . . ."

"No," I say, a moment of clarity washing over me. Or panic. Something telling me I need to get away from her immediately.

"Oh god," I say, "what am I doing? What the fuck am I doing?"

Absurdly, I laugh. The sound is so jarring that I see Ray recoil.

"I need to go," I say.

"Right, let me come—"

"No," I say, louder this time.

I struggle onto my feet and look down at her. Her eyes are wide, staring up at me confused. She looks hurt and it takes everything not to reach out to her.

"I need to get away from here," I say, my voice catching in my throat. "From this house. You."

"Me? Wait. Is this about . . . ?"

She gestures back at the terrace where Rachel is now on her feet hovering, clearly unsure about whether she should come over or not. I desperately will her to stay where she is.

I shake my head and open my mouth, but no words come out.

"I had no idea that you liked her, El. I'm sorry. I thought she was just your friend. I didn't really mean for anything to happen, but you made it so romantic out here."

She cracks a small smile, trying to bring me back to her, to lift the strange fog around us, but despite trying my best to hold it back, a tear slides down my cheek. Ray looks horrified.

"Please don't cry, please. I didn't know. I didn't know that you liked her. I won't see her again. I won't. Please don't get upset."

Ray's still kneeling down in front of me as though she's begging. I should feel powerful, but I don't. I feel smaller than ever, towering above her.

I bite my lip.

"I don't like her," I say, it comes out as a whisper.

"Well, clearly you do or—"

"No," I say, interrupting her, my voice breaking slightly.

I shake my head.

"I don't like *her*, Ray."

We're both quiet for a moment. She looks at me and then puts her head in her hands. I swallow and take a deep breath. Before she looks up, I start to walk away.

I think she might follow me. I hope she might: that she'll run after me and grab my hand and spin me around and kiss me and tell me she loves me and that everything will be all right. But when I get back to the house, she's just where I left her, kneeling in the dark.

CHAPTER FOURTEEN

I order a taxi and take the last train out of the village into London with my hastily packed suitcase and several tote bags bursting at the seams with my things. I have no idea what I've brought with me. It all happens so quickly that Will and Jamie don't even know I've left until I text them from the train.

Need to get away for a bit. Don't worry at all! I'm totally fine!! :) :)

Jamie immediately starts calling me, but I switch my phone on to Do Not Disturb. I can't talk to him now. I can't bear to talk at all. I stare at my blank phone screen and wipe off a smear of blood with my finger. I realize that my hands are shaking. I pretend not to notice the people staring at me, the girl in the flower crown and the bloody dress.

I didn't see Ray before I left. I can only assume she stayed in the garden. Maybe she went back to Rachel, although I don't really believe that she did. It would be OK, though, I tell myself. That would be OK. She isn't mine. We don't belong to each other. Not in real life.

I have never felt so awake. Never felt the need to live in reality so acutely. To feel the pain of it. To recognize the sheer bloody awfulness of it. But with reality, with the final dashing of my seemingly eternal hope, there's something else. The hurt is good. I need to hurt, I think, in order to heal. It's what Jamie said. I needed to get my heart broken and now I can move on.

When I arrive at Rob and Polly's flat, they both come out onto the street to meet me. They've changed out of their party clothes and are wearing joggers and hoodies, but Polly still has her makeup on. They must have only just got home. Rob takes all my tote bags without asking any questions and Polly wraps me in her arms when I burst into tears. She rocks me back and forth gently, stroking my hair.

"Shhh," she says. "Whatever it is, it will be OK. It will be OK."

I nod, because I have to believe that it will.

I sit in their kitchen, and Polly makes me a cup of tea while Rob gently tends to my hands, dabbing at them with an alcohol wipe from his first aid kit, removing tiny shards of glass with tweezers.

"Sorry," he keeps saying when I wince. "I'm sorry, El."

When Polly puts the mug of tea down in front of me, she gently lifts the flower crown off my head and smooths my hair down.

When Rob's finished with my hands, I realize that they're too sore to pick up my tea. I can't help but giggle through my tears when I catch a glimpse of myself in the mirror leaning up against their wall drinking through the rubber straw that Polly brings me so I don't have to hold my mug. So tragic that it goes all the way back around to funny. We all giggle and even then, in the recesses of my mind, hazy behind the heartbreak, I think, *I am going to be all right*, although it's gone in a flash, as quickly as it came and buried in a fresh wave of despair.

I try my best to wash my face without really looking in the mirror, I can't bear to look myself in the eye. When I get out of the bathroom, I hear Rob and Polly talking in hushed voices. I hover in the doorway, waiting for the whispering to subside, and when it finally goes quiet, I creep into the spare bedroom. It's small, more of a box room really, and I watch as my brother picks up a pile of his clothes from the floor, his book from the desk. A single camp bed is already made up with ancient blue sheets I recognize from our childhood home.

"Rob?" I say quietly.

He turns at the sound of my voice, but he doesn't quite look at me.

"I'm just grabbing a few bits, El, and then I'll leave you to it. Have you got everything you need? Polly's got some pajamas for you—I've left them . . ." He gestures to the pillow.

"Rob," I say again, biting my lip, not wanting to cry again, "have you been sleeping in here?"

He stops gathering his things, and when he finally meets my eye, he nods quickly.

"Oh no," I say. "Why?"

He takes a moment to answer, choosing his words carefully.

"It's been a bit of a tricky time," he says. "But we're working through it now."

I feel the shock of it trickle through me like ice. The idea of

Polly and Rob being anything other than rock-solid is impossible to me. They are the gold standard I hold all relationships up to. They are true love itself.

"What do you mean it's been a tricky time?"

He doesn't say anything, his fingertips tap anxiously on the back of his book.

"Is there someone else?" I ask. "Rob, did you meet someone. . . . Did you cheat on her?"

Even as I'm saying the words, I just know that can't be true. Rob pauses and then shakes his head.

"She cheated on you?" I whisper.

"It's complicated, El."

"Rob, did she?"

"It's complicated," he says firmly. "It's been very difficult, but these things are . . . it's never really as clear-cut as all that. I don't want you to think badly of her."

"But," I say, still struggling to compute, "you guys are perfect together. It's perfect. Why would she do something like that?"

"Nothing's perfect," Rob says gently. "You really don't know," he starts and then stops as though he doesn't quite know how to finish the sentence.

"You really can't judge," he says after a moment. "We've been together for a long time. Sometimes things like this . . . sometimes things aren't quite what they seem from the outside. It can be hard to hold it all together."

I nod. I'm surprised that I'm not angry at Polly. I'm heartbroken for them both.

"Why didn't you tell me?"

Rob shrugs, his bundle of clothes clutched to his chest.

"You've been so busy, and everything's been going so well for you at the house. I didn't want to worry you. Plus we're working through it, I just thought maybe . . . maybe you didn't ever need to know."

My bottom lip starts to wobble. I can't help it.

"No, El," Rob says, "this is what I mean, I didn't want to upset you."

"I'm not upset for me," I say, "I'm upset for you. I wish you'd told me. I'm so sorry. I could have been here for you. That's my job."

I've been so wrapped up in myself, in the house, in Ray that I never even noticed anything was wrong. It never even occurred to me that Rob might need me.

"It's not your job," he says gently.

"It is," I say, "it's our job. For each other. I've not been holding up my end; I've left it all to you."

We're both quiet for a moment.

"Are you going to be able to figure it out?" I ask. "Have you forgiven her? I mean, is she . . . is she sorry? Is it over?"

"She's sorry," Rob says, after a moment. "Yes," he says. "It's over. I believe her," he adds, anticipating my next question.

"Do you love her?"

"Yes," he says.

"And does she love you?"

"She says she does." Rob's smile doesn't quite reach his eyes.

"She does love you," I say firmly. "I know that she does. How could she not?"

Rob shrugs.

"I do too," I say.

"I know," Rob says. "I'm sorry you have to sleep in my sheets. I'll change them tomorrow."

"Gross," I say as he kisses me on the head on his way out. I wrap my arms around his waist and squeeze him extra hard.

I lie back on the camp bed in a pair of Polly's pajamas, my head spinning. I flick my phone off Do Not Disturb and see that as well as missed calls from Jamie and Will I have a message from Ray. I assume that by now she's filled them in on what happened.

I'm sorry. I'm so sorry. I can't believe that you left. I came to find you and you were gone. I don't even really understand what's happened but I'm sorry. I can't stand it that you're upset. I would never want to upset you ever. Please know that. Where did you go? Just tell me you're safe even if you don't want to speak to me. But please speak to me. Please.

A tear trickles down my cheek and into my ear. I don't wipe it away. It feels good to cry.

I'm safe. I'm at Rob and Polly's. I'm the one that should be sorry. You haven't done anything wrong. It's all me. I just need to be here for a while. Away from the house.

Away from you. I type it and delete it. Of course I can't say that to her.

Ray reads it immediately.

Call me? Or I can come and see you? I'll get the first train tomorrow.

I shake my head as if she can see me.

I need to just be alone for a while I think. I need a break to get my head together.

Are you breaking up with me, El?

I smile, I can picture her face writing it. I feel like she's smiling too. If she was with me in person, if she was here sitting on the edge of this bed, it would be enough to win me round. I'd laugh and she'd hug me and it would be enough.

How could I ever do that? I type.

You know where I am when you're ready to talk. I always want to talk to you. Anytime. You know you're my favorite person, El.

I know. We'll talk soon. Promise.

I press my phone against my wet ear to listen to a voice note from Jamie.

Oh god, El. I'm so sorry. I can't bear that you're heartbroken. Ray is beside herself, just so you know. When she realized you were gone she lost it. I've never seen her so upset. And she doesn't give a shit about Rachel. But you know that, really. It's not about that, I get it. I get it. I'm sorry my lovely, El. Ring me when you can. And come home. We'll figure this out. We're a family. A fucked-up family, but a family. I love you. I love you. I love you.

I send him a message back to tell him that I love him too. And that he has nothing to be sorry about. But I can't come home.

I sleep fitfully. I dream that a fox gets into the chicken coop while I'm gone and Edward, Bella, and Jacob are dead. Their beautiful, soft feathers tossed around the garden like they were nothing.

I wake up just before 7:00 a.m. My hands hurt and my head hurts. I feel like I've been punched in the chest. When I think of Ray going to my room and realizing I'd left, I feel as though I could throw up. Every single part of my body tells me to get up and go home. To see her. To hold her and tell her I'm sorry, I had a moment of madness and let's just go back to normal. That what we had was enough. Why couldn't I let it be enough?

There's a knock on the door, and Rob pushes it open, sticking his head round first and then opening it widely when he sees I'm awake. He's holding his phone, his hand covering the speaker and squinting as if he's only just woken up too. When he speaks, his voice is croaky.

"Hey, sorry it's so early. Erm, Mum's on the phone."

For a moment my mind draws a blank. I have quite literally no idea what he's talking about.

"Mum?"

"Yes."

"On the phone?"

"Yeah, apparently she tried to ring you but your phone's off, so she's . . ."

Rob shakes the phone in his hand and then walks across the room and passes it to me. I widen my eyes at him and mouth "Why?" and he shrugs.

I hold the phone gingerly up to my ear by my fingertips.

"Mum?"

"There you are, darling, I was worried."

Her voice is tinny and distant but despite that I can still hear how upbeat she sounds, the opposite of worried.

"Worried about what?"

"About you, obviously."

"Why?"

Mum sighs.

"Rob texted me last night to say you'd turned up at his house in the middle of the night, darling."

"Oh."

It hadn't occurred to me to get in touch with my parents. Or that Rob might. I wonder if he's told them about Polly. Who has he been leaning on if he hasn't been leaning on me? My stomach lurches. I take a couple of deep breaths and swallow hard.

"What happened, El? Life on the farm isn't what you thought it would be?"

Her voice is soft in that way that always conjures a lump to my throat. I close my eyes and swallow.

"It's not a farm, Mum," I say. I can't help but smile slightly as I say it.

"I know it's not, darling," she says. "Look, is this about Ray?"

I'm silent for a moment, trying to figure out when I might have mentioned Ray to Mum. As if reading my mind she says, "She's all you talk about every time we speak. Your dad and I do pick up on these things even if you think we're a bit useless."

I don't bother to protest: I do think they're a bit useless. Actually, that's a massive understatement.

"El, can I be frank with you?"

I close my eyes, bracing myself.

"Um, I suppose, if you really have to. . . ."

"You've been mooning about after that girl for too long."

"I haven't been *mooning* about. . . ."

"You've mooned about. And you're too much of a catch to just give yourself away to someone like that. Not getting anything back. You deserve better than that."

I can't help but laugh.

"What?" she says.

"You don't think I'm a catch," I say. "You think I'm boring."

I don't think I've ever said that to my mum before, but I'm too tired and everything's too messed up for me to care at the moment. I hear her gasp on the other end of the phone. I just know she has clapped her hand to her chest like she's in a soap opera.

"I have never in my life thought for even one second that you're boring. Where did you get that idea?"

"Don't worry about it, Mum."

And I know she won't.

"You know, Eleanor. One day someone is going to look at you and just think that you're the bee's knees. And then it will be up to you to decide if they're good enough for you. OK?"

I'm quiet for a moment.

"OK."

"What are you?" she says.

I sigh, staring up at the ceiling.

"I'm the bee's knees."

I hear my dad mumble something in the background, then: "Tell her that."

"Did you hear that, darling?" She doesn't wait for me to answer. "Your dad said I hope you know you can call us anytime—day or night. We are here for you. Even if we're not, you know, there."

"Right. Yes. Thanks."

I hear my mum sigh. She pauses, as if taking the time to carefully choose her words.

"I hope you don't feel . . . I hope you don't feel abandoned by us, El."

We're both quiet for a moment. I listen to her breathing, we both know she doesn't just mean right now.

"We could come home," she says.

"No," I say, and I realize I don't. I don't feel abandoned. She's calling me first thing in the morning. She's giving me pep talks about bees. I'm lying in my brother's spare bed. In what world have I been abandoned?

"I'm fine, Mum. Don't come home."

She knew I'd say that, I think, but still, the sentiment is nice. I think she might really have come.

"Right," she says, exhaling slowly, relieved, "now that I know you're alive, I have to go. Your dad and I are swimming with sharks today. Well"—she preemptively chuckles at her own joke—"the sharks are swimming with *me*."

I roll my eyes, but I can't help but laugh too.

"Good luck to them," I say. "Hey, Mum. Thanks."

"Oh, anytime, darling."

I smile as she hangs up. I probably won't hear from her again now until Christmas.

I open my notebook and carefully write at the top of a new page—*I am the bee's knees*. I stare at it for a moment, and then I underline it several times, my hand roaring with pain underneath the bandages.

Rob knocks gently and then comes and sits on the end of my bed. He places a cup of tea with a straw in it on the floor beside me.

"Did she tell you that you're the bee's knees?" he asks.

I nod.

"Me too."

"We are," I say. "And she's never wrong, is she?"

He nods into his mug of tea, a wry smile on his face.

"What are we going to do, El?"

"I guess," I say, "we should listen to our mother."

CHAPTER FIFTEEN

That first night, Rob slept on the sofa, but as it becomes apparent I'm not going anywhere anytime soon, Rob's belongings disappear from the living room and he moves back into their bedroom. I don't want to pry too much, but I watch them carefully, searching for deeper meaning in every single gesture. In the morning, before she goes to work, Polly reminds Rob to take his lunch, and he tells her to cycle safely, to let him know that she's arrived in one piece, and that feels like something uncomplicated to me, like love.

I unpack the contents of my tote bags into the cupboard, on top of the hoover and boxes of things they have no other place for. They wave away my protests and apologies. They tell me it's nice to have me, that I can stay as long as I like. I wonder if my presence makes things easier for them. One evening, just after we'd all said good night, Polly comes into my room and word-lessly hugs me. I feel her shoulders shaking, and I tell her it's OK, that we're OK. And I mean it. I love her too.

I assure them both that my staying is short-term only. That I'll have something else sorted soon. I lie awake at night won-dering what that might be. I ache with homesickness, for my messed-up commune family, for Ray.

On the Monday morning after the housewarming, I call in sick to work. I send Mona an email telling her I have food poi-soning and then I lie in bed all day until it's time to get dressed to meet Rozália. I don't want to let her down. Plus I know Lisa will never believe that I'm sick. Lisa doesn't believe in getting sick full stop.

I walk to meet Rozália. An hour and a half. I have my head-phones on for the entire time, blasting an inane podcast, men shouting over the top of each other to distract myself from my thoughts. I turn it up louder and twist the earbuds in farther and farther so that by the time I arrive at the coffee shop, the insides of my ears are burning.

I'm a few minutes early, so I get us a table inside by the win-dow. I order a hot chocolate. The barista keeps asking me ques-tions, and I say yes to them all, my brain fuzzy, not really able to take anything in. When my drink arrives, it looks like some-thing a five-year-old would order, covered in marshmallows, pink chocolate drops, a mountain of chocolate whipped cream. Ray would love it. Tears prick at the back of my eyes, which is ridiculous. She's not dead. She could come and have this hot chocolate tomorrow if she wanted to.

As I'm pulling myself together, tentatively dipping my spoon into the cup, Rozália appears. She looks at me for a moment before carefully pulling out the chair opposite and sitting down. A waiter puts a cup of black coffee in front of her, and she thanks him in Hungarian.

"Oh," I say, "Hungarian, is he?"

"Yes," she says. "Obviously."

I nod. Fair enough.

"Eleanor," Rozália says, looking at me with disgust—I think it's potentially her version of concern. "What is wrong with you?"

"What do you mean?" I say, putting a spoonful of cream in my mouth.

"You look like shit," she says. Her fingers are twitching, I know she'd rather sit outside so she can smoke but I'm freezing cold despite the warm summer evening. I realize this cream is the first thing I've eaten all day.

"I had a bad weekend," I say.

"The party didn't go well?"

I bite the inside of my cheek; it's raw now. My whole mouth is sore from grinding my teeth in my sleep, from chewing the skin on my lips.

"No, it didn't," I say. "Well, it did. It was a great party. Just not for me. I'm sort of temporarily back in London for the time being. Or maybe permanently. Actually, I have no idea what I'm doing."

Rozália looks at me for a moment. I reach down to pick a pink chocolate drop up and put it in my mouth. It melts on my tongue but tastes of nothing, just sickly sweet.

"A housewarming so bad that you actually had to move out of the house," Rozália says, swirling a teaspoon back and forth through her coffee.

"Yep," I say.

"So that must have had something to do with Ray," she says, matter-of-factly.

And because it's so obvious to her and because I'm tired, I just nod.

"Yeah," I say, "it's complicated."

"I'm sorry," Rozália says.

"Thank you."

We're both quiet for a moment.

"How are you doing?" I ask. "Have you seen any more of your brother?"

Rozália nods. "I feel bad," she says.

"Why?"

"Because I'm doing great and you're having a shit time."

"Rozália!"

"What?"

"That's all I want! I want you to be doing great. I want you to be happy. Nothing would make me happier than that. Honestly."

"Oh, right, OK," she says, as if that's news to her, as if I haven't spent the past few months expressing that same sentiment over and over. "So, yes. I have seen my brother. He came to my house, and I cooked him dinner." She pauses. "Well, I gave him leftovers from the restaurant."

I nod.

"And I'm seeing him again next weekend. And he might meet . . . you know that girl, who I bought a book for, who works at the RVT behind the bar."

"Yes," I say, trying not to show any kind of interest or excitement so as not to spook her from confiding in me. "I remember, Rozália."

"Well, I've been spending a lot of time with her, and he might meet her."

She says this all in a rush, every syllable running together, trying to get it out as fast as possible.

"That's fantastic," I say. "Honestly, that's the best news. How do you feel?"

"Fine," she says, shrugging and then after a moment, "nervous."

I nod.

"I'd be nervous too. But remember, they both care about you. So it'll be fine. It'll be great."

Rozália drinks her coffee and doesn't say anything.

"And how's the book coming along?" I ask.

Usually this question is met with a roll of her eyes and a stream of expletives about the restaurant taking up every single minute of her life, how she's going to die on the floors of that disgusting place, they'll work her to her bones. I don't believe anyone could possibly make Rozália work to her bones.

"Actually, pretty good," she says.

"Oh yeah?"

"Yeah," she says. "Well, I mean, I finished it."

"What?"

"I finished it," she repeats.

"Rozália, that's major news."

"Is it? I told you I'd get it done. I just needed my inspiration."

"So, can I see it?"

"If you really want to, I'll send it to you. Or I mean"—she gestures at her bag on the floor—"I could just show you now?"

"Um, yes, please."

I hold out my hand, and she reaches into her bag and produces a sketch pad.

"Oh," I say.

"What?"

"Nothing. I just assumed it would be on your laptop."

"It is," she says, looking at me like I'm clueless, as usual. "But I don't have my laptop. I have my sketchbook."

She passes it to me with a roll of her eyes, and when I open it, I can't believe what I'm seeing.

"Rozália," I say, "I didn't know you were illustrating it."

"It's a children's book," she says, "for children. Who look at pictures."

"I know, it's just I thought you were writing it, maybe someone else would do the drawings."

She laughs.

"Who else is going to do it? It's my story. Are you reading it or not?"

"Sorry, yes."

I flip through the sketchbook while Rozália watches me, her arms folded across her chest. I suspect that most people might be shy about showing people their work for the first time but not her. Then again Rozália is not most people.

She is an unbelievably talented illustrator, each page brought to life by her drawings, the pastel colors, the expressions on her characters' faces.

The story though, that is what makes me cry. I try not to. I know she'll hate it, but I can't help it.

I look up at her through misty eyes.

"It's about the chickens," I whisper.

"It's about this *one* chicken," she says, but her cheeks redden slightly.

When that chicken doesn't behave like all the other chickens—it likes different things, its feathers are the wrong color, it doesn't want to lay eggs—it's cast out from its family and has to find a new home, new friends, new family. The chicken is so sad, so lonely and frightened, that one by one it loses its feathers, a trail of them left scattered across each page.

I trace them with my thumb, lifting my jumper sleeve up to my face and wiping my cheeks, not wanting any tears to land on the paper.

The chicken escapes a fox, crosses a river, walks for miles, and ends up living in the countryside with an assortment of different birds—a goose, a swan, a peacock—who've all gone through the same thing and found each other. They take care of one another, and the chicken's feathers not only grow back but they grow back all the colors of the rainbow and instead of being cast out for being different, the birds are celebrated.

I close the book when I'm finished and shake my head at Rozália.

"Did you hate it?" she asks. "Is that why you're crying?"

I laugh and pass her sketch pad back to her.

"Are you kidding me? I love it. It's perfect." I take a deep breath, gathering myself. "This is such an achievement, Rozália. Are you proud of yourself?"

She makes a face, like she's embarrassed for me that I'm even asking that question. She shrugs.

"Well, I'm proud of you," I say. "I'm proud to know such a talented person."

She nods into her coffee cup, her cheeks flushed red, the first time I've ever properly seen her blush. She presses the back of her hands to her face, as if she can't believe it either.

Rozália has to leave early to go and meet her girlfriend, although when I refer to her as that she rolls her eyes at me.

"She's not my *girlfriend*, we're not labeling it."

"OK, sure."

Rozália pulls on her jacket and stands beside the table for a moment, like she doesn't want to leave me.

"Are you going to be OK?" she asks eventually.

"Yes," I say. "You don't have to worry about me. That's not your job."

"It is my job," Rozália says. "I'm your friend."

Before I can respond, she's gone.

I know that I can't keep away from the office forever, so the day after my meeting with Rozália I go back in. It's surprisingly easy to avoid Ray at work. I know her schedule, so I don't have to arrive at or leave the office at the same time as her. We pass each other on the stairs a couple of times, and she smiles and opens her mouth as if to say something but I just smile back, not quite meeting her eyes, and walk right past, as if I'm busy and have no time to talk. It's silly to pretend really because she knows I'm never busy. She knows I always have time to talk to her. I fantasize about her grabbing my arm, physically stopping me, demanding that I speak to her. But I know she would never do that because she's kind and respectful and she's giving me the space I asked for. The space that now feels like a gulf between us. She's getting farther and farther away.

I work from home on the first Thursday after the party, emailing Mona to tell her that I have a doctor's appointment so I don't have to face the sadness of missing the weekly admin audit meeting. Jamie messages saying he misses me and begs me not to hide away forever. I write back saying it won't be forever, but I don't really believe my own words. Truthfully I can't imagine ever sitting at that café and eating cinnamon buns and laughing with them ever again. The Thursday after that I quietly delete the meeting from my calendar altogether.

That lunchtime Jamie appears at my desk. I look behind him, warily.

"She's not coming, obviously," Jamie says. "She's listened to you, hasn't she? She's giving you space."

I nod.

"Come on, then, let's go somewhere different," Jamie says. "Get something fun to eat."

"I've got lunch," I say, gesturing at my crackers, my jar of peanut butter, and a plastic knife stolen from Pret.

"No," Jamie says, "you haven't."

We end up at a new Middle Eastern café on a nondescript street, far enough away from the office that I feel we can talk freely. All the way there Jamie tells me about Mustache Kyle, who he now simply refers to as MK: how he stayed over after the housewarming and how they've seen each other most nights since.

"He's just a good man," Jamie says, as we sit down at a plastic table with our falafel bowls. "And," he continues, "that's all I've been looking for."

"And he's really hot," I say. I realize that I didn't get a knife and instead of getting up to fetch one, I put an entire falafel in my mouth.

"He is so hot," Jamie says, following suit with the falafel. He continues to talk with his mouth full. "I just never really noticed it that much in the office, you know? But he's got that thing, like that quiet confidence. He genuinely doesn't give a shit what anyone else thinks of him."

I nod.

"And he makes me feel like that too, when I'm with him,"

Jamie says, "like I don't need to put on a show. I can just be myself."

I'm surprised when tears spring to my eyes. Jamie looks horrified, which makes them disappear as quickly as they came. I laugh as I wipe them away on my jumper sleeve.

"Sorry, J. That makes me so happy to hear. It's lovely. I'm just a bit delicate at the moment, so everything's making me cry. These are good tears."

"Right," Jamie says, dubiously. "So I guess that answers the question *How are you doing?*"

"I'm OK," I say, stabbing at a piece of pickled beetroot with my fork.

"You're obviously not," Jamie says.

"Yeah, I'm not. But I will be."

"What's your plan, El?" Jamie asks.

I look down at my bowl, spearing another falafel.

"I don't really have one currently."

"OK."

Jamie tips up his Diet Coke can and watches me, waiting for me to come up with something, to elaborate on how I intend to move forward with my life. I've got nothing.

"How's Ray?"

I hardly dare ask. I don't want to hear something I don't want to know. She's got a new girlfriend or she's absolutely fine, she's turned my room into a gym.

"She misses you," Jamie says, then shakes his head at me and looks as though he's about to say something else. He opens his mouth and closes it again.

What? I almost say. *Say it.*

My heart lurches in my chest.

"We all miss you," he says in the end.

"I miss you too," I say. I look away, not wanting to cry again.

Missing them doesn't even begin to describe the way I'm feeling, but I can't seem to find the words. It feels like I'm missing something more vital than my friends. It feels like I'm missing my family. My self. This safe little world I built around me where everyone shows up and loves me for who I am and thinks I'm fun and teases me when I'm not. I don't know how to live without it. I wish I could express all of that somehow.

"How's Will?" I say instead. "He texts me every day to give me a little update on village life, you know."

"He doesn't want you to forget."

"Forget what?"

"How good it is."

"I haven't forgotten," I say quietly.

I think about it all the time. How quickly I got used to the green space and the quiet and then took them for granted. How lovely it is to wave at Sally and her giant bear as I pass her window, to pause and watch the ducks in the stream when I walk over the bridge. What it's like to spend an afternoon pottering around in my own garden in the sunshine, planting seeds that I thought I'd get to see flower the following year and the year after that.

"Will's pretty good actually; he's been seeing a lot of Tess," Jamie says, interrupting my thoughts. "She's round ours most nights, which is great, she's a good cook. Everything's very organic and wholesome but nice. She loves things that have come from the earth."

"Sounds good for Will," I say. "Is she nice? Nicer than Melissa?"

"Oh god," Jamie says, "who isn't?"

"I'm so glad," I say. "That he's got someone like that. And that you have."

"You know we love you, El," Jamie says. "We want you to come home. We all do."

"I know," I say. "I'm sorry, I know."

We're both quiet for a moment.

"Sally was asking after you. She came round ours for a glass of wine the other night."

"Oh yeah?" I say. "What did you tell her?"

"I told her you were mending a broken heart but that you'd be back with us in no time."

I nod, biting my lip, desperately hoping that's true.

We meander back to the office, buying a bubble tea on the way, large enough to last us through the afternoon. Jamie describes mine as "an abomination": it's coconut flavor, but it's bright blue with yellow whipped cream and sprinkles on top. By the time we get back to the office I am already feeling shaky from the sugar.

I hug Jamie when we get to my floor, where we part ways.

"I'm sorry," he says. "I feel like it's my fault that it all got so fucked."

"It's not," I say, "it was already fucked. This had to happen."

He nods.

"You are going to make a plan aren't you, El? We'll get this sorted?"

"Yes," I say so assuredly that I almost convince myself, "absolutely."

I spend the afternoon at my desk, sipping my tea, checking in my phone camera if my tongue is blue (it is) and reading the plots of the most terrifying horror movies ever made off

Wikipedia, copied into Google Docs. I eat peanut butter off the plastic knife, straight from the jar, not caring that anyone can see me, running my blue tongue along the blunt, serrated edge. No one approaches me. I make no plans. In the brief lulls where I am copying and pasting a new Wikipedia page into my document, I let myself think of the house and of Ray missing me too and my stomach aches.

I pick up my phone and frown at it as I type so as to look busy and professional.

Hey Lisa, Rozália finished her book and it's the best thing I've ever seen. We need to help her get it published, but I don't even know where to start. Do you? El. x

Lisa replies immediately. I can just picture her now in her cat-eyed reading glasses, phone held a foot away from her face in its diamante case, tapping away with one talon-like nail.

Yes. I know everything. Leave it to me.

CHAPTER SIXTEEN

That Friday, nearly two weeks after I left the commune, I get another text from Lisa. I'm hoping it's because she's already got news about Rozália's book but no such luck.

Meet me in the pub at 7, I want to talk to you.

She means the pub at the top of her road. The only pub she ever goes to. I've only just got home from work, Rob and Polly are away for the weekend, a romantic weekend just the two of them, which I'm choosing to believe is a positive sign and not just them desperately needing a break from me. I was about to get into my pajamas, ready for a night of eating cheese and crying, but I suspect Lisa won't take no for an answer. I lie down on my bed for five minutes with my hands over my face, my fingers pressed into my eyes until I see shapes, and then I pull my jeans back on, put my headphones in and walk

the hour to meet her. When she sees me, she looks me up and
down and shakes her head grimly. I slump into the chair opposite her and put my hand to my hair, to tighten my ponytail. I
rub my fingers under my eyes, trying to remove traces of old
mascara.

"What are we going to do with you, darlin'?" she says, pushing a vodka tonic toward me. She's ordered for both of us, of
course. I get a waft of her perfume as she sits back, and of cigarettes which she smokes like it's her last day on earth. Her
bright pink lipstick is immaculate, her hair freshly bleached.
Gold jewelry adorns her thin wrists almost up to her elbows.
Her nails are long and painted bright red. I ball my hands into
my fists, my bare nails bitten-down stubs.

"What do you mean?" I say.

I take a sip of my drink and wince. It's strong.

"I mean exactly that," she says, watching me. "I mean, what
are we going to do?"

She takes two large gulps of her own drink and doesn't even
blink.

I shake my head.

"Look, did Rozália talk to you?" I say. "I know she's worried
about me, but I'm honestly fine, it's just . . ."

Lisa leans forward and places her hand on the table, not
hard enough to make the drinks wobble but hard enough to
make me jump.

"You think I don't know what's going on with my own
people?" she says, her eyes wide. "You think I don't have eyes
everywhere?"

I shake my head quickly and then change my mind and nod.

"I mean, yes, I do think you have eyes everywhere, Lisa.
Obviously."

She smiles and leans back in her chair again. "Of course, I do. And you know what I see?"

I shake my head.

"I see that you're as lost as the day you walked into my office five years ago."

It's such a surprise and so overwhelming to hear it out loud that I find my bottom lip starts to wobble. I bite it, not wanting to cry in front of her.

"Now, listen," Lisa says. "We've got a job coming up at the office. We've finally had a grant from those pricks."

She means the government.

"It's enough for a year, just. I need a coordinator. An office manager. Just an all-rounder to help me. I'm working twenty hours a day at the moment. I do everything myself. Can you coordinate people?"

I nod.

"Organized?"

I nod again. I want to tell her how much I love organizing things. All the notebooks I have for different things. But I don't. I don't want her to know I'm even sadder than she already thinks I am.

"I need someone I can rely on. Can I rely on you?"

"Yes," I say quietly, knowing that to be completely true. "You can, I promise."

She softens. "I know I can. You're good at what you do."

"I'm not really," I say.

"Not at your bloody stupid, paper-pushing, printing job, whatever it is you do."

"That's pretty much it."

"I mean you're good *here*. With me. At this. With the kids. You're a lovely presence; you make people happy; you're not intimidating. You won't believe this, but I've been told I can be a bit scary."

I open my eyes wide as if in disbelief and take a sip of my drink.

"Never," I say.

"All right," she says, "don't be bloody cheeky."

"Sorry."

"You want the job, then, yeah? It's not much money. I need you to find people like you. And I need you to carry on mentoring. It's going to be long hours. No bloody thanks. And a lot of time with me."

"I want it," I say, without hesitation.

I want it so badly that I can hardly believe it.

"Good," she says. "You know I'm not going to tolerate you having a face on at work."

"I don't have a face on," I say. "I'm fine."

"You get your heart broken?" she asks. She reaches out to touch her packet of cigarettes. She can't smoke in here but it's just a reassurance that they're there.

"Sort of," I say. I stir my drink with its wilting paper straw. "It's hard, isn't it," I say, "when you love someone?"

She sits back in her chair and nods.

"Yes," she says, her voice steely. "It's very hard."

I don't know the exact details of Lisa's life, but from what I've pieced together from conversations I've had with the other people who volunteer, I know that Lisa had a son who died a long time ago. I've never asked her about him, but I know he's the reason she dedicates her life to young people who don't feel they have a place in the world. The reason why she does everything in her power to keep them safe, to keep them here.

"Have you seen Rozália's book?" I say.

"I have," she says, draining her drink. "We've got a genius on our hands."

"Did it make you cry?"

Lisa barks with laughter. But, I notice, she doesn't say no.

"Listen," Lisa says, just as I'm about to leave, "I see you, all right? You've been different these past few months, you've had this fire in you. Don't let it go out. If she doesn't want you, fuck her, OK? Find another one."

I can't help but laugh even though I can see that Lisa's completely serious. I know she's right about the fire. It isn't out. I still feel it.

I'm not so sure about finding another Ray.

"This stupid thing you've been doing, this wild challenge or whatever it is . . ."

"Wait," I say indignantly, "so you *have* been speaking to Rozália about me!"

Lisa ignores me.

"You're just being who you always were. So you carry on with it or you don't but it's you, all right? You're not some new-and-improved version of yourself. Remember that. You're enough, yeah?"

Lisa points at me with her red talon, and I nod, not sure I even really understand what she's saying or why I'm crying again.

"All right," Lisa says, seemingly satisfied that her speech has done the trick, "bye, then, sweetheart."

Lisa sits back in her chair, and I realize that I'm being dismissed.

"You're not leaving as well?"

"I've got an evening of meetings just like this one," she says, looking at the massive gold watch hanging off her spindly wrist.

"What?" I say. "Giving pep talks to big broken babies?"

She smiles at me kindly as the barman puts another drink down in front of her. She pats his hand in thanks.

"I wouldn't be doing anything else," she says, "I love my broken babies. Now"—she points her talon toward the door—"out."

I nod and hurry off.

I walk home, Lisa's words ringing in my ears.

When I get back I take two slices of bread out of the freezer and put them in the toaster. There's an open bottle of red wine, so I pour myself a glass of that, something to do while I'm waiting. I sit down at the kitchen table and pick up my phone. I have another email from Bernard's dog hotel forwarded from my parents; I can see that they've sent it to Rob too. Bernard has been given a certificate for being the best behaved at mealtimes and they've attached a photo of him proudly accepting his award. Mum and Dad have actually written to us this time.

This is just the kind of thing you two would have won, we're getting it framed when we get home!!!!!

They follow it up with lots of crying laughing emojis. I can't help but smile. At Bernard's proud face. At the thought of his Good Boy certificate framed on the wall next to Rob's and my graduation photos, which, now that I think of it, take pride of place in the hallway of my parents' house. I've been hearing from my mum most days: often it is just a line of bee and knee emojis, but she's been doing the same for Rob. It's comforting. She doesn't want anything from me, no updates on how I'm doing, she just wants to remind me that she's thinking of me. That's fine actually, it's enough.

I open WhatsApp. I've archived *The Commune*, our group chat, because I couldn't stand to see it there, even muted. I open it up and it's flooded with mundane messages about picking up milk, remembering to call the electrician back. Will wrote in the group yesterday that Sally dropped a cake off as a thank-you for helping her with her garden—it's on the table, he and Tess have already cut into it, sorry.

And then a message from this morning that makes tears spring to my eyes—a photo of Jamie's open hand, and sitting in his palm is an egg.

Jamie: *An egg! One of the girls has laid an egg! They must be happy. That's what the chicken lady said. If they feel happy and safe maybe they'll lay an egg. And they have!*

Ray: *Amazing!*

Will: *Great stuff, J.*

Jamie: *Should we put it in an incubator???*

5 missed calls from Jamie.

Jamie: *Guys?!*

Ray: *No, Jamie. We don't have an incubator. What are you talking about?*

Will: *It's not going to turn into a chick, mate. We don't have a rooster. . . .*

Jamie: *Right, right. Of course. Panic over. I can take it out from under my t-shirt now then.*

Ray: *???*

Jamie: *Skin to skin! Ugh. You wouldn't understand.*

I know they'll see that I've read it all now. Nothing gets past Jamie. So instead of archiving it again, pretending that I haven't seen it, I write my own message. I ignore the toast when it pops up and focus instead on typing it out over and over until it's just right. As soon as the message is sent, I archive the group again, my stomach lurching at the idea of getting a response. I wipe away my tears and get up to pour myself another glass of wine.

Just to say that I am still here. I am so proud of the chickens and of you, J. You're providing such a lovely life for them. I miss everything about this. And I miss you.

CHAPTER SEVENTEEN

The feeling of handing in my two weeks' notice at the newspaper is just as sweet as I always hoped it would be. I finally get to send the email that's been sitting in my drafts pretty much since the day I started this job. I delete all the confrontational stuff, the lines about how they'll be sorry they ever overlooked my talents and how they'll regret it for the rest of their lives. It turns out that once freedom is in sight the desire to burn bridges drifts away. I'm moving onward and upward. This is September's wild thing.

Lisa was right. Perhaps I am not new and improved by my Wild Year, but my life is. The wild things come so naturally now that perhaps at some point I'm going to have to go more extreme—jumping out of a plane or joining a cult or something. Maybe they just won't register at all because it's how I live my life now. I move forward.

Mona is delighted for me, I think. I mean, it's actually impossible to tell. She calls me into her office for a meeting immediately after I send the email. I have to ask her where her office is on instant messenger, and she sends a crying laughing emoji back assuming I'm joking. I wander around the entire floor sticking my head around doors until eventually I find her in a room not much bigger than a cupboard. She is wedged behind a desk that definitely doesn't look like it should fit in there. I don't understand how she gets in or out.

"You look happy to be leaving us," she says seriously, looking up at where I'm hovering in the doorway, the only place to stand in her office.

"I am, Mona," I say. "I'm really happy to be leaving."

She nods; weirdly it seems to be what she wants to hear.

"Good. It's the most important thing. Much more important than rosters and spreadsheets," she says, waving her hand dismissively at the computer screen.

"I know. Thank you. You've been saying it all along."

She looks at me very seriously and points at the laminated piece of paper stuck on the wall above her head. In bright red bubble letters it reads:

Happiness is the new rich.

Kindness is the new cool.

I nod.

"Right, yes," I say, gesturing at the poster, "absolutely."

"Remember that," Mona says.

"OK," I say. "I will be rich with happiness."

"You will," she says, and for some reason when I leave Mona's secret office, I find that there's a lump in my throat. I swallow down tears, refusing to be moved by clip art.

I continue to walk a lot. Into the office and back to Rob and Polly's flat every day, which is nearly two hours each way. My calves are tight all the time. My feet hurt. The bottoms of my worn-out Converse are so thin that I can feel the individual grooves of the pavement through them. Sometimes I listen to loud podcasts about men doing terrible things to women, sometimes I let my heart ache, my feelings flooding through my veins until I feel like I could almost conjure them at my fingertips, billowing out like smoke, or ghosts.

I miss Ray. I don't think I knew what that meant before. To miss someone. I don't just miss her. I miss the way I used to think about her. The way I could slip seamlessly between reality and fantasy. Daydreams don't come so easily now.

She messages me a couple of times. Twice, precisely. Both times after I sent the message to the WhatsApp group.

I don't expect you to reply to this but I just want you to know I miss you too.

And then a couple of days later.

I know you won't reply to this either but I finally finished that book you gave me. Fucking hell. I might never sleep again. Thanks, I think? Anyway, I still miss you. We all do.

I read them over and over. She's right. I don't reply.

I try to stay off social media as much as possible, but during one slipup, an early-morning Instagram scroll as I sit at my desk, I see that Jamie has posted from @TheVillagePeople69 that the newspaper has finally run the feature on the house. I swipe through his post, reading the article in the little squares rather than going to his bio and clicking the link. I read Mustache Kyle's words about why the Instagram account grew in popularity so quickly, about what it's like to move out of the city, what it's like to live in the countryside when you're queer, when you're a person of color. I see that he's also interviewed Rafe and Jim. Got quotes from them about why they'd never live anywhere else now. I can imagine Jim's side-eye to camera at that remark.

There's a photo of Jamie holding a saw and standing near the chicken coop; he's wearing a plaid shirt that I'm sure he must have borrowed from Ray. I'm not sure what this photo is meant to depict—it just looks like he's going to hack the coop apart, albeit in a very handsome, rugged way. I pause at the next slide when I see myself on the screen. It feels like a shock even though, of course, I should have seen it coming. I remember now, Mustache Kyle pushing us all together, standing at the back of our house, the rainbow-flag chicken coop behind us. *Just act natural*, he'd said, as we all stood stiffly, forgetting where to put our arms, what a normal smile looks like.

In this photo we're in a row, Will standing with his arm loosely hanging around Jamie's shoulders, Jamie grinning broadly at the camera, his face turned slightly to the side, his best angle. He is clutching Ray's hand. Ray has her arm around me and instead of looking at the camera, she's gazing at me, a smile on her face, watching me as I adjust my flower crown. My head is tilted back slightly, laughing. I look so happy. I was so happy.

I open instant messenger and just as I'm about to message Jamie I change my mind and open the group chat with them both.

Eleanor: *the feature! mk did such a good job. are you happy, j?*

Jamie: *so happy! i love it. it does it all justice, i think. us and the house. the vibe is perfect.*

Ray: *j, the photos are gorgeous. you were right about the plaid. a look.*

Eleanor: *a strong look*

Jamie: *so, has it persuaded you to come back, el? the call of the wild?*

Eleanor: . . .

In the end, I just log off. I set my status to offline for the whole day. I pass Ray on the stairs in the afternoon though, and instead of looking at my feet and shuffling past, I hold my head up, catch her eye, and smile. She smiles back at me, her eyes wide with surprise.

Later that afternoon I have to do a handover with the new person they've hired to do my job. Anushka was a diversity scheme intern too. She's heartbreakingly eager when we first meet, but over the course of the couple of hours we spend together, her enthusiasm visibly dampens. She starts noting only every other thing I say and then puts her pen down altogether.

"It seems like a lot of spreadsheets," she says at one point.

"Oh, it is," I say. "But look, you can actually get away with doing three hours' work per day maximum, it's just a case of prioritizing tasks and replying to the big-ticket emails with things that make you sound extremely busy."

Anushka frowns at me as I start scrolling through my in-box for an example to show her.

"Will I . . . not be extremely busy?"

"Oh," I say, "do you want to be?"

She nods vigorously.

"Yes. This is what I've been waiting for. A real job in the newsroom. And they said . . . they said in my interview that there would be opportunities for me to do some reporting. . . . I've got loads of ideas for stories. . . ."

She looks at me expectantly. I open my mouth to explain that they told me the exact same thing when I started, but I find myself pausing. I really don't want to extinguish that last flicker of excitement she's clinging to. But I feel like she deserves to know the truth.

"I would say that the opportunities are pretty few and far between," I say, after a moment.

Anushka frowns.

"Like, how few?"

"Well," I say, "like so few that I haven't had a byline since I started this job four years ago."

Anushka exhales, her shoulders slump. It's awful seeing her enthusiasm wilting before my eyes.

"I'm sorry," I say. "I really am, but I don't want you to . . . I want you to go into this with your eyes wide open."

She nods at me. "Appreciate it," she says stiffly. She's clearly trying not to cry.

"But," I say, "for most of the time I've been here, I haven't really been my most productive self. Perhaps if I'd have been pushing myself, if I'd have been more of a self-starter like it sounds like you are, I would have got somewhere. So I'm not saying our experiences are going to be the same, I'm just saying that they're going to really make you work for it. No one is going to help you out."

"I can do that," she says. "Work for it."

"Good," I say. "Then maybe this is going to suit you much better than it suited me."

I go back to showing her the list of ways that people try to trick the annual leave system and all the staff who are the worst offenders. I tell her that all the admin staff have their own ways, that I've already taken thirty days of holiday this year and somehow have thirty left, which I'll take as pay when I leave, thank you very much. She looks horrified, but I know she'll thank me later.

"Hey, Anushka," I say to her in reception as she's leaving. She turns around from the other side of the barrier.

"Don't let the editors treat you like a PA, OK? You're not responsible for their individual problems. You're not responsible for their lunch or birthday presents or dry cleaning. If they give you any shit at all, you tell Mona."

She nods seriously.

"Mona seems quite scary," she says. "A bit intense . . ."

I nod. There really is no getting away from that.

"Mona is great," I say. "She'll look out for you. She wants you to succeed."

"OK."

She doesn't look like she believes me.

"Good luck," I say. "I hope this job is everything you want it to be. I really mean it."

On my last day I go down to the copier room one final time. I am going to photocopy my passport for Lisa and then sit with my eyes closed, enjoying the smell of damp and ink, the solitude of being an underground printing gremlin just one more time. I almost feel sad, as though I might miss it.

When I got to my desk this morning, I was fifteen minutes early. Never too late to show enthusiasm for the job. No one else had arrived yet, although Mona must have crept in at some point because there was a huge card and an average bunch of flowers waiting for me. The card had a teddy bear on the front, and it simply said, *I'm sorry*, not *I'm sorry you're leaving*. I think it might be a condolences card, actually. It had been signed by pretty much everyone on the admin team, and by the people I sit with. None of them really know me, so the messages were all the same, *good luck* and *all the best*. Mona's message is in the middle in huge, swirling handwriting—*Rich with happiness, Eleanor. Remember that*. Next to the average flowers, which were already starting to go limp, there was a small box of posh chocolates. I opened them immediately, scanning the back for one which wasn't filled with violet or rose or something else fragrant and disgusting. I put the caramel one in my mouth all at once and took a sip of my coffee, letting the chocolate melt on my tongue, enjoying the peace and quiet of the office. Maybe I should have come in early more often. Early bird catches the caramel and all that.

I have to add some more paper to the printer, and while I'm trying to dislodge some stray sheets, the machine makes such an ungodly noise that I don't notice someone else coming into the room until they're standing right beside me.

"El?"

I jump, spinning round with the huge block of paper gripped in my hands. I lift it in front of me to act as my shield, or my weapon.

Ray lifts up her hands in front of her face to defend herself.

"Sorry, sorry!" I say, chucking the packet of paper down on the floor. It lands with a thump by my feet which makes us both jump.

"I didn't know it was you. I thought you were a ghost or a murderer or something."

I've got to change up my podcasts occasionally, I'm clearly starting to get paranoid. My heart pounds in my ears, partly from the residual fear of thinking I'm about to be murdered and partly because I haven't been this close to Ray in weeks. She's wearing a smart white shirt that I don't recognize. It looks good. I realize that I can't tell her that now.

Ray lowers her hands and then fixes me with a stern look. She folds her arms across her chest as if still guarded in case I attack.

"You're leaving," she says.

I nod slowly.

"Today?" she says.

I nod again.

"Were you going to tell me?"

I pause, briefly considering sparing her feelings, but there's no point in lying now.

"No," I say quietly. "I wasn't."

I had assumed Jamie would tell her, which I guess I was right about. I just didn't expect that he'd leave it until today, or that she'd confront me about it.

She shakes her head at me. Her big brown eyes wide.

"Are you kidding me?"

She looks so hurt that I could cry.

"What have I done to . . . ? What have I . . . ?"

I know she wants to say *What have I done to deserve this?* but she won't. It's too melodramatic.

"Nothing," I say, saving her. "You haven't done anything. You don't deserve it. It's all me. I needed this clean break, but I know it hasn't been fair on you."

Ray shakes her head. She takes a step toward me, and I hold my breath, but she doesn't come any closer.

"I miss you," she says. "I just miss you so much."

"I know," I say quietly. It is silent down here now that the printer has stopped screeching.

"I'm sorry. But, Ray, it was killing me."

I feel free to speak openly now that I'm leaving. Now that I know what it's like to not speak to her for a few weeks. That it's possible even if it hurts.

"No," she says impatiently, as if I'm misunderstanding her. "I really miss you, El."

I frown slightly. "I know. I get it. This is so unfair on you. To lose your friend. I've lied to you. I'm sorry. I don't know what else to say. I'm sorry."

We're both quiet for a moment. I bite the inside of my cheek until I taste blood.

"I can't lose you," she says eventually.

"It'll get easier, it's just what I have to do for now, I really think—"

"El . . ."

Ray does step forward then, so that she's standing right in front of me. And as she does, the light goes out.

I gasp, and Ray grabs my arm, just like she did before, months ago, when everything was easier. Or so much harder. Except this time she moves her hands to my waist and pulls me to her so that her hips are pressed against mine. I can feel her heart thudding in her chest. As quickly as mine.

I think she's going to say something, but she doesn't. She leans forward so that her mouth is so close to mine that I can feel her breath on my lips. She hesitates for a moment, and my whole body floods with adrenaline. This is it. This one moment. For five years I have been consumed by the thought of Ray and her body and her lips this close to mine. I don't wait for her to kiss me. I'm sick of waiting.

I lean forward, closing the gap between us, and before I get a chance to overthink it, I do it. I kiss her. For one heart-stopping moment, she hesitates, caught off guard maybe, but then she kisses me back, tentatively at first and then, her hand moving from my waist to the small of my back, harder, her tongue pushing against my lips, opening my mouth. I wrap my arms around her neck and pull her closer. At some point the light flickers back on, but neither of us registers it. She pushes me back gently so I'm resting on the copier, and she nudges her leg between my thighs, at which point I'm pretty sure I'm going to faint, or perhaps even die.

After a while her kisses slow, and I can feel her smiling against my lips. My heart sinks into my stomach. I can't bear for this to have been a joke to her. A test to see how she feels.

"What?" I whisper. "Why are you smiling?"

She kisses me again, just a brush against my lips. A reassurance. It is somehow even more intimate than before.

"Ray," I say. I tuck my fingers into the belt loops of her jeans and pull slightly so her hips are tilted toward me.

"Yes." She looks down at my hands and smiles, letting me adjust her, leaning in.

"What does this mean?"

"What does what mean?"

"Ray."

"Eleanor."

"Does this mean you feel the same way?"

"Well, you haven't actually explained to me what you feel. I've had to figure it out from a very confusing conversation on our lawn when you were covered in broken glass and from many long conversations with Jamie who thinks he is the authority on everything. He keeps saying you are 'gay for Ray,' which is actually a slogan I'm keen to adopt."

I'm going to kill him.

"What have you deduced, then?"

"That when you told me you had a huge crush on me that night on the roof, you meant it."

I close my eyes and take a deep breath.

"So you do remember."

"Of course I remember. But, El, you had a boyfriend. And you stayed with him after that. And you never mentioned it again. I just thought maybe you were a bit infatuated with me but that it wasn't that deep. Maybe I was just a bit of a novelty."

I shake my head. I could laugh at how wrong she was.

"I could never think that. You're not a novelty," I say.

"Well, I know that now, obviously. You stuck around. I've never had such a good friend in my life."

She lifts our joined hands to her mouth and kisses my fingers, setting every single nerve ending on fire.

"So, did you have a huge crush on me too?" I say.

"Honestly?"

I grimace, bracing myself. "Erm, only if it's nice. Wait. I mean, yes. Be honest."

"I don't know. Yes, I mean, obviously. But I hadn't properly let myself think that way about you. You were with someone else. You were so smart and serious and you made me laugh. I thought, *This girl is just not an option for me*. Then I suppose I just thought of you as this brilliant friend who I love spending all my time with. I mean, who I want to be with literally all the time, who I think about all the time. When you walked away at the housewarming, it was like a ton of bricks just landed on me. I think I've been very stupid for a very long time."

I shake my head.

"You're not. You haven't been stupid. I'm just very clever and smart."

She smiles.

"I've been good at pretending," I say. "Most of the time even I thought everything was fine just as it was."

"I'm sorry," Ray says.

"No, Ray."

"No, I am. I shouldn't have dismissed you. I should have known that you don't say things you don't mean. I'm meant to be your best friend."

"You are," I say.

"I'm your best friend?"

"You're my best everything, Ray."

She looks at me then in a way that makes it impossible to believe we were anything other than this to each other.

She kisses me again, her hands moving up the back of my shirt. I feel her finger tracing my spine, and my whole body shivers. I hear myself make a sound somewhere between a moan and a gasp; it sounds like someone struggling to breathe, which is true. It makes Ray kiss me harder. I move my fingers from her belt loops, down her thighs and then back up, where I pause, my thumb brushing over the button at the front of her jeans.

She stops and reaches down to take my hand. Not removing it, but not letting it go any further either.

"El," she says, smiling, leaning in to kiss my neck just behind my ear. "We really can't."

"Why? It's my last day and if you get fired, then we can just stay at home and do this all day."

The word *home* lingers in the air around us but neither of us choose to acknowledge it, not wanting to burst this bubble around us.

"Tempting," she says. And then, she gently pulls my hands away and lifts one up to her mouth to kiss it. "But no."

"Does it feel weird to kiss me?" I say.

"No," she says quickly, and then, "Well, maybe. Good weird. Hot weird. I actually think it's weirder that we haven't been doing this the whole time. Why? Do you think it's weird?"

"No," I say, mentally putting *hot weird* onto my list of things about this moment that I'll think about forever. "It feels like what all kisses should be like. Like I never want to stop."

"Do you know what I want to do?" Ray leans forward so she's speaking in my ear, her leg between my thighs suddenly applying so much pressure that I'm in danger of swooning again.

I shake my head, not sure I'll actually be able to stay upright on hearing the answer.

"I want to take you out for a drink. I want to sit across a table from you and have you tell me all about yourself. Really properly now that everything's out in the open."

"Oh," I say, trying not to be disappointed. I mean, I really do want all those things. "We can do that."

"And then I want to come back to yours—"

I interrupt her.

"Sorry but . . . I'm staying with Rob and Polly at the moment, and I don't think it would be very cool if I . . ."

"Right, OK." She pulls back and smiles. It's the kind of smile that makes my knees go weak. The smile I've spent years daydreaming about.

"So then I want you to come back to mine. And we can do all the things you're thinking about right now."

She slips her fingers under the front of my T-shirt, her fingertips tracing along my hips and she leans forward and kisses me gently.

I hold my breath. I literally don't think I can speak, apart from that I hear myself whisper "Oh god" against her lips.

"Would that be OK?" she says, pulling back to look at me.

I nod. I feel like I'm having a fever dream. The idea that Ray wants to do any of the things I'm thinking about makes me come over all light-headed. I feel in genuine danger of swooning and having to be carried out of here on a stretcher. A major statement on my last day.

"Can we go right now?" I say.

She laughs.

"No, I've got to go and work for another couple of hours. And so have you."

"I don't think I can wait."

"What's another few hours?" she says. She kisses me on the cheek.

"I've really got to go," she says. "Jamie's going to think I've got trapped down here."

"Ray," I say to the back of her head as she turns, still clutching her fingers in mine, waiting until the last possible second to let go.

"Eleanor," she says, turning back to look at me.

"Am I what you've been looking for?"

She frowns slightly, trying to figure out what I'm talking about.

"You said after you broke up with Kirsty that you were looking for something else. Something better. Is that me? Or are you still looking? I just . . . I have to be sure."

She smiles at me. She knows now, how my whole heart is in her hands.

"There's nothing more to look for, El. How could there be anything better than you?"

I nod, and when she leaves, I lie down on the grungy floor in the basement for one final time, cover my face with my hands and burst into tears. There is no more fitting way to say good-bye to this place.

CHAPTER EIGHTEEN

There is no fanfare when I leave my desk. The people who sit near me are in meetings or on the phone, pretending to be busy, which feels about right. What would I have even said to them? *It's been a pleasure to sit near you in silence for four years?* I pack up my desk, the green-tea bags I never drink, the almonds I've never snacked on, the twelve notebooks I've used one page of, and put them all in a tote bag the company gave us instead of our pay raise this year. I pick up my limp flowers and put them in the tote bag too. A shower of petals fall onto the desk, and I sweep them up and throw them into the bin on my way out.

When I get down to reception, I unclip my pass from my lanyard and hand it in at the desk. I take one last look at the photo, but there's nothing to see, I've faded to a ghost. I could be anyone.

When I turn around, I see that Ray is sitting waiting for me, and my heart leaps. She isn't even pretending to read, she's just leaning back in her chair, one leg resting across the other, looking at me, a huge smile on her face. I had known she was going to be there but there's still a part of me that hadn't really let myself believe it, just in case I'd dreamed the whole thing. It was a distinct possibility; I have fantasized about Ray in the basement before. Multiple times, actually.

She stands up when I get to her, and we stop still in front of each other. I'm suddenly unsure about what to do. Would we normally hug? Are we going to kiss again? Did we really kiss before? I'm worried I'm going to do something awful like try to shake her hand, but she saves me by leaning forward and kissing me on the cheek. I catch Reggie the security guard's eye behind Ray's head, and he rolls his eyes as if to say, *Finally.*

"Hi," Ray says.

"Hi," I say.

"So we're officially no longer colleagues," she says.

"No," I say, "just friends."

"Just friends," she repeats, grinning. "So, my friend, fancy getting a drink with me?"

I nod.

"Yes, please."

We end up in a bar in Soho drinking too-expensive cocktails. It's gloomy inside and lit only by candles and the dim amber lights under the shelves behind the bar. When Ray is getting our drinks I quickly message Rob and Polly to tell them not to wait up, that I'm out for drinks with a friend, then I delete the word *friend* and type out *Ray*—I'm out for drinks with Ray. She orders us dirty martinis even though I know she would secretly prefer something pink and sweet.

She grimaces when she takes a sip of her drink. I relish it, so strong it makes my eyes water.

"Do you hate it?" I say, setting my glass down. "Why didn't you order something else?"

"I'm trying to impress you," she says. "It's not very sexy to drink something with cotton candy in it, is it?"

She stares longingly at the table across from us, where a man and a woman both have cloudy pale pink drinks in tiny glasses lined with popping candy. They're delighting in it, giggling with every mouthful, their phones out, capturing the magic.

I burst out laughing.

"What?" she says, indignant.

"Do you know how many times I've watched you drink ridiculous cocktails like that?"

"You wouldn't fancy me more if I was all suave and sophisticated?"

I look at her, emboldened by the gin on an empty stomach.

"I couldn't fancy you more if I tried."

Ray grins.

"OK, we're getting you more of these," she says, gesturing for the waiter to come back.

We intend to go somewhere to eat, but we end up staying in the tiny bar drinking and ordering all the tiny food they have to offer. We eat a bowl of olives, some fancy pretzels, things just about substantial enough to mean that we don't end up on the floor but also don't interrupt the flow of the evening. Ray orders the popping candy cocktail and when the waiter comes over he puts it down in front of me and gives her my martini.

We wait until he's gone to swap them around.

"Here's your girly drink for girls," I say as I push it toward her.

She smiles and takes a sip.

"What is the thought process there, do you think?" I say.

Ray rolls her eyes.

"He called me 'sir' earlier, which, you know, I don't mind but"—she gestures at herself—"if you look closely, I am quite clearly not a sir, or like, if in doubt, don't do it, you know? Why sir or madam at all?"

"Exactly," I say. "What's something gender-neutral people could use instead? Mate?"

"Hun," Ray says immediately, and I burst out laughing.

"What? I love being called hun," she says, laughing too. "Anyone can be a hun."

"All right," I say, "I'll remember that."

We get closer throughout the evening, our knees touching. I slip my foot in between Ray's and leave it there, tangled up with her underneath the table. At one point, halfway through our third drink, she reaches down and puts her hand on my knee, moving her thumb back and forth almost absentmindedly while she's talking, and I honestly have no idea what she's saying. After a while she clocks that I'm not listening and smiles.

"Are you OK?" she says.

And because I'm a bit drunk and I'm deliriously happy I say, "I feel like I'm dreaming."

Ray grins and pinches the soft skin just above my knee gently.

"Real?" she says.

I nod. "Real."

We drink the last of our cocktails slowly. I'm aware of time creeping up on us, of when Ray's last train is and the fact that we haven't really discussed what we're doing after this yet. Did she really mean it about coming home with her? Was that just copier room talk? If Ray's thinking about it too, then she's doing a good job of hiding it. She looks completely at ease, as if we do this all the time.

"Should we maybe head off?" I say eventually, when there is not a single drop left in my glass. When people at the tables around us start to leave. Our tea light is just about to burn out.

"Sure," Ray says. When the bill comes, we split it. She tries to insist it's on her because it's my last day, but I refuse. I don't know why it feels so important to pay but it does. She doesn't argue too hard; the cocktails really were extortionate.

I hesitate, standing on the pavement outside the bar. If I'm going back to Rob and Polly's, then this is where we need to part ways and Ray really needs to get a move on.

"El," Ray says, always good at reading my mind, "will you please come back with me?"

"OK," I say, not even taking a pretend second to think about it.

"OK?" she says.

"Yes," I say, taking her hand and starting to drag her along behind me "but we need to hurry if we're going to make it."

We end up running through the station when we get to Liverpool Street, leaping onto the train just as the doors are closing. We walk through carriages full of drunk businessmen sloppily eating McDonald's and parents with their hyped-up kids who've been out in the West End until we find one right at the back of the train all to ourselves. We throw ourselves down in the seats, pink and breathless, brimming with adrenaline.

"We made it," I say, and instead of replying, Ray reaches out, pulls me toward her and kisses me. Not a gentle kiss. A kiss like she's been waiting to do it all night and she just can't hold on any longer. She reaches up, her hands in my hair and pulls gently on my now-loose ponytail. I gasp and she stops kissing me and I feel her smiling against my lips.

She pulls away but keeps her hand at the back of my neck.

"I've told you that I love your hair like this, right?"

I nod.

"You told me once when we were on the tube," I say. I realize I might need to be careful with how much I reveal regarding my near photographic memory of moments with Ray so as not to spook her. I could probably provide times, dates, what I'd eaten that day, the weather.

"That's right," she says. She shakes her head, taking me in, and I squirm, conscious that if I'd known this was going to happen today I might have chosen a different outfit. Something other than the same pair of tights for the third day in a row, for example. The ponytail was not a fashion choice, it is because tomorrow is hair-washing day. Then again, Ray has seen all my outfits, all the different versions of me. Well, nearly all of them.

I feel more like a teenager for the rest of the train journey than I ever actually did when I was in high school. Ray and I put our feet up on the seats in front of us, intermittently kissing and giggling about nothing and everything. At every station we hold our breath, hoping that no one gets on our carriage. Thankfully the doors stay closed, we're left alone. We test the waters with each other. Her hand creeps up from my knee to my thigh until her fingertips have slipped under the hem of my skirt. I reach under her shirt, trace my thumb along her hip.

When we arrive at our stop, we're the only people who get off, and we walk up the empty platform holding hands. It's a cold evening but I don't feel it.

Ray tries to insist that she's going to cycle us both home on her bike, but I put my foot down.

"Ray, no. We will die."

"Don't you trust me?" she says. She's so cocky, leaning on her handlebars, grinning at me. I could so easily say yes to anything she asked of me.

"Do I trust you with my life after four cocktails?" I say. "No. I don't."

"Yep," she says. "Fair enough."

We call a taxi instead and sit in the back in the dark. Ray reaches out her hand to me and traces circles on my wrist with her thumb while she chats to the driver about his night. I stare out of the window at the familiar view, which takes on a dream-like quality, a blur as we speed past. The stars and the trees in the wind and Ray's hand in mine.

Walking up the garden path to the house feels surreal. It's as if I've never been away. When Ray opens the front door and I hear the sound of music coming from the living room, Jamie's cackle, I realize, my stomach flipping, that it feels like coming home.

"I'm back," Ray yells. We kick off our shoes, throw our bags down, and then she takes my hand again and leads me through to the living room.

"Hiya," Jamie says. He is sitting next to Mustache Kyle on the sofa, one leg draped over his. Mustache Kyle is wearing gray jogging bottoms and a white T-shirt. The kind of clothes I suspect he didn't wear over here. The kind I bet he keeps here because he stays over so often. There's no sign of Will; I wonder if that means he's at Tess's house.

"You're back late, we were just starting to—" Jamie stops when he looks up from his phone and sees me standing next to Ray.

"Oh my god," he says, pushing himself off Mustache Kyle and standing up.

"Hi," I say, lifting my free hand to wave. Jamie's eyes are wide, and I grin at him, trying to convey a thousand things at once.

"What are you doing here?" Jamie says. "I mean, I'm so happy you're here." He walks toward me for a hug. I wave at Mustache Kyle over Jamie's shoulder and he dutifully waves back, clearly confused about why my being here is causing such a stir.

"I'm, um . . . visiting," I say, looking at Ray.

"Overnight visiting?" Jamie says, raising his eyebrows, looking between us and grinning.

"OK. Night, Jamie!" Ray says, starting to pull me out of the living room.

I follow her, but I look back behind me and open my mouth at Jamie, a silent scream of joy. He silently screams back, stamping his feet on the ground, raising his hands above his head, cheering me on.

"I'm so happy!" he mouths at me.

"Me too," I mouth back. My heart swells. I've missed him so much.

He blows me a kiss, and as we start walking up the stairs, I hear him saying loudly to Mustache Kyle, "About fucking time!"

The door to my bedroom is closed, and it's hard to believe that behind it is nearly everything I own. I have done such a good job in the past few weeks of compartmentalizing that I almost forgot that I had existed here. That I still exist here. I had never considered coming to collect my things. Or moving back in. I just sort of believed that while I wasn't here this house simply didn't exist.

We walk past my bedroom and into Ray's, and when she closes the door behind us, it suddenly feels like we're entirely alone. As if this room is separate from the house, from the other people in it, from the world itself. It's exhilarating and terrifying. She switches on a lamp on her bedside table, and it emits a low glow.

"Sorry," she says, "are you hungry? Thirsty? We basically haven't eaten anything all night. We can go back downstairs. . . ."

"No," I say. "I'm fine."

By which I mean, I don't want to leave these four walls and you, ever. You are everything I need. But that is potentially a bit intense right off the bat.

"OK," Ray says. She smiles and sits down on the edge of her bed. She gestures for me to come and sit down next to her. I do go over to her, but in a moment of boldness, enhanced by the feeling that in this room we've somehow entered a parallel universe, I sit on her lap instead. I wrap my arms around her neck, my legs across hers. She shifts slightly, so she's holding me up. She has one arm around me, resting on the top of my thigh.

"Hi," I say, looking down at her. She smiles at me.

"Hi," she says back.

"I can't believe this is really happening," I say.

She's quiet for a moment, looking at me.

"Me neither," she says. "But I also can't believe this hasn't ever happened. You know it's not just you. I've thought about this before too, El."

"Really?" I say. My eyes light up at the idea of Ray thinking about me.

"Obviously," she says. "You were quite literally the girl next door."

She nods at the wall separating my room and hers.

"All the times I was sleeping in there," I say, "I used to lie there and think about coming in here; I used to dream about it."

"Really? What did you dream about, specifically?" Ray says, her hand at the hem of my skirt. She keeps slipping her fingers underneath it and stopping, flattening it down again. It's maddening.

I bury my head into her shoulder, I can feel my cheeks reddening.

"Lots of things," I say into her neck.

"OK," she says, "so when I told you today we could come home and do whatever it is you were thinking about . . ."

"Ray," I say, squirming. I shuffle in her lap, and she sits back on the bed, pulling me closer.

"Tell me," she says. She kisses me then, biting my lip gently. "I want to hear you say it."

"I can't." I whisper. "I really can't. I'll die."

Ray laughs.

"You'll die?" she whispers back.

"Yes."

"So, what?" she says. "I just have to guess."

I nod. My heart lurches in my chest. I have never felt so alert to all my senses in my life. I'm aware of every single nerve ending, every single pulse of blood running through my veins.

Ray shuffles forward so that she's sitting on the edge of the bed and puts her hands on my waist, shifting me so that I move from her lap and I'm standing up in front of her, in between her legs.

She runs her hands up my thighs until they reach the waistband of my tights, and I close my eyes briefly, thanking the universe that I'm not wearing the pair that come all the way up to my bra. She looks up at me and I nod, giving her permission. She gently pulls them down, and for the first time in my life, I manage to gracefully step out of them. She pulls me back onto her lap so that I'm facing her, my thighs either side of her, my skirt pushed up. I bend down to kiss her and undo the top few buttons of her shirt, running my hands over her shoulders, through her hair. I can barely concentrate as her hands run over my bare thigh. She adjusts me slightly, her hand sliding between my legs, tracing lines at the edges of my underwear, her thumb drawing circles on me. I stop kissing her and bury my face into her neck. She smells like she always does, of her perfume, of her shampoo, of her—but it's different up close, when it's not fleeting or part of a fantasy. It's better.

"You OK?" she asks, into my ear.

"Yes," I say, breathless. I could laugh. I'm not OK. I feel like I'm about to pass out.

"OK," she says, and in what feels like one movement, she shifts my underwear to the side and pushes her fingers inside me.

I wrap myself around her even more, my arms around her neck. I'm grateful that she's holding me tightly because I can feel that my legs are shaking. My face ends up on her bare shoulder, and I bite it gently at first, and then harder. I'm trying to be in the moment, to not picture Jamie and Mustache Kyle standing outside the room, listening.

Ray gasps and I look at her.

"Sorry," I whisper.

"No, I'm fine," she says, "it's good." She shakes her head slightly as if she can't believe what she's seeing and then she kisses me again, hard. And I've never felt more sure that it isn't just me. The electricity I've been feeling all this time. It's both of us.

Time moves differently in Ray's room. Or it doesn't exist at all. We stay up for hours: sometimes we're frantic, as if this could all be a dream and we might wake up at any moment. Sometimes we're slow and deliberate, like we have all the time in the world. At one point she looks down at me and says, "You have no idea how fucking long I've wanted to do this," and I make her say it again and again until it sinks in. It's everything I had thought it would be and then nothing like I thought it would be at all.

At one point, when Ray and I are lying under her covers, her arms around me, my leg between hers, she laughs, quietly.

"What?" I say.

"Guess what time it is," she says, pushing a stray strand of hair away from my face.

"Um, two?" I say.

"It's nearly six," Ray says, nodding at the digital clock on the bedside table behind my head.

"Oh my god," I say and laugh too. "This has got to be some kind of record. Like I have literally never stayed up doing this *all* night. Have you?"

Ray hesitates, and I immediately say, "Don't answer that."

She leans forward, kisses me, and rolls onto her back. I sit up slightly next to her, adjusting myself on her pillows. I peer down at her, still not really believing it. That I'm here with her. That it's really Ray lying next to me.

"El," Ray says, "you're staring."

"Sorry."

"Did it live up to whatever you were thinking about for all this time?" she says. She's asking in her normal way, a self-assured smile on her face, but I know what she's really asking me. Is she as good in reality as my idea of her.

I nod and press my finger gently into the bruise forming on her shoulder.

"It doesn't even compare," I say, watching her skin turn white and then purple.

"So," she says, "what now?"

"Um," I say, "well, I would really love a glass of water or maybe like, an energy drink."

Ray laughs. "I mean what now? Like, what are we doing? Are you going to move back home now?"

I lie back in the bed next to her, looking up at the ceiling. I don't say what I'm actually thinking. That if she wanted to, we could just live in this room forever, maybe only leaving to get married or you know, for a snack.

"I don't know, Ray. Is it a bit intense for me to move home? Is it a bit soon? Or does it feel like we're doing things in the wrong order? People don't move in together immediately, do they?"

Ray looks at me like I'm mad and shakes her head.

"What?" I say.

"You're worried about doing things in the wrong order?"

"Yes!"

"El, we know each other better than most married couples do. We've lived together already. You know pretty much everything about me. I think I know you pretty well."

She takes my hand and brings it to her lips.

"I know," I say, watching her. "But it was different before."

"Why?"

"Because we were just friends then."

"And what are we now?" Ray says.

"Um." I'm quiet for a moment. "I don't know. I mean I don't know what you want, maybe if you just want to be friends, we can see how it goes. . . ."

Ray laughs and rolls over onto her side to face me. She prods me gently in the side.

"What do *you* want, El?"

I pause before I answer, so practiced in not telling her the truth that it takes a moment to remember that now I live in this new world where I can actually say how I feel.

"I want you. All of you. I don't want to be your friend," I say.

"And do you think I want to be your friend?" she asks, her finger tracing the butterfly on my hip.

I look down at her and smile despite myself.

"Maybe," I say, shuffling down so I'm facing her. The tips of our noses touching.

"El."

"Ray."

"I don't want to be your friend. OK?" she says. "I'm all in. Are you all in?"

I nod and exhale slowly. Five years of holding my breath. I've been all in from the moment I met her.

EPILOGUE—NEW YEAR'S DAY

I wake up with a sour taste in my mouth. It's the taste of red wine and no water. The taste of three helpings of treacle tart and not brushing my teeth properly. The taste of regret.

I open my eyes, squinting into the bright, winter sunlight. I didn't remember to close the curtains last night—well, this morning. The first thing I see on the wall opposite the bed is the soft-porn woman drinking a cocktail, tanned and smiling, mocking me. I vow that if I am ever able to get up from this bed the first thing I will do is tear her down.

There is a stirring next to me, a low groan.

"Are you awake?" I try to say, but I find that my voice is gone. I cough quietly, trying to clear my throat.

"Are you awake?" I try again, but it's no clearer: it comes out a raspy whisper, cracking in the back of my throat.

Ray turns over; she has one arm over her eyes but opens them slightly to peer at me. She smiles and pulls me to her. I settle beside her so my head is resting on her chest. She smells of woodsmoke and cigarettes. Different kinds of fire.

"Say something else," she says into my hair.

"I can't." I try to say it in my normal voice but virtually nothing comes out.

"You're all husky," she says, "I like it."

"Ray," I croak, "I think I might be dying."

I hold the back of my hand to my forehead as if to take my temperature.

"Do you think it might have something to do with all the wine? And the singing?" Ray says.

"The singing," I whisper, closing my eyes. "I was doing karaoke with Jamie."

"You were," she says, kissing the top of my head. "It was quite special."

"Not Dane Bowers and Victoria . . ."

"Oh yes,"

"And was I?"

"Dane? Of course."

I groan and pull myself up to look at her.

"How do you look this good in the morning?" I say. She has a gray sweatshirt on because this room is always freezing, but she must be a little warm because her cheeks are pink. She has circles under her eyes but in a sexy way, like she's been awake all night.

"I don't," she says. "You're just blinded by lust."

"Blinded by lust?" I laugh. "Where have you got that from?"

She reaches out and taps her finger on top of a book I got her for Christmas. It's about the hair burglar.

"What? It says he was blinded by lust?"

She nods.

"Like you," she says, grinning at me.

"I swear I don't make wigs out of women's hair and wear them," I say.

"Hmm," she says, pushing me down and rolling over so she's on top of me. "I think that's exactly what a hair burglar would say. I'll have to be careful with you."

She pins my hands above my head and just as she does there's a knock on the door. Jamie's head immediately appears.

"Oh, fucking hell," he says, shielding his eyes. Ray lets go of my hands, moves to sit next to me. I shuffle so that I'm sitting upright.

"Do you ever stop? The things we hear. Have some respect for God's sake, it's New Year's Day. *And* it's Sunday. A day of rest if ever there was one."

"Jamie," Ray says, "typically if you knock on someone's door you wait for them to say 'come in.'"

He ignores her.

"So girls, once you've finished shagging . . ."

"We're not . . . ," I start to say.

Jamie holds his finger up to stop me.

"Once you've finished shagging, I would like to propose that we meet for breakfast, and then I would like to propose that we go for our New Year's Day swim. Get it over and done with."

I laugh and then stop abruptly when I see that he's serious.

"Um, no, J, obviously not."

I gesture to the window, encrusted with frost.

"That's not what you said last night," Jamie says.

I turn to Ray, and she shrugs like she can't help me.

I throw myself back onto the pillows and realize slowly,

crushingly that they're right. Flashes of the previous evening burst into my mind. Tess telling us how when she was growing up it was her family's tradition to go swimming in the sea on New Year's Day. Me telling her how special that is. Telling her about swimming in the pond and describing it as "life-changing" and "a spiritual experience," without revealing that I didn't get in or, crucially, that I am deathly afraid of all ponds and pond life. I distinctly remember saying that it will be "just like the plunge pool" at Center Parcs. I have never been to Center Parcs in my life.

"Was this . . . was this my idea?" I say, my voice sounding hoarser by the second.

"It was, babe," Jamie says. "And now we're all going swimming in the freezing-cold pond because of you. So get out of bed, make everyone some toast, and get your bikini on."

I nod. Suddenly so aware of my dry mouth that the pond is briefly appealing, as though it might quench my thirst.

I am never drinking again.

I crawl out of bed and head downstairs, promising Ray a cup of tea. I pull out a seat at the dining table and put my head down, not yet able to make it all the way to the kitchen. The dining room is a mess. I think this means that our New Year's Eve dinner party was a success.

The multicolored taper candles in old wine bottles are still sitting in the center of the table, streaks of luminous wax running down the sides and pooled at the base. The candles were the only light in the room last night, the glow illuminating the place settings, dried red-and-orange flowers in ceramic vases, linen napkins with brushed brass rings. The whole house smells like cinnamon and cloves: diffusers in each room have been pumping out the scent since November 1 (before that it was pumpkin spice), and I don't know that it will ever smell like anything else now. Christmas is firmly lodged in the walls, the floorboards, the curtains, the fabric of the house.

Last night we had Mustache Kyle and Tess (who are basically permanent residents of the commune now), Sally, Rafe, and Jim round for a dinner party. Sally told us it's the first year she's been invited to do something on New Year's in over a decade. The four of us wrapped our arms around her in a group hug so tight that she had to scream to be let out. When we released her, she was dabbing her eyes.

We each had to contribute a dish, which meant we ate a vegetable curry, lasagna, and a butternut squash salad, with a cheesecake for dessert. The table was heaving. We all ate a bit of everything. We all drank a lot of everything. Around 9:00 p.m. things start to get a little hazy, memory-wise. I know that Jamie brought out the karaoke machine he was sent for free after he uploaded our video from the village hall on his Instagram, and there was a lot of singing. I know that we switched on the TV for the countdown but that Ray had already kissed me five minutes before, in the dark kitchen, pressed up against the wall, so that at midnight we could hold hands with Sally and kiss her on both cheeks.

Rafe and Jim walked Sally home just after midnight, and we'd had a moment when MK and Tess were in the kitchen, attempting to start clearing up, when it was just the four of us.

"I'm so glad we did this," Will said, pouring himself one final glass of Baileys. "I wouldn't want to be here with anyone else."

"God, yeah," Jamie said, "imagine if you had to live here with Melissa? What a nightmare."

Will laughed. It was an easy laugh. He's doing OK. We've

built our own tight-knit world now, such a secure bubble that it's easy to forget about Melissa, that Will's life was so different only six months ago—that all our lives were.

"Maybe not a nightmare," Will said. Ever the gentleman, even about Melissa. "But this is perfect. It was meant to be for us, don't you think?"

"Yes," I said, sticking a spoon into the treacle tart Sally made. "It was meant to be. I've never felt so at home."

There is a half-full jug of water on the table, which I drink directly from. It's chilled because the room is so cold and it tastes of bitter lemon, the wedges still in there. I spit a pip into my hand.

I can hear voices coming from the living room, so I creep into the kitchen, not wanting to have to make tea for everyone, but wherever he is in the house, Jamie can always sense when the kettle is being switched on.

"You doing tea, El?" he yells from the living room.

I close my eyes, mustering up the energy to yell back.

"Yes," I say weakly. I'd be surprised if someone could hear me if they were standing right next to me.

I pick up my phone from the kitchen counter. The screen is filled with notifications. Oh god, I've obviously been drunk texting. I message Jamie.

I can't speak. Yes, I'm making tea, who else wants one?

Everyone, please. MK has oat milk and one sugar. Chop chop!

While the kettle is boiling, I lean against the countertop and scroll through my phone. Worse than drunk texting it turns out. Drunk voice notes. One to Rob and Polly who spent last night at home, just the two of them, one to my parents, one to Lisa and to Rozália. I press play and hold my phone between my ear and my shoulder while I fetch mugs out of the cupboard. When I open it, a fleck of blue paint floats down onto the counter, slowly, like a feather. Sometimes the house crumbles in such a lovely way.

Rozália! HAPPY NEW YEAR! I just want to say again that I am so proud of you. You've had an amazing year and I know next year is going to be even more amazing. It is going to be YOUR YEAR. I just know your book is going to get published and you're going to change LIVES, Rozália. It's such a powerful message, so POWERFUL. Oh god, that chicken, and when its feathers fall out . . . sorry . . . no I'm fine . . . no I'm not crying . . . sorry, Jamie's asking if I'm crying. Anyway. Hope you're having a great night and you're safe and I'll see you on Monday.

Rozália replied at three in the morning, when I was already fast asleep.

Ha, you're drunk. And yes, you were crying. Happy New Year, El. I think things are getting better for us both, right? We're moving up. Thanks for everything. Even in hard times I've always been able to laugh at you.

I'd like to think she means *with you*, but I know Rozália only says what she means. I pour water over the teabags and warm my hands over the steam. A slug wiggles its way across the floor, but I don't have the energy to deal with it, so I just watch its silver streak shine on the cracked tiles.

It feels absurd to be pulling off my hoodie and my warm pajamas to put my swimsuit on. I feel on the verge of tears but pull myself together given this is my own fault and Tess keeps thanking me profusely for the "great idea." Every time she does, the rest of the group glares at me.

"Won't we need wetsuits?" I'd croaked to Tess, over our cups of tea.

"No," she laughed. "I promise you'll be fine; you just get in for a couple of minutes and then you'll be on a high all day."

I doubt it somehow, but I've made my bed and now I must lie in it. My cold, watery, frog-spawn-filled bed. On some level I'm not surprised that this idea surfaced when I was drunk. I've been turning it over in my mind over the past few months ever since I got back to the commune. The pond is the one wild thing that conquered me. But that was before I knew that anything was possible. Surely now I am the wild thing that will conquer the pond?

I stand in front of my giant mirror (Facebook Marketplace strikes again) shivering, before quickly pulling on a pair of leggings and then a pair of jeans over the top. I put on three jumpers to be on the safe side. When I'm finished wrapping up I can barely move my arms and beads of sweat are starting to form on my upper lip.

While I'm waiting for Ray to get ready, I sit on the floor and look at the mini Polaroid pictures inserted into the frame of the mirror. For Christmas, Ray's nan bought her one of those pastel-colored cameras that print out little photographs. Ray has never expressed any interest in having one, but it's turned out to be a total hit, best present of the year. Jamie loves using it to get flattering pictures for the Instagram account and now we have lots of tiny memories pinned up all over the house.

There is a photo of the four of us standing in our garden around the bonfire on Fireworks Night, clutching sticks with marshmallows on the end of them. I'm grinning from ear to ear, too hot in my bobble hat and gloves. It was unseasonably warm, but we all got wrapped up anyway and lit a fire when we got inside.

There's one of my parents and Rob and Polly, sitting in front of our fireplace the weekend before Christmas. Mum and Dad's first visit to the house. They loved it here. Polly is leaning into Rob, and he's laughing at something she's just said. I don't know if they're back to normal yet, whatever that is, but they're on the mend, or they seem to be anyway—from the outside. They're trying.

"You're glowing," Mum had said on that trip, gripping my shoulders as she left. "Well, you actually look very pale. But still, somehow you're glowing."

"It's a year of being wild," I'd said. "It suits me."

"I don't know about being wild," Mum said, pulling on her enormous leopard-print coat that Jamie had been wearing most of the day. "A year of being happy maybe."

Annoying how someone who appears so oblivious always seems to manage to hit the nail on the head.

"Enjoy your Christmas cruise, Mum," I'd said, kissing her on the cheek. My dad was in the car warming up the engine, talking to Rob about petrol or gears or whatever it is they're into.

"I'll call you," she said. "From the ship, when we're all settled in."

"Sure," I said.

"No, I will," she said firmly. "I will call you, honey."

I nodded.

"OK. I'll call you too."

There's a photo of Ray and me on Christmas Day taken by her nan. It's blurry, we're out of focus, our faces streaked across the tiny square. But you can see that we're laughing, mouths open, eyes squeezed shut. I'd spent Christmas morning with Rob and Polly as usual and the afternoon at Ray's nan's house. Ray's nan had grabbed me in the kitchen while I was helping clear up and said, "You know it was always El this, El that. I'm glad she finally saw sense."

We set off back to the commune that night in Ray's new old beat-up car. The roads were empty, and we drove with the windows down, singing along to Christmas songs. When we got home we stood in the garden and listened to the sound of nothing. Pure silence. We sat in the nook, fairy lights twinkling, firepit roaring, hands clasped together, not believing our luck.

We meet Rachel at the bottom of our street. She's in the village for one more day having spent New Year's with her family before heading back to London tomorrow. When I moved back to the commune the first thing I did was message her to try to apologize and assure her I'm not (in Jamie's words) "full crazy" but more crucially, to make amends so that we could continue to frequent the Swan. Essential.

It turns out that Rachel was as mortified as I was. She was drunk and Ray was there (Ray's ego was quite bruised on hearing this detail) and her head was all over the place. We moved on, or we've tried to. We're in the process of moving on. Hence why it only feels right to invite her to endure a terrible swim with us given that we only know about the pond because of her.

"I can't believe it's you suggesting this," Rachel says as we walk up ahead from the rest of the group. "After the fuss you made last time."

"I know," I say, "but I'm a big believer in second chances."

I decide not to mention the influence of several bottles of wine.

"Very brave," she says, smiling.

"I am, famously, very brave."

The trudge to the pond warms us up pretty quickly. I have to remove two of my three jumpers after only a few minutes of walking. When I take my bobble hat off, I'm pretty sure that steam comes off the top of my head. It's one of those perfect winter mornings, blue sky, the ground crisp, breath like a puff of smoke in front of your face every time you speak. I can't help but notice, though, a large dark cloud looming. A bad omen if ever I saw one.

We don't waste any time when we arrive at the pond. Tess starts shouting health and safety instructions, to get into the water slowly, to only stay in for a minute, to wrap up the moment we get out. She and Rachel go up ahead with Will trailing behind them like a man walking the plank. What have I done to my poor friends?

It hadn't occurred to me that it might actually be danger-ous to swim. I realize I've been holding on to the hope that the pond might have frozen over and that we wouldn't be able to get in but no such luck. I take a few deep breaths. It's fine. Maybe I'll have a brief heart attack but that's OK, who hasn't?

Tess, Will, and Rachel are the first ones to brave it. They sit on the jetty side by side and slowly lower themselves into the pond. The sound, I'd imagine, is the same as if they were being dipped into a pot of boiling water. Agonized screams, deep gut-tural howls. I'm certain that at one point, Will actually yells, "Help."

Once they're in the water though, they're laughing in be-tween gasps for air.

"Come on, guys," Tess calls out, "quickly, you're going to get freezing cold standing there."

"Do you want me to film you, J?" I say, holding out my hand for his phone.

"Um," Jamie says, staring at his phone as if he didn't even realize it was in his hand. "Actually, no."

He drops his phone onto the blanket, and MK grins at him, jumping up and down slightly to try and stay warm, his arms across his chest.

"Let's keep this one just for us," Jamie says.

The four of us walk up the jetty and sit in a row, elbows knocking into each other, our toes dangling into the water. The sun is now entirely hidden by the dark cloud. The water is black.

Jamie and MK go first. They both yowl and shriek before splashing off in the direction of the others. Jamie vows that he'll "never forgive me for this."

When it's just the two of us left Ray looks at me and shakes her head slightly, in disbelief that this is happening, that I'm making us do this. That we're not tucked up in bed, cozy and dozing or lounging by the fire, enjoying the cold day from the warm indoors. We sit side by side on the jetty, shivering. I close my eyes. I know what I have to do—water spiders or no water spiders. I say a silent prayer to the Goddess of Ponds and Disgusting Pond Life, asking her to keep me safe, and take a deep breath.

I let myself drop, my shoulders plunging under the icy water. The cold momentarily takes my breath away, sending a rush of adrenaline through my chest. I panic for a moment, not trusting that the human body can function at this temperature, but I kick my legs and start treading water. Nothing touches my feet. Nothing goes in my mouth. The goddess has heard me. My head stays above the surface—I'm able to breathe. I reach up with shivering hands and grip Ray's dangling ankles.

She bursts out laughing, trying to kick me off. "Don't you dare," she says through chattering teeth.

"I won't," I say breathlessly, holding out my hand to her. "I won't if you get in right now."

She shakes her head. But then, after a moment, she closes her eyes, takes a deep breath and drops into the water, sending ripples all around me. She looks at me, eyes wild, white knuckles gripping onto the jetty.

I kiss her fingers with my blue lips.

"It's never as bad as you think it's going to be, is it?" I say, as we push off together, swimming toward the others.

"What isn't?" Ray asks, her pink shoulders bobbing along next to mine.

"Jumping in."

The dark cloud gets lower and lower. It starts to rain just as we're thinking about getting out of the water. Torrential rain, so fast and hard that we laugh. At how somehow, despite being submerged in water, it makes us feel even more drenched, at how beautiful and surreal the moment is. Alone, surrounded by trees and birds and swimming in a freezing pond in the pouring rain. I feel a sudden euphoria, to be here with these people, with Ray. That this is my life. That I got in the water.

Eleanor's Wild Year Diary

JANUARY

I did ten tequila shots in one night and then threw up ten tequila shots about an hour later. I thought getting drunk on a school night was going to be an easy one, but I have to be honest, this was a rough start to the Wild Year. Went out on a Wednesday night date to a bar where they only serve tequila. I don't like tequila. Now I like it even less. Will never see my date again. They have blocked me on everything which is more than fair. I wish I could block myself. 3/10.

FEBRUARY

I got a tattoo! I really did it! I now have a tiny butterfly on my hip. It hurt but in a good way, I think I could have stayed there

for hours. Perhaps I have found my wild thing niche and will
become one of those people who is tattooed head to toe. Perhaps
not though because it is very expensive and I am in my overdraft
already. 8/10. Would tattoo again!

MARCH

Took MDMA for the first time last week. Briefly thought I was
having the time of my life but it's taken me three days to write
in this journal because I've been too sad to pick up a pen. I
don't think drugs agree with me. 5/10. Glad I did it. Glad I
don't have to do it again.

APRIL

Threesome month! Underwhelming. Did not actually have sex,
which I believe is usually considered essential to the full threesome
experience. I did kiss two people in one evening though. Quite
wild, actually. Good work overall. 6/10. Would not repeat.

MAY

Made a decision to move out of London (bye, Amelia!) and
into a commune in the countryside. Sort of no idea how this will
work logistically but it does mean I will be housemates with Ray.
Quite wild in a potentially catastrophic way. Let's see! So far
8/10 (nearly all marks for excitement of moving out of Amelia's,
docked two for having to pack).

JUNE

Actually left London and moved into a dilapidated commune in the countryside. With Ray. Maybe the wildest thing yet. 9/10 (I love it but you have to leave room for improvement and actually the house does need a lot of improvement).

JULY

I sang in front of a room full of strangers (at karaoke, had not just lost my mind) and actually enjoyed it.

Also went on a date with Sabine, stayed up all night and met Ray at Polo Bar at 6:00 a.m. Jamie says this doesn't count, but I think it does and it is not Jamie's Wild Year, it is mine. 7/10—feeling pretty pleased with myself.

AUGUST

I didn't swim in the pond. It felt like a failure at the time but maybe the real failure would have been growing spiders on my brain?

I told Ray how I feel (sort of) and moved out of the commune. Maybe temporarily. Maybe forever. 0/10. I don't even know why I'm still doing this. What is the point of being wild alone?

SEPTEMBER

I quit my job! I quit my stupid, stupid job! I will never lurk in a basement again! I should have done this a long time ago, but it really doesn't matter because I've done it now. I'm going to work with Lisa instead, which is terrifying and brilliant. Everything else is shit but this is wonderful. I feel very lucky. Lisa says I've got a fire inside me and it's to do with me and nothing to do with Ray. 6/10. All 6 points are for excitement about new job. Nothing else to be excited about.

OCTOBER

OK, so I did end up lurking in the basement just one more time. And I'm so glad I did because it meant I kissed Ray. I kissed Ray. I kissed Ray. I kissed Ray. And she kissed me back. This might be a fever dream but if it is I hope I never wake up. 100/10. I don't care. Numbers don't make sense anymore. The world is upside down.

NOVEMBER

Not a fever dream! Real! I moved back to the commune. Maybe it's too soon. Maybe it's a risk. I guess that is what makes it wild. It's good to be home. 1000/10. Truly I have given up with the numbers.

DECEMBER

OK, so technically I am writing this on January 1. But I'm counting swimming in the freezing cold as December's wild thing. This is my Wild Year. I make the rules. Probably I wouldn't ever swim in the icy pond again. But maybe I would. No hard and fast rules. No nevers.

I guess what I'm saying is, next year, although I don't actually have to be wild, I'll try my best to be, because look where I was. And look where I am now.

ACKNOWLEDGMENTS

Firstly, thank you to Emma Finn—my first reader and biggest champion. I am so very lucky to have an agent whom I trust both to do the best for my work and to always want to gossip. The ultimate combination. Thanks also to everyone at C+W, who are so supportive and make their authors feel like part of one big team.

Thank you to Hillary Jacobson for loving this book, seeing its potential, and working so hard to find it a great home. I am so very lucky to have you on board.

Thank you to my editors, Emma Capron at Quercus and Anna Kaufman at Vintage. You both came to this project with so much love and understanding for these characters, and I am very aware of how lucky I am to get to work collaboratively with you both—thank you for making the book so much better and for making the process so much fun.

Thank you to everyone at Quercus for always doing such a phenomenal, creative job but especially Joe Christie, Lipfon Tang, and Aje Roberts. Also, thank you to David Murphy, Isobel Smith, Chris Keith-Wright, Tara Hodgson, Frances Doyle, Hannah Cawse, Sinead White, Rachel Wright, and Lorraine Green.

Thank you to everyone at Vintage but especially Edward Allen, Erica Ferguson, Nicholas Alguire, Sophie Normil, Madeline Partner, Julie Ertl, Karen Niersbach, and NaNá Stoelzle.

Thank you to Emma Hughes, Bethany Rutter, and Emmett De Monterey for being great colleagues and friends in this very silly industry. Laughing with you about things that would otherwise make me cry makes it all doable. Also, the gossip is unparalleled—thank you. A special mention to Lily Lindon, whom I will always thank forever in everything because no one has the receipts you have. Wow, you could really end me. Thank you for being such a kind friend and for giving really good advice even if I mostly ignore it. How fortunate I am to have been publishing my little gay story at the same time as you. Thank you, Ailbhe Reddy, for being both the wild crush and the wonderful friend. When I first heard you say "Wild Fings" in your flawless English accent, it made it all real.

Thank you to all my friends who are also my family for making me laugh more than anyone else in the world, especially this year. All I want to do is move into a commune in the countryside with you, start a rosé farm, and create a new and exclusive gay enclave (complete with token straight benefactors). This book is purely an exercise in manifestation. It is a love letter to you. And to rosé.

Thank you, Jen, always. If we do it right, you'll be in the commune next door, coparenting the animals.

The biggest thank-you to my family—Mum, Dad, and Sarah—for being there, for making everything funny, for being the kind of unbreakable safety net people dream of. Without you, none of it is possible.